WHERE THE

Heart

LEADS

OTHER BOOKS AND BOOKS ON CASSETTE
BY ANITA STANSFIELD:

First Love and Forever

First Love, Second Chances

Now and Forever

By Love and Grace

A Promise of Forever

Return to Love

To Love Again

When Forever Comes

For Love Alone

The Gable Faces East

Gables Against the Sky

Home for Christmas

A Christmas Melody

The Three Gifts of Christmas

A Star in Winter

Towers of Brierley

TALK ON CASSETTE

Find Your Gifts, Follow Your Dreams

WHERE THE *Heart* LEADS

a novel

ANITA STANSFIELD

Covenant Communications, Inc.

Cover painting by LeConte Stewart, courtesy of Williams Fine Art.

Cover design copyrighted 2001 by Covenant Communications, Inc.

Published by Covenant Communications, Inc.
American Fork, Utah

Printed in the United States of America
First Printing: August 2001

08 07 06 05 04 03 02 01   10 9 8 7 6 5 4 3 2 1

ISBN 1-57734-848-6

Library of Congress Cataloging-in-Publication Data

Stansfield, Anita, 1961-
     Where the Heart Leads / Anita Stansfield.
         p. cm.
     ISBN1-57734-848-6
     1. Physically handicapped women–Fiction. 2. Mormon women–Fiction. 3. Physicians–Fiction. 4. Utah–Fiction.
I. Title

PS3569.T33354 W45 2001
813'.54–dc21
                                                    2001037203

This book is dedicated to all the men
who have faithfully read my stories,
diligently putting up with being harassed about
reading romance novels.
Your wives and girlfriends love you for it.
And so do I.
This one's for you.

I know that I'm a prisoner
To all my father held so dear.
I know that I'm a hostage
To all his hopes and fears.
I just wish I could have told him
In the living years . . .

—Rutherford & Robertson

PROLOGUE

Boston—1894

Jonathon Brandt entered his mother's bedroom to see the early morning sun beginning to penetrate the sheers hanging at the windows. Sara glanced up, and the sleeplessness in his sister's eyes barely masked her anguish, an anguish that he shared completely. Their mother's life was now being measured in hours, and he and Sara took turns remaining at her bedside for every moment. Everything, beyond eating and getting the minimum sleep, had been put completely on hold.

"Anything?" he asked, wondering if there had been any change.

Sara lovingly touched their mother's forehead and gently straightened her dark, curly hair against the pillow. "She woke up for a minute about an hour ago. She asked me who I was. I told her, and she smiled and went back to sleep."

Jon pressed his fingers to his mother's throat, checking her pulse. He sat beside the bed and took her hand into his. Its coldness startled him and he found it difficult to speak. "It won't be much longer now." Sara looked up with huge tears emphasizing the desperate pleading in her eyes. Jon had to look away. All his years of medical training and experience were useless. He cleared his throat and added, "You should get some sleep. I'll wake you if anything changes."

Sara said nothing. She just climbed onto the huge bed and lay close beside her mother. Jon focused on his mother's face, attempting to soak up her image, almost as if he could drink enough memories in the next few hours to carry him through a long desert trek. He found himself trying to contemplate the enormity of life and death, but the uncertainty of what lay beyond this moment forced his mind elsewhere. If he troubled himself over questions without answers, he'd lose what little reason he had left.

Jon's reverie was broken when Phillip Brandt entered the room, dressed to go out. Jon sat up straight and watched his father sit quietly on the edge of the bed. With a tenderness that defied his brusque nature, Phillip touched the face of his wife of more than thirty years, then pressed a kiss to her brow.

"Good-bye, Carol," he whispered. "You know how I love you."

She showed no response beyond the barely audible sound of her strained breathing.

Phillip stood up, gazed once more toward his wife and moved away. Jon resisted the urge to scream what he was thinking. *That's it? Your wife is dying, you haven't been in this room for hours, and that's all the time you have to give?* Instead he followed his father into the hall and demanded in a quiet voice, "Where are you going?"

"I have patients to see, obligations to meet."

"There are other doctors who can see to those patients, just as they have been seeing to mine. You can't take one day off work to be with her while she's dying?"

Phillip Brandt straightened his tie and gazed at the wall. "She's not there anymore, Jon. I've said my good-byes. She knows I love her."

"Well, it's a good thing somebody does," Jon said. Phillip glared at him.

"You'd do well to keep your opinions to yourself, son, especially when you have no idea what you're talking about."

"I know that your medical practice is more important to you than the fact that your wife will likely not be here when you get home today."

The subtle hurt in Phillip Brandt's eyes quickly disappeared behind a hardened expression—one Jon knew well. "Considering that you care *nothing* for your medical practice, I won't even expect you to understand." He glanced toward Carol Brandt, resting peacefully, then added with definite sarcasm, "I know I'm leaving her in good hands."

While Jon was attempting to get past the familiar hurt and confusion enough to retort, Phillip hurried down the stairs. The slamming of the front door infuriated Jon, but its finality forced him back to the reason he had approached his father in the first place. He pushed an urgent hand through his wavy brown hair and tugged at it, as if doing so might somehow aid him to think clearly. He looked through the open doorway of his mother's room to see Sara leaning on one arm, looking distressed. He hurried to the bed and found his mother awake, her eyes full of concern. He wondered if she'd overheard the angry conversation in the hall. In spite of it being a typical exchange between his father and him, he didn't want his mother's final moments to be marred by such animosity.

Jon forced a pleasant demeanor and sat beside her, taking her hand into his. He found its coldness a stark contrast to the warmth in her expression. "Where's your father?" she asked in a strained voice.

"He's . . . gone to the office," Jon said, forcing his voice to remain free of the bitterness he felt.

She looked more relieved than upset before she closed her eyes, as if it was just too much effort to hold them open. She sighed and squeezed his hand. "You've taken such good care of me," she whispered and briefly opened her eyes to smile at Sara. "Both of you. I couldn't ask for better children."

"There was never a better mother," Jon said. "Caring for you has been a pleasure."

"Jon," she said, looking briefly at him before she closed her eyes again, "you must make peace with your father. I know he can be difficult, but you must try to understand."

Jon wanted to tell her that he'd spent years trying to understand. He wanted to tell her that his father's harsh attitude and lack of acceptance were impossible to get beyond. But she knew all of that, and this wasn't the time to delve into pointless conversation.

Her grip tightened on his hand, and her eyes opened, urgency showing in them. "Jon," she said doggedly, "you must promise me . . . you'll not argue with him any more. He loves you. He's only wanted . . . what's best for you. Promise me."

Jon couldn't remember the last time he'd had a civil conversation with his father. He wasn't sure he knew how, especially when his father's approach was so condescending and unyielding. How could he promise something so impossible? But how could he *not* promise what she was asking on her deathbed? He glanced at Sara as if she could provide the answer. She nodded firmly and her eyes clearly said that if he didn't promise, she'd be tempted to slap him. He looked back at his mother, fully aware that every bit of her strength fed the urgency of her concern.

"I promise," he said firmly.

Carol Brandt closed her eyes, inhaled deeply, and smiled. She immediately drifted back to sleep with another deep breath. Sara let out a panicked gasp, as if she feared it was over. But their mother's breathing became perceptible and they both sighed with relief, not wanting to let go any sooner than absolutely necessary.

Sara slept intermittently, often lifting her head to make certain her mother was still breathing. While she did so, Jon calmly observed his mother's peaceful rest, although he could feel her hand in his becoming steadily colder. Jon had seen death more times than he could count. He knew the signs, and he knew it wouldn't be much longer; but he couldn't begin to understand how he was going to keep his promise to his mother.

CHAPTER ONE
Running West

Less than an hour after his mother's funeral, Jon tossed a suitcase on his bed and haphazardly filled it with his belongings.

Sara appeared in the doorway. "What are you doing?" she asked, her voice raised in both panic and accusation.

Jonathon glanced quickly toward his sister and kept packing. Just looking at her somehow magnified the pain. If the black dress and her swollen eyes weren't enough to remind him of his loss, she was the spitting image of their mother.

"Jonathon!" she said when he didn't answer. "Tell me what you're doing."

"I'm leaving," he insisted quietly, remaining focused on his task. "I've got to get out of here."

She gasped and sunk into a chair near the door. "Why?" she asked breathlessly. When he said nothing she added, "What's brought this on?"

"Don't pretend to be surprised. You know as well as anybody how much I hate it here. I stayed for Mother. If you must know, I did it *all* for Mother. But she's gone now. And none of it matters anymore. I have to get out of here."

"You're serious," she said, gasping again.

He paused a moment to catch her expression and shook his head. "You think I'm packing this thing just to entertain you? Of course I'm serious."

"But . . . why the rush? Surely you can take some time to—"

"Time will only put me in a position where I'll end up breaking that promise I made. I've managed to keep my mouth shut long enough to get through the funeral. I can't expect myself to remain disciplined much longer when he's criticizing me every chance he gets."

Sara's expression made it clear that she understood, and she obviously didn't have any alternative solutions. She protested softly, "But what about . . ."

"What?" he demanded when she hesitated.

"What about me?" She stared him down. "Don't you care if you ever see me again?"

"What about you? I love you, but you have a life here, Sara. You have friends. You have Mr. . . . Hartford, or whatever his name is. And I'm certain Father will keep you plenty busy."

"And what about Father?"

Jonathon glared at her. "What *about* Father?"

"When you made that promise, I'm certain Mother didn't want the solution to be your running away. You can't just up and leave him . . . while he's grieving."

"Forgive me for my insensitivity, Sara, but I really don't care."

"You *are* insensitive. And selfish, too."

"*I'm* selfish? Oh no, my darling sister, I'm just the one with enough self-respect to know that staying would only make a bad situation worse. Maybe one day you'll realize that you can *never* make him happy. You can *never* be good enough. And that is after you've spent your whole life struggling to do just that—to just be . . . *good enough.*" He sighed and turned to rummage through his dresser drawers. "I stopped trying a long time ago. What I did I did for Mother. I stayed for Mother. There's nothing here for me now."

"But . . . Jonathon . . . the funeral barely ended an hour ago. Surely you can take some time to—"

"I should have packed before I went to the church. I could have been gone by now."

He heard her sigh, then sniffle, and he forced himself not to look at her. "Where will you go?" she asked.

"I don't know exactly. I'm going west. California, probably. I think I'll stop in Utah and see Aunt Ellie. After that . . . well, I don't know. I'm just going west."

"You're not just *going* anywhere, Jon. You're running. I may be your baby sister, and you may think I put up with too much, and maybe you're right, but I do know one thing—you can't run away from what's eating at you. If you ever hope to find any real happiness, eventually you're going to have to turn around and face it head on." When he said nothing she added in a tone of resignation, "Are you hearing me, Jon? You can't run from your problems."

"Thank you for that gem of advice, Sara. You think I've never heard that before?" He fastened his suitcase and moved toward the door. "I'm not running from my problems. I'm starting over. Simple as that."

"Wait," she said, and he hesitated in the doorway. "Don't forget this."

Jonathon turned slowly to see her holding up his medical bag. He was about to tell her that he wouldn't be needing it, that it represented something he hated—that it had always been *the* sore point between him and his father; but she quickly continued, "Or are you running from this, too?" He glared at her, but she added with a degree of warmth, "If you come across someone in trouble on your journey, you might wish you had it. Besides, Mother gave it to you. She would want you to take it."

Jonathon reached out and grabbed the bag, tersely thanking her.

He hurried down the stairs of the fine home that had seen each day of his childhood, brushing away any possible sentiment that might hold him back. He ignored his sister's footsteps following close behind, but her hand on his arm made him hesitate.

"I'll miss you, Jon," she said gently. "You must be careful."

He turned to see her tear-stained eyes filling with fresh mist. "There's no need to cry over *me,* Sara. I'll be fine. And so will you."

"You'll write?"

"Of course. As soon as I'm settled I'll let you know."

Sara nodded and bit her lip. "Is there anything you want me to tell Father?"

"Just tell him . . . good-bye for me. And tell him to treat you well." He set down his suitcase in order to touch her face. "You're a good woman. You deserve to be treated well."

Their embrace was brief, but fraught with emotion. She was all he would miss. Looking into her eyes once more he felt a moment's hesitation, but it was quickly squelched by the fear that their father would return home before he had a chance to get around the corner. He had little beyond angry memories of his father as it was; he didn't want an angry farewell that would only mar his final memories of his mother. He had to leave here. *He just had to.*

* * * * *

As the train jolted, Jon came abruptly awake and reoriented himself to his surroundings. The rhythmic jostling of the train held a certain comfort, and he closed his eyes again, relishing in the freedom it offered. The growing distance between his father and him felt painfully good, the painful aspect being that he would have far preferred to feel some minuscule sorrow in thinking he might never see his father again. As it was, the very idea was pleasant, if not utterly relieving. An endless string of arguments catapulted through his mind, with hardly a pleasant memory to soften them. In contrast, he couldn't recall his mother ever raising her voice to him, ever speaking unkindly, ever behaving in a way that made him wonder if she loved him. Her love had been pure and rich and real. And it was for her that he had patiently, and penitently, tried to please his father, certain that one day a magical healing would take place. But it never had. And eventually Jon had come to accept that he would never be able to find value in his father's eyes. Of course, his mother had compensated greatly. Carol Brandt had been Jon's anchor. She had kept his feet on the ground and his heart believing that there were good things to be found in this world. But she was gone now. The illness had come on suddenly and taken her with little warning. And the only grain of hope Jon found in losing her was the way her death had severed the wearing threads that kept him bound to his father. Her death had been painful, but the freedom it offered him was a poignant gift.

Startled by the hot tears leaking through his closed eyelids, Jon hurriedly wiped them away and forced his mind to the future. The train ticket he'd purchased would take him to some obscure town in central Utah, the closest station to his aunt's home. Thinking of Aunt Ellie dried his tears and brought an unconscious smile to his lips. He'd not actually seen her in at least ten years—or was it fifteen? But his memories of her were warm and bright, and her regular letters had been a radiant spot in his life. Across the miles her written words had expressed a keen interest in him—one that had made it easy for him to pour out his feelings and struggles in the letters he'd regularly sent in return. He'd always been baffled that she had the same blood, the same upbringing, as his father. But rather than questioning the contrast, he'd simply been grateful for her presence in his life—however distant. The prospect of now being able to see Ellie, and spend some time with her, assuaged the hovering ache he felt with his mother's absence, and he concentrated on his destination.

The time it took to travel the continent astounded Jon, and he completely lost track of the days while he drifted in and out of sleep at irregular intervals. He felt certain his body was making up for the complete exhaustion from the endless hours he'd spent near his mother's bedside. He hadn't wanted to miss a single moment with her once he'd realized the end was imminent.

With thoughts of his mother he drifted to sleep, but was startled awake by a deep voice speaking close by. When he realized the conductor had been addressing him, he said, "I'm sorry. What was that?"

"It's your stop, young man. Less than five minutes."

"Thank you," Jon said, and sat up a little straighter. He focused on the view out the window with suddenly more interest than he'd felt over the endless miles of scenery they'd passed previously. He'd heard Utah described as desert and mountains; but what he saw was a stretch of hills, small ones merging into mountains, covered with sagebrush and cedar trees.

The grinding of the train coming to a reluctant halt prompted an edge of nervousness in Jon. It only took a few minutes to get his bags, but he wasn't sure how to get his bearings. As the train pulled away, his view of the area broadened. He turned and looked all around, feeling somehow comforted by the awe he felt at his surroundings. Every direction he turned there were mountains. What he had first considered mountains from the train window, he quickly redefined as large hills in contrast to the distant blue peaks he could see in the opposite direction. He turned a full circle three times, and had to say it aloud, as if it might be more convincing. "Mountains every direction. Incredible!"

Jon finally focused on his surroundings in closer proximity, and he wondered exactly where to go from here. The address on his aunt's letters had simply been: *Eleanor Jensen, Sterling, Utah*. Well, he was in Sterling. But now what?

"Excuse me," he said to a couple of middle-aged men that were standing nearby and chatting. "I wonder if you could help me. Are you from around here?"

"That we are," one of them said with a wide smile and an extended hand.

Jon put down one of his bags to receive the solid handshake.

"What might we do for you?" the other one asked, shaking Jon's hand as well.

"I've come to visit my aunt, but I have no idea where she lives, and—"

"Who might that be?" the first one asked, hooking his thumb behind the strap of his sun-faded overalls.

"Eleanor Jensen . . . Uh, Mrs. David Jensen."

"Of course," he said with a little laugh. "I'll tell you what, son. I've got a quick errand to see to, and then I'm headed out that way. I'd be happy to give you a lift as far as the fork. And then it's just a hop, skip, and a jump from there."

"Thank you," Jon said. "I'd be most grateful."

The two men exchanged a quick farewell and Jon followed his benefactor to a rough, flat-bed wagon, hitched to two work horses.

"You can put your bags in the back there," the man said, motioning briefly with his hand while he climbed onto the seat at the front.

"Thank you," Jon replied, and set his bags amongst an odd array of sacks and boxes. It was evident this man had come into town to stock up on a number of things. He climbed onto the seat only a moment before the horses jerked the wagon forward and Jon grabbed hold of the board he was sitting on.

"So, what might your name be?" his new acquaintance asked.

"Brandt," he answered. "Jonathon Brandt."

"You're not from around here," the man said.

"No," he said, not having to wonder if it was so readily evident; his clothing alone had made him feel terribly out of place among what few people he'd seen. And he'd quickly picked up on the distinct clip in his voice that sounded so different from the voices he'd heard chattering around him at the station. "I come from Boston."

"Whew! Long trip. And you say you're a nephew to Ellie?"

"That's right," Jon said, finding some comfort in hearing the familiarity of her name.

"Well, it's mighty fine to have you here, son. Would she be expecting you?"

"No, the trip was a bit impulsive. Even if I'd written a letter, I likely would have beat it here."

"Could be," he said.

"And what might your name be?" Jon asked.

"I'm Brother Mortensen," he said. "But you can call me Ernest."

"It's a pleasure to meet you, Ernest," he said. "Call me Jon."

Ernest halted in front of a small house on the outskirts of town. "I'll just be but a minute," he said and jumped down.

He pulled a box out of the back of the wagon and Jon asked, "Can I help?"

"No, thanks. I got it."

While Jon absorbed the stretches of rich, green fields surrounding him, he contemplated the way this man had introduced himself. *Brother* Mortensen. Until now he'd actually forgotten that Ellie's reason for settling here was her marriage to a Mormon—and her subsequent conversion to his faith. She mentioned a little about their customs and beliefs occasionally in her letters, but Jon had honestly forgotten. For him, religion was something he'd participated in to please his mother. And while he might call himself a Christian, he was personally indifferent as to whether or not God took any interest in his life at all. He had nothing against God, beyond the fact that it had been one more disgruntlement between his parents. While his mother had firm beliefs and took religion seriously, she had mostly lived it passively—at least on the surface—because his father had taken the view that religion was mostly nonsense. He only kept up with minimal involvement for the sake of public appearances—he'd wanted the outside world to see him as a religious man. Jon viewed this attitude as hypocrisy, and had long ago decided that taking a passive stand himself was the best way to keep the peace.

But now Jon had landed himself in the middle of a Mormon community. He suddenly wished he had paid more attention to what little his aunt had written regarding their beliefs and customs, just so he could know what kind of people he was dealing with. He certainly didn't want to offend anyone, but neither did he want to be expected to somehow become involved.

Jon pulled a cigarette out of his pocket just as Ernest emerged from the little house, empty-handed, and walked toward the wagon. He sensed some disdain in the subtle glance he was given as Ernest climbed onto the seat, which prompted him to ask, "Mind if I smoke?"

"I don't mind," Ernest said, "but I'll warn you, most of the people around here won't take kindly to it. You'd do well to indulge in the habit privately."

Lesson one, Jon thought. *Mormons don't smoke.*

"Don't mean to be offending you," Ernest said, starting the horses forward. "I just—"

"Oh, I'm not offended," Jon insisted. "I'd rather know up front than offend someone else."

Ernest chuckled, seeming pleased with Jon's attitude. "I grew up with smoking in the house," he said. "So it doesn't bother me. But then I joined the Church as a youth and gave up that sort of thing."

"Then I take it you weren't born around here," Jon said.

"Nah. I come from Kentucky, myself. Been here just about forty years, though. Started out in Manti—that's about six miles or so from here—then a bunch of us settled out this way, oh, about twenty years ago, I guess it's been."

"You like it here," Jon stated.

"I do, yes."

"You have family?"

"My sweet Martha and seven children. Only got two left at home, though. The others have married and moved on."

Ernest rambled on about his children and grandchildren, while Jon wondered how far from town Ellie lived. But he didn't feel impatient. He was enjoying the scenery, the distance from Boston, and yes, even the company. He liked Ernest and was glad he'd managed to ask the right person for directions. If he hadn't gotten a ride, it would have been an awfully long walk.

When a lull came in the conversation, Jon lit another cigarette and asked, "So, what else should I not do around here—besides smoke?"

Ernest chuckled comfortably. "Well, do you chew?"

"No," Jon said.

"That's good. It's kind of hard to spit tobacco without drawing attention to yourself." Jon chuckled and he went on. "Cussing doesn't go over very well, either."

"That's not a problem. My mother never allowed it."

"Good for her. Would she be Ellie's sister, then?"

"No," Jon said, hating the way his mood fell with the question. "Ellie is my father's sister. I've not seen her since I was a kid, but we've kept in touch through letters."

"Will you be staying long?"

"Hard to say," Jon said, not wanting to sound committed one way or the other. "Anything else?"

"What?"

"That I shouldn't be doing?"

"Well," Ernest chuckled, "if you're looking for drinking and women, I'm sure you can find 'em, but if you're looking to be respected by the community, you'd do well to stay away from such things."

"I'll keep that in mind," Jon said. The women wouldn't be a problem. He'd always taken the attitude that he'd rather wait for the right one to come along, as opposed to wasting his time with women who were either brainless or simply out for a good time—or both. And while he was rather fond of wine with dinner, and an occasional brandy, he could live without it. And he certainly wasn't looking to go out and get drunk.

"Well," Ernest said, pulling the wagon to a halt, "here's where you get off." Jon glanced around and could see nothing beyond a lane going off to the right, which disappeared over the curve of a hill. He wondered over the definition of *a hop, skip, and a jump,* as he viewed the distance of the lane. He jumped down as Ernest added, "It's the house at the end of the lane. Can't miss it."

"Thank you," Jon said, lifting one of his bags from the back of the wagon.

Ernest handed him the other one, apparently taking notice of it as he asked, "You a doctor?"

Jon fought off the urge to feel defensive. "Not really," he said, wishing he'd left the bag in Boston. But he reminded himself of what his sister had said: *Mother gave it to you. She would want you to take it.*

He was startled by Ernest's warm laughter. "Either you are or you're not, son. Which would it be?"

Jon hoped to close the argument firmly when he stated, "I'm qualified to be a doctor, but I never wanted to be, therefore I don't consider myself one."

"Suit yourself," Ernest said, apparently unaware of the terse undertone in Jon's statement. "But if there's one thing the world doesn't have enough of, it's doctors. We know that well enough around here."

Great, Jon thought with sarcasm. *If word gets out that I'm a doctor, I'll have no peace for as long as I'm here.* He reminded himself to be gracious and ignored the comment, holding out a hand. "Thank you for the ride, Ernest. It's been a pleasure getting to know you."

"And you, young man. Enjoy your stay now. I hope to see you around."

Jon nodded and began walking up the lane before Ernest pulled away. The noise of the wagon wheels quickly dissipated in the distance, leaving in the silence only the rustling of a faint breeze and the occasional chirping of birds. He couldn't help but admire the tranquility surrounding him. The late summer day was only slightly too warm for comfort, but after a hearty walk over the rise of the hill he was decidedly thirsty.

A moderate two-story home, painted white, appeared through the trees and he moved on eagerly. But by the time he got to the head of the long dirt drive leading to the house, he could see another house a little further up the lane. Not recalling exactly what Ernest had said, he felt momentarily confused. Impulsively he headed up the drive of the closest house, figuring if it wasn't Ellie's, perhaps he could at least get a drink of water to get him through that last stretch of the lane. The term *neighbor* took on new meaning here in contrast to the neat rows of houses lining the streets in his Boston neighborhood.

Closing in on the house, he noted how the rough ground merged into rich lawn, with no definite border in between. Bushes of roses in several colors intermingled with each other until they met with the porch, where potted plants marked the path to a large swing hanging at one end. Jon liked the feel of the house and could well imagine his aunt living in such a place. As he approached the door he could hear piano music playing. He paused a moment to listen, marveling at such obvious talent. He'd always loved music, always been touched by it. Hearing it now reminded him of Sara, although he ventured to say that she was not nearly so fluid with the piano as what he was hearing now. He felt an indescribable tingle rush through him just before he lifted his hand to knock. When the music continued he knocked louder and it stopped.

"Come in!" he heard a feminine voice call. Jon set his bags on the porch and barely had the door open before he heard that same voice again. "Hello Ellie. You can leave the plums on the table. Mother's out in the garden."

The music began again immediately. Jon closed the door and peered from the hallway into the parlor where he could see the profile of a young woman seated at an upright piano, her long fingers moving furiously over the keys. Her blonde hair waved back off of her face and into the thick knot that was pinned at the back of her head. Jon was intrigued with her playing, but forcefully interrupted his own contemplation in order to make his presence known.

"Excuse me," he said loudly and the playing stopped abruptly. She turned startled eyes toward him, so he quickly added, "I don't mean to alarm you, but I'm not Ellie. However, I think you've already answered the question I came to your door to ask, so I'll just be on my way . . . but . . ."

"But what?" she asked when he hesitated.

"I . . . uh . . ." Jon heard himself stammering and wondered why his initial desire to just hurry along had vanished.

"May I help you?" she asked with a warm trill of laughter, as if she found his staring at her somehow humorous. But seeing her face break into such a genuine smile only heightened his fascination. She almost had an unearthly glow about her, enhanced by a vivid sparkle in her green eyes. While he was tempted to believe that he'd seen her somewhere before, he knew it was impossible. He never would have forgotten such a face.

Hearing the silence grow long he forced his voice past the lump in his throat. "Forgive me," he said. "You're playing just . . . well, it's very good . . . very touching."

"Thank you," she said. When he didn't go on, she added, "You were saying . . ."

"Oh, yes. I was looking for Ellie Jensen's home. I was a little confused over the directions, and I wasn't certain if it was this house or the one up the lane." He fidgeted with the hat in his hands. "But as I said, I think you've already answered that question, so . . . I should just be on my way and—"

"But?" she said expectantly.

"Excuse me?"

"When you first came in, you said 'but' and you never finished the sentence. Is there something I can do for you?"

Jon thought quickly. "Oh," he chuckled, "I think I was just going to bother you for a drink of water, but I don't want to impose, or—"

"It's not a problem." She erupted with that genuine laughter again and he couldn't help but smile. "The kitchen's just around the corner. There are some clean glasses by the water pump. Help yourself."

"Thank you," he said, and he hurried to get himself a drink, while the piano music resumed. It was a melody he didn't recognize, but he liked it. He couldn't help noticing the tidy coziness of the house, and he felt reluctant to leave. With his thirst satisfied he quickly returned to the parlor, reminding himself that he had no business being here and he'd do well to move along.

"Thank you again," he said, and the music stopped. "I'll be on my way and—"

"Is Ellie expecting you?" she asked, turning more toward him on the bench and folding her hands in the lap of her dark skirt.

"No," he said and glanced down, "but I'm hoping she'll be glad to see me anyway." Looking up again, he noticed she seemed more curious than concerned at having a strange man in her home. He stepped forward and held out his hand. "Forgive my lack of manners. My name is Jonathon Brandt. I'm Ellie's nephew."

"Really?" she said and her face lit up even more—if such a thing was possible. She shook his hand eagerly and added, "Would I dare guess that you're from Boston?"

"That's right," he said, and grinned, hesitantly letting go. Her handshake was warm and firm, especially for a woman.

"Ellie's mentioned you occasionally. You exchanged letters quite regularly, I believe."

"That's right," he said again, his pleasure increasing.

"I'm Maddie Jo Hansen," she said.

"Maddie Jo," he repeated, liking how it felt to say it.

"Actually," she laughed, "it's Madeline Josephine, but everyone calls me Maddie Jo."

"It's a pleasure to meet you, Maddie Jo. Or maybe I should call you Miss Hansen."

"Maddie Jo is fine," she said. "Actually, Maddie isn't such a mouthful. And we don't hang on formalities around here."

Jon felt himself smile, and admitted, "I wish I could say that Ellie had told me all about *you.*"

"Well," she laughed softly, "I'm certain she has better things to write than gossip about her neighbors."

"On the contrary," he said, "I must get her to tell me everything about you."

Something subtly darkened in her eyes before she turned them down and he wondered if he'd offended her somehow. She quickly looked back up, her eyes smiling again as she said, "You might as well have a seat, Mr. Brandt. Ellie's supposed to be along any minute. I think I'd like to see her surprise when she meets my new friend."

"Are we friends?" he asked, taking a seat close to the piano.

"If you're related to Dave and Ellie, then we *must* be."

"Then you should call me Jon."

"Very well, Jon," she said. Following a moment of silence she erupted with some nervous laughter that made him wonder if she felt as awkward as he did. He couldn't help hoping that meant she was as intrigued with him as he was with her.

"Listen, Jon," she said, "you might be able to do me a very big favor."

"Anything," he said, wishing it hadn't sounded quite so dreamy.

She laughed again. "The thing is . . . Ellie is somewhat mischievous, and a bit of tease."

"Really?" he asked. At her surprise he added, "I mean, well, I haven't actually seen her since I was . . . I don't know . . . it's been years. We've kept close through letters, but I'm certain there are many aspects about her that I don't know."

"And the other way around too," she said. "But that makes it even better."

"What?"

"What I want you to do."

"And what's that?"

"Well, let's just say I owe Ellie a little surprise. And since she's not expecting you. . ." She laughed again. "Do you think she'd even recognize you?"

"I don't know." He laughed with her. "I guess we can have some fun finding out."

"Yes, I believe we can. Before she gets here, maybe we could . . ."

A knock at the door stopped her and she put a hand over her mouth to suppress a giggle.

Jon whispered, "Do you want me to hide or—"

"No," she whispered back, "just . . . go along with me, okay?"

"Okay," he said.

"Come in," she called and the door opened. "Is that you, Ellie?"

"It is indeed," a woman's voice called and the door closed. She whisked quickly past the parlor with a bushel basket against her hip. "I'll just set these in the kitchen and—"

"And then you can meet a friend of mine," Maddie called.

Ellie returned only seconds later, wiping her hands on her long apron. "Hello," she said with a bright smile, her eyes focused curiously on him. Her hair was streaked with gray and her face had become lined. But she was the same Ellie. The smile that lit her eyes was something he could never forget. Jon felt so glad to see her he was hard pressed to keep from jumping to his feet and hugging her. But he smiled in return and waited for the surprise to unfold.

"This is my neighbor and dear friend, Ellie Jensen," Maddie said.

Jon rose and held out his hand. "Hello," he said as she slipped her hand into his.

"And you might be . . ." Ellie said more to Maddie, waiting for the introduction to be completed.

Maddie laughed and said, "Doesn't he look just a little bit familiar?"

Ellie squinted and scrutinized him closely without letting go of his hand, as if holding it might enlighten her. "Uh . . ." she said, "you're . . . Melvin . . . Melvin . . . what was the last name?" Maddie laughed and she added, "You're Melvin . . . that boy who used to live out by the mill and moved to Provo when you were twelve."

"No," Jon laughed and Maddie laughed with him. He felt certain if he said more than one word at a time, his accent would give him away.

"Not even close," Maddie said. "Come on, Ellie, think."

"I've really met you before, eh?"

"Yes," Jon said.

Maddie laughed, as if she were having the time of her life.

"You think this is funny?" Ellie said as if she were angry, then she laughed as well.

"It is, indeed," Maddie said. "I haven't had this much fun since the time I woke your rooster up in the middle of the night and had you cooking breakfast at three in the morning."

Ellie looked mildly alarmed only a moment before she laughed. "If that's the last time you had any fun, we've got a problem, young lady. That was years ago." She added to Jon, "And there she was, peeking through my window in the middle of the night, just watching me work and laughing."

Jon chuckled while he absorbed Maddie Jo Hansen once again.

He recognized that sparkle in her eyes now; it had a mischievous root. Her spunk and mischief made her all the more attractive.

"Now, don't change the subject, Ellie," she said. "You must tell me where you've met my friend before."

"You look awfully familiar," Ellie said to Jon, "but I'm afraid you've got me stumped." To Maddie she said, "Give me a hint."

"He's just arrived from Boston."

"Boston?" Ellie echoed in a raised pitch. "I have family in Boston. Maybe you'd know them."

"Maybe," Jon said with a chuckle. Maddie's laughter increased dramatically and Ellie looked into Jon's eyes with a skeptical search.

"Ellie," Maddie finally said, "I'd like you to meet my new friend, J—"

"No, don't tell her," Jon said. "First I want to know if she remembers caramel apples on the Fourth of July, and—"

"Jon?!" Ellie shrieked as he laughed. "Jon!" she said even louder. "Is it really you?"

"It really is," he said as she jumped into his arms. He lifted her feet off the floor and turned circles while they laughed together.

"I don't believe it," she said as he set her down and helped steady her balance. "What are you doing here?"

"I came to see you," he said. "What other reason could there possibly be?"

"Okay. But what are you doing . . . *here?*" She glanced around.

"He stopped to find out which house was yours," Maddie provided.

"And we became fast friends," Jon said.

"I just can't believe it," Ellie said, taking a seat as if she'd suddenly become weak in the knees. "Well, I certainly don't want to interrupt whatever the two of you might have been . . ." She hesitated just a moment, and Jon barely caught Ellie giving Maddie an inquisitive glance. When he turned toward Maddie, her expression was completely innocent. But Ellie's voice was subtly unnatural as she added, "However, I do have a lot to do at home, so we'll just have to pop back in tomorrow."

"That would be wonderful," Maddie said brightly and held out a hand toward Jon. "It was a pleasure meeting you, Jon. I hope you'll stay around long enough that we can get to know each other better."

"I hope so, too," he said, bending to kiss her hand rather than settling for a cursory handshake. Their eyes met before he slowly let go, and he had to tell himself that love at first sight was a ridiculous notion.

"Is there anything you need, dear?" Ellie asked Maddie with a slight ring of concern.

"No, of course not," Maddie said. "I'll see you tomorrow."

Jon followed Ellie out the door and picked his bags up off the porch.

"I was wondering who those belonged to," she said, leading the way across the lawn to a buckboard she'd obviously come in.

"You came to pick me up in style," he said.

Ellie laughed. "If I had known you were here, I certainly would have. But honestly, I'm not carrying a bushel of plums all the way up the lane. It was less work to harness the buckboard."

Jon set his bags inside and helped Ellie up. She laughed for no apparent reason as he sat beside her.

"What?" he asked, laughing also.

"I just can't believe you're here. It's incredible."

"I hope it's not a problem," he said. "It was kind of impetuous. I didn't figure sending a letter would make much difference if it got here the same day."

"Of course it's not a problem. And your timing's good. Everybody's healthy at the moment, and Dave Jr. just left for school, so we have a spare room. I mean . . . we've always got the guest room, but it's a bit tight. You can use Dave Jr.'s room."

"Anything is fine," Jon said. "It'll be a joy just to spend some time with you, but I don't want you fussing over me or letting me hold up anything you're doing. And if there's anything I can do to help, don't be afraid to say so."

"Oh, I won't be afraid to say so. Me and Dave can put you to work, no problem. But I won't have you lying to me."

"Lying to you?" He nearly gasped. "When have I ever lied to you? I haven't told a lie since I was four years old, and—"

"Then don't be telling me that coming here was impetuous. You've been talking about coming for ten years. Leaving Boston's been in your blood at least that long. Sounds premeditated to me." She smirked and winked at him, and he realized she was teasing him. "I'd say it's about time you lived up to your word and came to see your old auntie."

"Old?" He looked around. "I don't see anybody old."

"Well, maybe you should get your eyes checked," she said, and laughed.

Jon unharnessed the horse while Ellie rambled about how different he was going to find life on the farm. She talked about the chickens and goats and cows and the names she'd given them, and he found her chatter perfectly delightful.

Walking together toward the house, she said soundly, "It's so good to have you here, Jon."

"It's good to be here," he said.

"But I have to ask . . ." She stopped and turned to face him. "What happened?"

"What do you mean?"

"You've been threatening to go west for years. Why now?" Jon looked down, attempting to gather his words, but she added, "What are you running from, Jon?"

He looked up sharply. "I'm not running, Ellie. It was time to move on. Simple as that." She looked mildly alarmed, as if she'd grasped the implication. Did she know there was only one occurrence that could have broken his ties with Boston? He responded to the expectancy in her eyes by saying, "Mother died."

Ellie sighed deeply and her eyes darkened. "I'm so sorry, Jon. What happened? I had no idea."

"The illness came on suddenly. There was little warning, and little time to notify anyone. By the time we realized she wouldn't recover, she was gone in a couple of days. I left right after the funeral."

She sighed again. "How's my brother taking it?"

"It's difficult to know, Ellie. To me, he didn't seem any different while she was sick, or after she was gone. I'm certain he's grieving in his own way, but he won't let anybody close enough to share it."

Ellie nodded, showing a concerned smile. She moved on toward the house and Jon followed. "So, what are your plans?" she asked, opening the door while he carried his bags into the kitchen.

"I don't have any, to be quite honest."

"You still got a notion to settle in California?"

Jon refused to admit aloud that he didn't have near as much of a notion as he had before he'd met Maddie Jo Hansen. He was more inclined to let time tell if what he'd felt in her presence might have any promise for him. He just smiled and said, "I don't know, Ellie. Maybe I'll like Utah so much, there won't be any need to move on. We'll just have to see."

Ellie smiled broadly, as if the idea gave her great pleasure, then she led him upstairs to Dave Jr.'s room. She left him to get settled in and freshen up. Jon put some of his things into the empty dresser drawers and laid a hand over the pieced quilt on the bed. He admired the fading wallpaper, covering the ceiling that slanted almost to the floor, and adding a cozy look to the room. He walked over to peer through the gabled window that jutted outward from the house. His heart quickened. Through the trees he could see the two-story white house where he'd encountered Maddie Jo Hansen. And he smiled.

CHAPTER TWO
Plums and Frogs

Maddie craned her neck for a final glance through the curtains at Jonathon Brandt as he helped Ellie into the buckboard. Her heart quickened all over again and she tingled recalling his overt interest in her. Long after her mother came in from the garden, and they worked together at the kitchen table to sort the plums Ellie had brought, Maddie's mind continued to wander back through her encounter with Ellie's nephew. She unconsciously laughed, and was startled from her thoughts when her mother did the same.

"What is it, dear?" Sylvia Hansen asked.

"What do you mean?" Maddie responded, feeling almost guilty. A part of her wanted to harbor this feeling inside of her forever, as if it could be preserved and left untainted.

"I don't know where your mind is, but you've had a silly grin on your face ever since I came in."

Maddie laughed again. There was no reason to keep any secrets from her mother. "Well," she drawled, "I met a man."

Sylvia glanced around the kitchen and down the hall, making Maddie laugh again. "Did this man appear out of the woodwork, or something?"

"Almost," Maddie said. "He just . . . walked in the front door."

Maddie soothed her mother's alarm by quickly recounting the circumstances of Jonathon Brandt's arrival. She found it impossible to keep working as she fully concentrated on describing this man who, for the first time in years, had brought any measure of excitement and diversity into her life.

"His hair is brownish, more dark than light; slightly wavy, hangs over his collar a bit, combed back off his face. And his eyes . . . Oh, mother . . . his eyes. I think they're hazel, and they sparkle when he smiles. He smiled a lot. He wore a bowler hat, although . . . I didn't actually see him wearing it. He was holding it. You don't see bowlers around here very often."

"No, you don't," Sylvia said, a smile teasing her lips. Maddie was encouraged by her mother's obvious pleasure.

"And his clothes were fine. It's evident he's well educated and comes from a fine family."

"He's from Boston, you say?"

"That's right. And you can hear it in his voice. I really like the way he talks, especially the way he said my name, and . . ." Maddie heard herself heave a long sigh and became suddenly self-conscious. "Listen to me rambling on," she said, forcing herself back to sorting plums. "You must think I'm terribly silly."

"I think it's good to see you so happy. Perhaps you'll have an opportunity to see more of Mr. Brandt while he's in town."

"Perhaps, but . . ."

"But?"

"Oh, Mother, there's no point in pretending that any such interest could ever come to anything."

"And why not?" Sylvia pressed gently. "He may end up being as decent as he seems."

"I believe he is decent; I can just feel it."

"You always were a good judge of character."

"Not always," Maddie said sadly. "But . . ." she sighed, "decent or not, I know he's not a member of the Church."

"Are you certain?"

"Well, hasn't Ellie said that she's the only member in her family?"

"Yes, but that was a long time ago," Sylvia said.

"I think if one of her relatives had been baptized she would have mentioned it. I doubt little could thrill her more."

"I'm sure you're right."

"But I believe Mr. Brandt smokes."

"Really?" Sylvia didn't seem as concerned as Maddie thought she should have been.

"He had that aroma around him, you know, the way the Peterson kids always smelled because their dad smoked."

"Yes, I know."

"But he probably just doesn't know any better," Maddie said.

"Maybe we could be a good influence on him." Sylvia smiled almost mischievously.

"Perhaps," Maddie sighed, "but as it stands, Father wouldn't appreciate such a man showing an interest in me."

"I know your father can be difficult, Maddie, but you're a grown woman. You must follow your own heart. You can never be sure what good might come out of a difficult situation."

"Yes, but. . ."

"Listen, honey," Sylvia took hold of Maddie's hand across the table, "you can't just assume that Mr. Brandt would find your situation distasteful, just because others have."

"Well, I would just prefer he never find out."

Sylvia sighed. "A relationship certainly can't go very far in that light."

"Relationship?" Maddie's laugh was void of any humor. "The best I can hope for is some temporary diversion. So, what's the point? I simply don't want him to know."

"He'll find out eventually."

"Better later than sooner. If nothing else, maybe if he gets to know *me* before he finds out, well . . . I'd just prefer he didn't know."

Sylvia sighed. "Whatever you say, but . . . you should keep an open mind."

Maddie persisted with her mundane task while her mind wandered back to her brief visit with Jonathon Brandt. And once again, she couldn't keep herself from giggling a little.

* * * * *

Jon quickly felt comfortable in his aunt's home. She gave him a quick tour of the house and yard and he noticed that in spite of visible differences, the cozy mood and tidiness reminded him a great deal of Maddie Jo Hansen's house. And he liked it.

They visited while she prepared supper, and he helped by cutting some vegetables that she added to a simmering broth. Her husband, Dave, came in from the fields with their sons, Fred and Joe. Both were gangling teens, similar in height and build, and both strongly resembling their father. All three had the same lean build, sandy-colored hair, and light blue eyes. Throughout supper Jon was assaulted with questions, and he quickly felt comfortable with Dave and the boys. As soon as the meal was finished, he excused himself to the backyard for a cigarette. His mind wandered to his encounter with Maddie Jo Hansen and his heart quickened. At the moment his deepest hope was to see her again—as quickly as possible.

Jon returned to the house to find Fred washing dishes and Joe drying them.

"May I help?" Jon asked.

"They've got it taken care of," Dave said with a little smile toward his sons. "We don't want you denying them the opportunity to learn to work."

"I think we've learned that pretty good, Papa," Joe said facetiously.

"Yeah, I'd say," Fred echoed.

"I don't want you to deny me the opportunity to work for my room and board," Jon said to Dave. "As long as I'm here, you must have something to keep me busy."

"I'm certain we can come up with something," Dave said.

"If you're not opposed to woman's work," Ellie said, still clearing the table, "we've got plums coming out of our ears. We'll be working like mad tomorrow to get as many of them preserved as we can before they spoil."

"Just show me what to do," Jon said. "I'd be glad to help."

"It doesn't take much talent," Ellie said. "The first thing you need to do is get a good night's sleep. We'll be leaving early."

"Leaving?" Jon echoed.

"We'll be doing it at the Hansens'. Sylvia's kitchen's bigger, and we just work better together. We've been doing it this way for years."

Jon couldn't help smiling. "How pleasant," he said, and Ellie laughed.

"I can see right through you, Jonathon Phillip Brandt."

"Me?" he asked with exaggerated innocence.

"What's this all about?" Dave asked.

"I think Jon's taken a fancy to Maddie Jo," Ellie said with a little wink, and Jon felt his smile deepen. He wasn't about to deny it.

"Really?" Dave said, seeming pleased, but Jon noticed a rueful glance pass between Joe and Fred. He was distracted from it when Dave added, "She's such a sweet girl. You just might be good for her, Jon."

"And the other way around, perhaps," Ellie said with another wink.

In response to her teasing, Jon purposely stared at her and moved deliberately closer, as if he'd seen something horrible.

"What?" she gasped and touched her hair. "Is there a spider? What?"

Jon got close enough to touch her ear and said with a scolding tone, "Shame on you for lying to me, Ellie Jensen."

"What are you talking about?"

"You told me there were plums coming out of your ears." He clucked his tongue with mock disgust as she laughed and playfully hit him. Dave and the boys were obviously amused.

When the kitchen was all cleaned up, Dave said to Jon, "Won't you join us for scripture study?"

"Uh . . . sure . . . I'd love to."

"He has no idea what you're talking about," Ellie said.

"But I'm always open to an adventure," Jon admitted.

Jon sat with the family in the parlor and listened while Dave read aloud from a book of scripture. He'd grown up attending church and hearing countless stories from the Bible, but he quickly realized that he must have missed something. During a break, while Joe went to get his father a glass of water, Jon said, "I don't recall ever hearing that story before. We must have had a different Bible."

"Actually," Dave said as if the question pleased him greatly, "this book is more of a companion to the Bible." He held it out to Jon, who took it and kept his finger between the pages where Dave had been reading.

"The Book of Mormon," Jon read aloud from the cover. He was glancing through the pages when Joe returned with the water.

"Why don't you read for a few minutes?" Ellie said. "Dave just can't get rid of that frog in his throat since that last cold."

Jon gave his aunt a comical glare. "Plums in the ears. Frogs in the throat. You people are strange out here in Utah."

Fred and Joe laughed heartily and Jon added, "You even have your own scriptures."

"That's right," Ellie said. "So read. Start where he left off." She pointed to the place and Jon cleared his throat.

"But behold, every man that lifted his club to smite Ammon, he smote off their arms with his sword. . ." Jon hesitated. "Is this true?" he asked Ellie with a skeptical glance.

"It is," she said so firmly that he was taken aback.

"I love this part," Joe said. "It gets better. I like it when the servants take in all the arms Ammon cut off to show the king."

Jon chuckled. "Okay. Where were we?" He continued to read, feeling himself drawn into the story, and he enjoyed the warmth he felt with his aunt's family. He was disappointed when Dave called study time to a close. And while he felt a bit awkward kneeling with the family while Dave offered a prayer, he couldn't deny that it was a nice way to close the day.

When Joe and Fred went off to their rooms to turn in, Jon escaped to the yard for a cigarette. He came back to find Ellie still seated in the parlor, reading from the Book of Mormon. He felt compelled to linger with her a few more minutes before going to bed, but they ended up talking until nearly midnight, and he went to bed with so many thoughts churning around in his mind that it was quite some time before he actually slept.

He was awakened early by Ellie's knock at his door, and her sweet voice calling, "Breakfast is nearly on. Then we've got to be going." Jon groaned when he couldn't see even a hint of daylight, then he recalled that they were going to see Maddie Jo Hansen. He was suddenly filled with energy. He put on his most casual clothes, but when he went down to breakfast it was quickly evident he was overdressed. He determined that if he was going to be staying more than a few days—

which seemed feasible as well as favorable—he'd do well to buy some different clothes.

The sun was barely showing itself when Jon and Ellie climbed onto the wagon—one very similar to the one Ernest had driven—and headed toward the Hansen home. There were three more bushels of plums loaded into the back, and Ellie had consented to let Jon drive.

Jon carried a basket of plums into the Hansen kitchen and found Maddie Jo seated at a large table, busily cutting plums in half and removing the pits. Just seeing her again filled him with a childlike excitement. He returned her smile and set the basket down, saying eagerly, "Hello, Maddie. You're looking lovely this morning."

"Thank you," she said, turning her eyes down. With the back of her hand she brushed a stray wisp of blonde hair from her face. "How are you settling in?" she asked, looking at him again.

"Great," he said. "At this rate, I might never want to leave."

She broke out in that sweet little laugh of hers and he sat down across from her, taking up a little knife to imitate what she was doing. He also decided that he genuinely liked Maddie's mother, and he felt certain she liked him, too. Sylvia Hansen was a little shorter than Ellie, and about the same age, he guessed. Her mild features and dark hair, pulled back tightly, showed almost no resemblance to Maddie's, but they shared the same sparkle in their eyes.

The hours of the morning passed quickly while Ellie and Sylvia bustled around the kitchen, and Jon and Maddie cut and pitted an endless supply of plums. They all talked and laughed in a way that made Jon feel completely at home and comfortable. It was easy to imagine that he'd been living on a farm and preserving plums his entire life. Boston seemed pleasantly distant and obscure.

The kitchen filled with steam and the pleasant aroma of simmering plums. Jon learned they were making plum jam, plum jelly, and just plain bottled plums. And of course, they'd be having plum upside-down cake for supper tomorrow.

Jon marveled at the way his initial attraction to Maddie deepened through their conversation. She was bright and intelligent, and when he mentioned that he and Ellie had stayed up until midnight discussing the Book of Mormon, he was amazed at her knowledge of the book and its origination. Listening to her discuss her feelings on the matter, he felt a shift taking place within himself on matters of God and religion. He took a break only once for a cigarette, but he appreciated the few minutes it gave him to allow his impressions of Maddie Hansen to settle into him. In briefly pondering her attitude on theology, it occurred to him that while he would have classified his mother as a religious woman, Maddie was more spiritual. He made a mental note to further analyze the difference and went back in the house to find Maddie gone. He resumed his task for a short while until Ellie asked him to go out with her to the yard where he helped her do a cursory sorting of another bushel of plums, setting aside the ones that weren't yet ripe enough to be preserved.

They went back in the house to find Maddie seated at the other end of the table, making some sandwiches with thick slices of bread, cold roast beef, and cheese. They all sat together to eat lunch, and Ellie took the liberty of telling Sylvia and Maddie everything she knew about Jon. She teased him about his mischief as a child, and expressed appreciation for his diligent letter writing that kept her feeling close to her brother's family, even though he rarely ventured to write a letter. Jon was completely comfortable with the conversation until she said, with pride in her voice, "And Jon is a doctor."

He attempted to glare at her, but she simply smiled and focused her attention on Sylvia and Maddie, who were listening with absorbed interest. She told them all about his years of education, and the thrill she'd felt when he'd finally earned his medical degree. And she told them details that he'd actually forgotten about some of his experiences working in a prestigious hospital in Boston. It was evident that Sylvia and Maddie were impressed, which made it all the more difficult for him to admit, "You know, Ellie, that's all well and good, but I've put that behind me now, and—"

"What do you mean by that?" Ellie demanded, as if he'd told her he would be shaving his head and joining a monastery.

"I mean . . . I just don't think it's really me."

"Then what exactly did you intend to do with the rest of your life?" Ellie asked firmly.

Jon warded off his temptation to get defensive and sought for something to lessen the tension. "I don't know," he said lightly. "Maybe I'll become a farmer and grow plums."

Sylvia and Maddie both laughed, but Ellie didn't seem impressed. He was glad the subject changed when Sylvia said, "Jon, if you're finished eating, could you bring in another basket while we hurry and get lunch cleaned up?"

"I'd be happy to," he said, and hurried outside. He had a cigarette while he was at it and returned to find Maddie once again pitting plums.

"Well," he said, sitting across from her and resuming his work, "now you know everything about me. Tell me about you."

"There's not much to tell," she said. "This is where I was born. Life is pretty simple here."

"You've spent a lot of time with the piano," he said. "Time well spent, I might add."

"Thank you," she said. "I enjoy the piano."

By asking questions, Jon learned that she was an only child. That along with farming alfalfa, her father made furniture, and he was presently away taking a load of furniture to Provo to be sold—a trip he took regularly, twice a year. He'd return just in time to start on the final hay cutting of the season.

"So, do you help with that too?" he asked.

"What?" she said, seeming alarmed.

"Cutting hay."

"No," she turned her eyes down and seemed slightly nervous, "I mostly stick to the kitchen."

"So," Sylvia said from across the kitchen, "have you read any of that book yet?"

"Book?" Jon asked, disoriented.

"You said earlier that Dave had given you a copy of the Book of Mormon. I was wondering if you'd read any of it yet."

"Only what I read out loud with the family last night," he said, "but I'll get right on it."

While Jon's mind wandered, Ellie started in on an observation Dave had made recently on somebody in the book named Abinadi. If nothing else, he thought, his reading the book would give him something to talk about with Maddie and her parents. He was pleased to see that Sylvia seemed to like him, and she didn't seem concerned with his obvious interest in Maddie. He hoped her father would be equally agreeable when he returned. He wondered how particular Mormons were about courting and marrying other Mormons. *Marrying?* What was he thinking? He'd barely known her a day. But she smiled at him and he found the idea ludicrously delightful. He tried to imagine himself settling in Utah and becoming a farmer. He chuckled at the thought, but didn't find it necessarily distasteful. Maddie silently questioned the reason for his laughter. He just smiled and shook his head to let her know it wasn't important, then he wondered how they could manage to communicate silently when they were practically strangers.

Jon was distracted from his thoughts when the room became suddenly silent. He glanced up to see Sylvia and Ellie whispering near the stove. A few minutes later, Ellie said, "You're doing a fine job there, Jon, but I think Dave could probably use some help out in the field. Why don't you take the wagon out to the north section and I'll walk home when we're finished."

Jon wanted to protest. He wanted to insist that he stay here and be with Maddie every waking moment he could get away with. But he forced himself to be gracious and dignified as he rose to his feet, saying, "I'll work where I'm most needed. Would you like me to come back for you?"

"No, that's fine," Ellie said. "Thank you, anyway."

"Will we be doing plums again tomorrow?" he asked, wishing his voice hadn't sounded so urgent.

"No," Ellie said, "what few aren't ripe yet won't be ready for three or four days at least."

While something felt mildly unnatural, Jon didn't question it. He concentrated instead on the desperation he felt to see Maddie again as soon as possible. A quick glance at her left him relatively certain that she shared his desire. He cleared his throat gently and hurried to say, "It's been a pleasure, Maddie. I wonder if I might come by tomorrow and pay you a visit."

He liked the way her face brightened and she erupted with that laughter he was coming to love. She shot a brief glance toward her mother, as if for approval, and he wondered if she was younger than she looked. He took a glance at Sylvia and his aunt, and sensed that they were pleased. "I'd like that very much," she said.

"What time would be convenient, then?" he asked, washing his hands at the water pump.

"How about ten in the morning?" Maddie suggested.

Jon turned to Ellie and asked like a child, "Will I be done with my chores by then, Aunt Ellie?"

"If you get up early enough," she said with a wink. "Go on. Get out of here." He smiled and moved toward the door, and she added, "And thanks for your help."

"It's been a pleasure," he said. To Sylvia he added, "It was nice meeting you, Mrs. Hansen. Thank you for lunch." To Ellie he said, "I'll see you this evening." And then bowing slightly toward Maddie, "And I will see you in the morning."

"I'll be counting the hours," she said with a little laugh, and he couldn't help but smile again.

Jon couldn't find Dave and the boys. He wondered if he'd misunderstood where Ellie had said they would be, or if he was just confused on the layout of the farm. But he could have sworn she said the north section, and he had figured out which way was north once he'd learned that the distant mountain peaks were to the southwest. He finally returned to the house and found them in the barn, joking and laughing more than doing anything productive.

"What are you doing here?" Dave asked. "I thought you were in on the plum project."

"I thought so, too," Jon said, feeling something uneasy prickle at him. "Ellie said she thought you could use my help in the north section."

Dave looked confused but simply chuckled and said, "She must have been mistaken. We finished there yesterday."

Jon nodded and managed a smile, wondering why the women had wanted to get rid of him. He forced the thought away and asked, "Well, is there anything I can do?"

"Sure," Dave said, "me and Fred were just heading out to repair a fence, and Joe's going into town to pick up a few things. Maybe you could go along with him. You can help him load the grain, and you mentioned you might want to pick up a few things."

"Sure," Jon said, feeling about as needed as a hole in the head.

Jon enjoyed his little excursion with Joe, although he discovered there was nowhere in town to buy the practical clothing he was hoping to acquire. Joe mentioned that they had to go to Manti to get anything beyond the most basic items.

"If you're taking the wagon," he said, "you got to plan a whole day to get there, back, and do your shopping."

"I'll just have to set a day aside and do that," Jon said.

The ride home was mostly silent, in contrast to the ride out where Joe had talked nonstop. The silence spurred Jon to speculate more on the uneasiness he'd felt about being sent away with a flimsy excuse. He decided that at the first opportunity he'd just come right out and ask Ellie, rather than stew over it. Knowing he couldn't do anything about it at the moment, he thought about his appointment with Maddie in the morning, and once again he asked himself if he could spend the rest of his life farming in a Mormon community. He laughed and reminded himself to give such a decision more than a day's thought.

Jon felt anxious to talk with Ellie, and he was relatively bored without anything to occupy his time, so he was disappointed to find that Dave was taking care of supper and Ellie would be late. He was grateful to find that Dave wasn't a bad cook, and he helped the boys with the dishes. When it became evident that study time and prayer would wait until Ellie's return, Jon took a lamp to the back porch and read from the Book of Mormon where he could smoke as much as he needed to assuage his nervousness. While his motives in reading the book were far from religious, he couldn't help being intrigued.

When Ellie finally returned, there wasn't a moment to speak with her privately before the family gathered to read and pray. As soon as the *amen* was spoken, she declared exhaustion and excused herself to go to bed. Jon knew he'd never sleep if he didn't get some answers and he quickly said, "Could I talk to you for a minute first? I won't keep you long."

"Sure," she said and pulled a shawl around her shoulders, leading the way to the front porch.

"What is it?" she asked, sitting on the step as if she had all the time in the world, when a minute ago she'd declared she had to get some sleep.

Jon sat beside her and put his elbows on his knees. He cleared his throat and forced his voice past a sudden bout of nerves. "I just have to know if I've done something inappropriate, or . . . well, I try to be sensitive to what's going on around me, and I didn't think I was out of line, but . . ."

"I have no idea what you're talking about, Jon. As far as I can see, you've been perfectly appropriate. Is there something specific bothering you?"

"Yes, since you asked. It makes little sense to me that I was sent to help Dave when he didn't need any help. And you probably could have come home a couple of hours ago if I'd stayed to help *you.*"

She looked at him sharply and he knew he'd hit on a sore point—if only he understood what it was.

"Well?" he said when she looked away but said nothing. He sensed she was choosing her words very carefully. "Have I done something wrong?"

"No, Jon, of course not. There are simply some reasons why it would be difficult for you to be at the Hansens' for too long, and I thought it would be best if we finished without you."

"*Reasons?*" he questioned. "What reasons?"

"It's really not my place to say, Jon. But I can assure you that it has nothing to do with you."

Jon sighed. "Well, okay. I don't like being left in the dark, but I do feel better knowing I wasn't being stupid or something."

"No," she laughed softly and put her hand on his arm. "You were a perfect gentleman." She paused and said, "You like Maddie Jo, don't you."

He laughed. "Yes, I do . . . very much, I think."

"And she likes you, I believe. I think you could be very good for her."

"You do?"

"Yes, I do. But I think you're going to have to be patient."

"Patient?" he echoed. But her eyes repeated what she had already said: *It's really not my place to say.* He attempted to be patient now and let it drop. "You'd better get some sleep," he said. "I don't want to keep you up past your bedtime *again.*"

"If you must know, I thoroughly enjoyed being kept up past my bedtime. We'll do it again sometime."

"When you're not so worn out."

"Precisely," she said and came to her feet. Before she went in the house, she put a hand on his shoulder and added, "It's really good to have you here, Jon. I hope you'll stay a good, long while."

Jon put his hand over hers and looked up. "The feeling is mutual, Ellie. Thank you . . . for everything."

She smiled. "I'll see you in the morning."

"Ellie," he said as she opened the door, "will you please let me know if I do something out of line?"

"I will," she said, "but I'm not terribly concerned. As I told you, you've been a perfect gentleman. Oh, and . . . thank you for not smoking in the house."

He chuckled. "Not a problem. Mother wouldn't allow it. I didn't figure you would appreciate it, especially when you don't even believe it's right."

"How did you know that?" she asked.

"Ernest told me . . . or words to that effect."

"Ernest Mortensen?"

"I believe that was his name."

"Oh that's right," she said. "You mentioned that he gave you a ride from town. Well, good night."

"Good night," Jon said. He sat on the porch for a long while, marveling at the silence of the night air and the brilliance of the stars, so unlike the streets of Boston. He finally stood up and took a deep breath, concluding that he could really get used to this kind of life.

When Jon found it difficult to sleep he read some more in the Book of Mormon and found he was actually enjoying it. He fell asleep while Nephi was making swords to defend his people and dreamt of his mother sitting in the swing on the Hansen's front porch. He woke up missing her, but the smell of breakfast cooking and the distant sound of Ellie's voice soothed his ache. The prospect of seeing Maddie later this morning spurred him to get cleaned up. He was determined to have a wonderful day.

After breakfast Dave and the boys set out to the fields, but Ellie insisted that Jon's help would be more appreciated in the kitchen before he went to visit Maddie. They chatted while they worked, and Jon felt as if they'd been talking this way forever. He reminded himself that in a way they had. Their letters back and forth through the years had truly been a strength to him. And he was grateful to be here now.

Just before he left to see Maddie, he ventured to ask, "Hey, I was thinking I'd like to ask Maddie out for a picnic or something, but I . . . well, do you think that's a bad idea or—"

"I think it's a wonderful idea, and if you're trying to ask for some help with the food, I'd love to. Tomorrow would be good, since we'll probably be finishing plums the day after."

"Great," he laughed. "Thank you."

"You're welcome," she said, "but . . ."

"But?" he asked, not liking the way her countenance fell.

"As I said, Jon, I think it's a great idea. I think it would be good for her. But Maddie might be hesitant. Don't get discouraged if it takes some effort to talk her into it. And it might take some time."

"Time? How long?"

Ellie laughed softly. "We'd love to keep you around until next summer."

Jon narrowed his eyes as if to ask her to clarify that, but she only laughed again. He wondered just how patient he was going to have to be.

"You'd better hurry or you'll be late."

Jon found Maddie sitting in the swing on her porch, right where he'd dreamt of his mother sitting. He hoped that was a good omen.

"Good morning," he said, stepping onto the porch.

"Good morning," she said with that smile that lit up her face.

He hesitated a moment, since the only other place to sit was next to her in the swing. He was just wondering if she might invite him into the house when she patted the seat next to her and said, "Won't you join me. It's really quite comfortable."

Jon sat beside her and found it to be plenty roomy. He chuckled with pleasure at the way it moved beneath him. He set it to a gentle rhythm and heard her laugh, musing that she felt nervous too.

"So," he said, "I bet you were up pretty late with those plums."

"It wasn't so bad," she said. "Cleaning up the mess is the worst part. But it was a fruitful day."

Jon chuckled at the unintended pun. When she apparently realized what she'd said, she laughed again. *He loved the way she laughed.* It was rich and generous and it lit up her eyes.

"How about you?" she asked.

"My day was all downhill after leaving here," he said, omitting any further explanation.

Following an awkward silence she asked, "So, are you really a doctor?"

Jon sighed. "I really am, although, as I said, I just don't think it's really me."

"Forgive me," Maddie said, "but . . . becoming a doctor takes years of education, and Ellie says you've been working in a hospital for quite some time. How can you be so diligent in pursuing something if it wasn't what you wanted to do?"

Jon swallowed the emotion connected to the question and simply answered it. "My father is a doctor, and he's very good at it. Being his only son, he very much wanted me to follow in his footsteps. I never wanted to be a doctor, and I always made that clear. My father's not known for being kind and sensitive; in truth he was always harsh and . . . dare I say . . . controlling."

While he was trying to gather his words to go on, she asked, "So why did you do it?"

"I did it because my mother wanted me to do it. She loved my father very much, in spite of his . . . challenges. And she would have done anything to please him. She was an angel . . . loving, kind, and generous to the heart. She understood how I felt, but she wanted me to please my father. I did it for her."

"Then you must not regret it," she said.

Jon was startled by the comment and had to think about it. "No, I don't suppose I regret it, beyond feeling that the years were somewhat of a waste. And I still don't know what I want to be when I grow up."

Maddie laughed. "You could become a farmer and grow plums."

Jon looked into her eyes. "I'm seriously considering it."

She apparently caught the serious undertone in his statement, because she looked down abruptly.

"Your mother died recently," she said.

"That's right."

"Tell me about her."

It was easy for Jon to talk about his mother, and subsequently he ended up talking a great deal about his father and some of the difficulties that had come between them. She listened attentively, offering compassion and perspective. He was amazed at how she could find something good in every situation.

After sitting in the swing for well over an hour, Jon suggested, "It's a beautiful day. Why don't we take a walk and you can show me the—"

"It sounds wonderful," she interrupted in a voice that seemed somehow unnatural, "but I am rather tired and . . . I should be going in soon anyway, and . . ."

"All right," Jon said. "Perhaps another time."

"Perhaps," she said without looking at him. Her normally bright countenance was dark and clouded. His conversation with Ellie came back to him, and he knew there was something strange taking place of which he was completely ignorant. He just didn't know how to ask.

When the silence became strained he felt certain he ought to be leaving, but he couldn't go without saying, "Listen, Maddie, I've had this urge to go on a picnic ever since I got here. I can't say why. I just have." He chuckled and felt pleased to see her smile. A degree of light returned to her eyes. "Maybe because there's just so much open space around here for such things. But . . . well, Ellie agreed to help me put some food together. Would you go on a picnic with me? Tomorrow maybe?"

That glimmer of light in her eyes faded into a deeper darkness. "It sounds lovely, Jon, but I just . . . can't."

"Why not?" he asked and she looked pointedly away.

Jon blew out a long sigh of frustration and attempted to think on how to handle this. He recalled Ellie telling him that Maddie might be hesitant with the idea, and it might take some effort to talk her into it. But he couldn't do that if he didn't understand her reasons for declining. He wondered what Ellie knew that he didn't.

"Listen, Maddie," he said, instinctively taking hold of her hand. It felt cold in contrast to her warm handshake the previous day.

She glanced at their clasped hands and smiled softly. But she still wouldn't look at him. "If there's a reason you feel uncomfortable with me, all you have to do is say so."

"Oh, no," she said, her alarm evident. "I enjoy your company very much, Jon."

"Okay." He sighed with some relief, but had to ask, "Is it because I smoke?"

Her alarm deepened, but she simply said, "No. I mean . . . I don't agree with it, and I would think that you should know better, but . . ."

"Know better?"

"Your being a doctor and all. You should know it's not good for you."

Jon wondered what he might have missed in medical school, but he let it go and listened as she went on. "I appreciate your not smoking around me, but it would never keep me from being your friend."

"Or going on a picnic with me?"

She smiled slightly and shook her head.

"Okay," he said, "is it because I'm not a Mormon? Is there some rule about sweet Mormon girls not going on picnics with men like me?"

She laughed softly, albeit tensely. "I don't have a problem with it," she said. "My father might not agree, but it's evident you're a decent man with a good heart. That's all that matters to me—at least as far as . . ."

"As what?" he pressed.

"Well, admittedly . . . we're just visiting on the porch and preserving plums together, but if you were . . ."

"What?" he asked again.

"Never mind," she insisted.

"No, please tell me."

"Well, when it comes right down to marriage . . . if I were to ever marry . . . it would be in the temple. But that's hardly relevant when we're just . . ." She blushed visibly and turned her face further away.

Jon took a moment to try and read between the words. Then, in his curiosity, he had to clarify one point. "So, I take it that *the temple* is where Mormons get married, and you're saying if I wanted to marry a Mormon girl, I—"

"That's hardly relevant," she insisted. "As I said, I don't have a problem with your not being a Mormon."

"Okay," he drawled, wondering what the implication was. He just had to say, "In light of what you said earlier, I'm having to assume that it's not a problem because you would never consider marrying a man like me, or . . ." She shook her head frantically before he could find a way to tactfully ask her reasons for saying: *if I were to ever marry . . .*

Before he could figure her reasoning, she said, "You're a wonderful man, Jon. This has nothing to do with you."

"Does it have to do with your father?" he asked.

"What do you mean?"

"You said your father might not agree. I have to assume you mean he might not agree with your seeing a non-Mormon."

"Well, I'm certain my father would have plenty to say about that."

"Great," he said with sarcasm. "I can hardly wait to meet him."

Maddie laughed slightly, but her expression sobered quickly when he asked, "Is it because of my age?" She looked confused, and he clarified, "Do you think I'm too old?" He didn't know how to politely ask how old she was. While he guessed twenties, he wondered by her concerns if she simply looked and behaved older than her years, and her youth made their associating improper.

"I shouldn't think so," she said.

He wanted to shout: *Then what is it?* But he simply tried to mull over any other possibility he could think of, reminding himself of Ellie's admonition to be patient.

"I know," he said, "you're like . . . a Mormon nun."

"A what?" she asked, but at least she looked at him and smiled.

"You've taken some kind of vows or something to remain single and not associate with men and—"

"No, Jon." She laughed softly. "There's no such thing as a Mormon nun." She sighed. "Forgive me. I know I'm being difficult, but . . . you must believe that the problem is with me. And I truly wish it could be different. I'd love to go on a picnic with you . . . but I just can't. I would enjoy having you come back tomorrow and visit, however."

Jon forced back his curiosity and disappointment. "I'd like that very much," he said. "Would the same time be all right?"

"Yes, of course."

She thanked him for his visit and he walked home. Each time he glanced back she was still sitting in the swing; then the lane turned and he lost sight of the front of the house.

CHAPTER THREE
The Truth About Maddie Hansen

When Jon arrived at the house he temporarily considered home, he sat on the front step and lost track of the time while he attempted to figure out the conversation he'd just had with Maddie. He was startled by the door opening behind him, and a moment later Ellie sat close by.

"I take it your picnic idea didn't go over very well."

"No," Jon chuckled and shook his head, "but then, you knew it wouldn't." He turned and looked at her pointedly. "Why?"

"Why what?"

"Why did you know it wouldn't? What do you know that I don't know?" She sighed and he turned away. "Oh, that's right. It's not your place to say."

"Well, I've been giving that some thought, Jon. Maddie asked me not to tell you, but Sylvia and I both agree that her reasons for keeping it from you are . . . well, not very logical; downright ridiculous, in truth. It's only a matter of time anyway before you find out . . . when the whole town knows."

Jon felt his heart quickening as he absorbed his aunt's grave countenance. Did Maddie have some dreadful disease? Is that why he hadn't seen her exert much energy? Why they hadn't wanted him around for extended periods of time? Why she'd been too tired to take a walk? Was she dying? He unconsciously pressed a hand over his heart at the thought. The very idea caused him such pain that he had to admit he was already far more emotionally involved with Maddie Hansen than he'd ever been with any woman. But then, no woman had ever made him feel the way she did. He'd never met anyone like her.

"What do they know?" he demanded.

Ellie looked into his eyes and opened her mouth to speak. She hesitated and swallowed. "The truth about Maddie Hansen is . . . well . . ."

"Wait," Jon said, holding up both hands. He hurried to make some sense of what he was feeling. With confidence he said, "If Maddie didn't want you to tell me, then you shouldn't. Whatever it is, I think Maddie should tell me herself." He stood up abruptly.

"What? Right now?"

"Sure, why not?"

"Well, for one thing, she's probably having lunch, which is what we should be doing. And maybe you should think this through a little more before you go barging over there and demanding answers."

"I had no intention of barging or demanding in any respect."

"Fine," she said, standing beside him, "but let's eat and . . . give it a little time, okay?"

"Okay," he reluctantly agreed.

While Ellie set lunch on the table, she told Jon that Dave and the boys had taken food with them in order to take advantage of daylight in the fields.

"Maybe I should have gone with them."

"There's no need for you to feel like you have to work, Jon. In fact, I think you've been working too hard for too many years. Why don't you just take some time to let life catch up with you."

He wanted to question her on that, but she asked him to sit at the table and she offered a blessing on the food. They ate in silence until Ellie said, "I know you've always gone to church, Jon, but I have to ask . . . Do you believe in prayer?"

"What do you mean?"

"Just what I said."

"Well, I suppose I do. I've never given it much thought."

"Then . . . you don't pray . . . personally."

"No. Should I?"

"Couldn't hurt. That's certainly up to you. I just wanted you to know that ever since I saw you and Maddie Jo together, I've . . . well, I must admit I've been praying that you could make a difference for her. Just keep that in mind."

Jon nodded, wondering why her statement left him feeling an almost tangible warmth. Following several minutes of silence, he said, "I get the feeling Maddie's father is . . . difficult."

"Why do you say that?"

"Oh, I don't know. I've heard very little, actually. I just get that feeling."

"Glen Hansen is a good man, Jon. Make no mistake about that. But he's very protective of Maddie, and he's very stubborn. If you must know, he reminds me a great deal of my brother."

"Father?"

"That's right."

Jon scowled, silently retorting with a sarcastic, *That's just great!*

As if she'd read his mind, Ellie said, "The good thing about that is . . . well, I think you could gain some understanding of the situation with Maddie and her father by looking at the situation with your sister."

"Sara?"

"She's the only sister you've got. And your father has always kept her tightly under his wing. I don't believe he's ever intended to make life more difficult for Sara. In truth, he's just been overly protective, especially since she had that bout with rheumatic fever."

Ellie got up to clear the table, leaving Jon with far too much to think about. He helped her with what he could, then went out to wander in the yard. His mind kept going to what Ellie had said about prayer. He wondered why she was hinting that he ought to start praying. Couldn't hurt, he thought. Making certain no one was around, he glanced heavenward and simply said, "Alright, God, if you're listening," he hesitated, feeling awkward and uncertain, "it would be nice if my visit with Maddie Jo Hansen went well. Ellie thinks I could help her. Maybe I can. Maybe she can help me, too. Either way, a little help would be nice. Thank you. Amen."

* * * * *

Mid-afternoon Jon knocked at the Hansens' front door. He knocked again but got no response. Unwilling to give up that easily, he wandered into the backyard and felt some relief when he found

Sylvia working in the garden.

"Hello, Mrs. Hansen," he said.

She looked up at him and grinned. "Oh, hello," she said and he felt more relieved that she was pleased to see him.

"I . . . uh . . . was hoping to talk with Maddie. Is she . . ."

"I think she might be resting. If you'll wait here a minute, I'll just go and see."

"Thank you," he said, and watched her disappear into the house.

More than ten minutes later she finally returned. "Maddie's in the parlor. Why don't you go on in?"

"Thank you," he said again, and he entered through the kitchen door where he'd come and gone several times the previous day.

"Hello," he said, entering the parlor to see her sitting prettily on the sofa.

"Hello." Maddie smiled up at him, marveling at the way just seeing him could make her heart pound.

"Forgive me for bothering you again today, but . . ."

"Oh, you would never be a bother," she said, wishing it hadn't sounded so wistful. "Please have a seat."

"Thank you," he said and opted for the sofa, right next to her, even though there were other options. He took her hand and she seemed pleased. Then he forced himself to get to the point.

"I realize our conversation earlier was . . . strained. And I must confess that it left me a bit confused. So, I've come back hoping to just clear up any confusion and get it over with." He wondered if the crease in her brow was a result of confusion or concern. He pressed on. "I must admit that there have been a number of things that just don't quite add up with the situation here. Ellie's made it clear that there is some issue here that I'm not aware of, but she tells me it's not her place to say. However, it's also evident that I'm the only one in town who *doesn't* know. That's understandable, my being a stranger here and all, but . . ."

Maddie heard pulse-beats in her ears, making it difficult to keep her head upright with the dizziness. A tight knot gathered between her eyes and she pressed her fingers there, willing it to go away before she burst into tears and humiliated herself further.

"Well . . . I've come to the conclusion that I really need to know what's going on with you, Maddie, but I don't want to hear it from gossip or hearsay. I realize we haven't known each other long, but it's evident that we've become fast friends."

Maddie felt his grip tighten on her hand. She attempted to turn her face away but he touched her chin to make her look at him. While his touch ignited something warm and sweet in her, the insistence in his eyes let her know she couldn't go on pretending. She had to tell him the truth. And she had to accept that she'd probably never see him again.

"Please, Maddie," he said, "tell me." When she squeezed her eyes shut but said nothing, he asked, "Why don't you want to tell me?"

"There was only one man who ever showed any interest in me at all," she said and tears leaked from beneath her closed eyelids. "Everyone else just steered clear of me, never bothering to become interested."

Jon couldn't believe it. One man? She was so beautiful, and talented, and thoroughly pleasant to be with. Were the men in this community blind? He kept to the point and asked, "And what about this one man?"

"He just . . . told me he couldn't live with it." Maddie forced herself to open her eyes and look at him. Reasoning that he'd already seen her cry now and she might as well just get it over with, she admitted, "I didn't want to tell you because I've enjoyed your company so thoroughly and . . . I've never met anyone like you and, well, I didn't want you to stop coming—or worse, come because you felt sorry for me . . . but then eventually you would have to tell me that you couldn't live with it, and . . ."

"First of all," he said, "I can't decide whether or not I can live with it if I don't know what *it* is. And secondly, if you've never met anyone like me, then it stands to reason that I'm not going to be like that other man."

Maddie couldn't help smiling at him. She wiped at her tears and had to admit, "You're so sweet, but . . ."

"But?" She only looked down and he pressed, "Just tell me and get it over with."

He watched her draw her shoulders back and lift her chin. "I can't walk, Jon."

Jon took a moment to absorb what she was saying. And a

moment was all it took. He felt incredibly relieved as everything suddenly made perfect sense. And he'd convinced himself so completely that she was dying of some dreadful disease; this seemed so insignificant in contrast.

Maddie turned away and squeezed her eyes shut, not wanting to see the shock and pity on his face. She was startled when he said, "And?"

She turned toward him in surprise. "And what?"

"Is that it?"

"What do you mean: *is that it?* Did you hear me? I can't walk."

"I heard you," he said. "Does that somehow make you less of a woman? Does it mean you have any less to give to the world than any other woman?"

"Perhaps," she said crisply, hating the way his question hit such a sore point for her. "Every woman I know works hard; they help in the fields, in the gardens. They cook and clean and do whatever needs to be done. I am capable of doing so little."

"No, what you're capable of is different, Maddie. If you didn't live in a farming community, I believe the differences would be much less apparent. Being different doesn't make you any less valuable, Maddie."

Maddie looked into his eyes, in awe at how thoroughly warming his words had been. The warmth increased when she saw the sincerity behind them. *He really meant it.*

Jon saw something warm and hopeful rise in her eyes, and he wondered how she could believe that her inability to walk made that much difference. He saw her eyes cloud over again and asked, "What else?" She looked confused and he insisted, "Something else is bothering you. What is it?" She hesitated, and he said gently, "Maddie, please talk to me."

"I'm sorry," she said and sniffled. "You're very sweet, Jon, but I can't help believing that it's only temporary and—"

"Temporary? Listen to me, Maddie. I can't predict the future, or where this relationship may lead us. At this point I'm not certain how long I'm even staying in Utah, but that does not make anything we might share temporary. We will always be friends, at the very least. And with any luck . . . maybe we will be much more than that."

Jon heard the words come out of his mouth and wondered when he had become so presumptuous. He was relieved to catch a glimmer of warmth in her eyes that seemed to echo what he'd said. But once again, they clouded over. Searching her eyes he asked, "What exactly did *this man* do that's made you so afraid to tell me what you're feeling?"

When tears appeared on her face again, he knew he'd hit on the problem. "You can't blame him, really, he simply pointed out that he needed a wife who could work with him and . . . give him children and—" Jon gave a disgusted sigh, but she went on before he could find a retort. "But it's true, Jon. I can't be a wife and mother, and I don't want you to think that I might be hoping you would . . . well, I mean . . ." She blushed visibly and turned away.

"Maddie," he said, once again touching her chin to make her face him, "listen to me carefully. Taking you on a picnic is not a marriage proposal. But under the circumstances I'm not going to pretend the prospect of that possibility has not crossed my mind. I think you're an incredible woman and I very much want to get to know you better. Now, speaking in generalities, I don't believe that a good wife is determined by her ability to work in the fields or stand over the stove. I would think that good conversation, genuine caring, a loving heart, and a good head on her shoulders would be far more important. And giving birth is the least of what constitutes motherhood, Maddie. There are many children in the world who are lacking in love and guidance. I doubt you would have to look far to find opportunities for mothering."

Maddie looked at Jonathon Brandt's hand in hers while she allowed the things he'd said to settle into her heart. Did he have any idea how thoroughly and completely he had soothed her aching heart and given her a hope she'd let go of years ago? If she never saw him again, she would be forever changed by his influence. As it was, she couldn't help hoping that their futures might be intertwined. She looked into his eyes, unashamed of the tears on her face. She couldn't help laughing to see the perfect acceptance in his expression. He just made her so thoroughly happy.

She was wondering where to begin to tell him that she hadn't been this happy in years, when he shrugged his shoulders and asked, "Would you go on a picnic with me tomorrow?" She laughed again, and he added, "We don't have to be gone long. I'm sure I can manage to carry you to the buckboard."

"I'd love to," she said, and he laughed with her.

"No buts?"

"No buts," she insisted.

"Now listen," he felt the need to clarify, "I know there are probably things you need help with . . . personal things . . . and it wouldn't be appropriate for me to help you. So you've got to be honest with me and tell me what you can and can't do, and what you might not be comfortable with. We can take your mother if . . . What's wrong?" he asked, noting her horrified expression.

"It's just so . . . embarrassing to be discussing such things with . . ."

"Forgive me," he said. "I don't mean to make you uncomfortable. But, well, I am a doctor. I'm accustomed to being very straightforward on such matters."

"Of course. Well, I suppose I'll get used to it. I can manage just fine without my mother if we're not gone more than a few hours."

"Good," he said decisively, "I'll pick you up at eleven."

"I'll be counting the hours," she admitted. He stood to leave and she kept hold of his hand. He looked down at her and she added, "Thank you, Jon."

"No," he said, pressing her hand to his lips, "thank *you.*"

Maddie found it difficult to keep from letting out a loud whoop the second Jon closed the front door. She watched through the curtain until he was out of sight, willing her heart to slow down. *She couldn't believe it!* Jonathon Brandt was like an angel sent from heaven. She wondered what she had ever done to deserve having such a caring, sensitive man come into her life. She prayed it would last, that his attention to her was not short-lived. It was easy to imagine living out the rest of her life with such a man, but she cautioned herself against getting carried away. She couldn't count on such things, especially looking at the differences in their lives. However long it lasted she would make the most of it, and maybe, just maybe, it could last a lifetime—perhaps even forever. She didn't find it difficult to imagine Jon embracing the gospel eventually. He was such a good man, with a good heart.

"Is he gone?" her mother asked, startling her from her reverie.

"Yes, but . . ." she couldn't suppress a little laugh, "he's coming back tomorrow to take me on a picnic."

Sylvia smiled brightly. "That's wonderful, darling. I take it you told him."

"I did, and he was so sweet and gracious. Oh, Mother. I never imagined that such a man existed." She glanced out the window. "I only pray that it's not too good to be true."

Sylvia sat beside Maddie and took her hand. "You're a good woman with a lot to offer, Maddie. Surely God would bless you with the love of a good man."

Maddie glanced down, hating where her thoughts wandered.

"What is it, darling?"

"I fear Father won't see the situation that way."

"I know your father can be difficult, but he's only concerned for your well-being."

Maddie smiled and nodded, but she knew deep inside that her father's concerns for her went far beyond what was necessary. She didn't understand them, which made her fear that he would never understand this need she had to break free from the confinement of her life.

She finally came to the conclusion that her father wasn't here, and for the moment, she would make the most of the situation. Surely when he returned he would be able to see how thoroughly happy Jonathon Brandt had made her.

* * * * *

Jon walked into the house and found Ellie rolling out a pie crust. She looked up eagerly.

"How did it go?"

"Very well, actually. We'll be going on a picnic tomorrow." He laughed for no logical reason. "And we got all that other nonsense straightened out."

"That's wonderful," she said. "I really didn't figure you'd have a problem with her condition."

"It's not a condition, Ellie. She doesn't have some chronic illness or terminal disease."

"All right then," she chuckled. "I didn't figure you'd have a problem with the situation."

"No, I don't."

"And I'm glad it's all out in the open."

"So am I."

Ellie nodded toward a letter sitting on the corner of the table. "That came today from Sara. She was writing to tell me of your mother's death." Jon picked up the envelope and touched his sister's handwriting. "She asked if we'd seen you; said you'd left in a hurry. Apparently your father was very upset."

"I expected him to be."

"You didn't even tell him good-bye."

Her tone was in no way critical, but he still felt the need to defend his point. "No, I didn't tell him good-bye, Ellie. If I had believed we could have had any degree of a warm farewell, I would have gladly told him good-bye. As it is, I know beyond any doubt that it would have simply turned into one more argument. He could not accept that I was an adult, capable of making my own decisions. He wanted to control my every choice, Ellie, and it would have eventually destroyed me. I stayed as long as I did for Mother. I've known for years that the best way to keep peace with my father was distance. Leaving quickly just alleviated certain . . . complications."

"I'm sure he never meant to hurt you, Jon. At heart, he really is a good man."

"That's what Mother always said. And I just had to trust that she knew what she was talking about. Personally, I saw little—if any—evidence of anything that wasn't harsh and difficult." When Ellie made no comment he said, "I've always wondered how you and my father could be so thoroughly different. You had the same upbringing, same parents, same struggles."

"Yes, but I believe we come to this world with our personalities. It's not what happens to us that molds us, Jon. It's what we do with what happens to us. We grew up poor and struggling, and our father was a difficult man. For me, I was always able to appreciate what we *did* have. Phillip could only see what we *didn't* have. And he deeply resented it. He worked very hard to become a doctor, and to become one of the best. I think he just wanted you to do the same, to ensure you would never go without. But you're right. He's not sensitive and caring, and he has many personal struggles. Deep down, however, I believe he has a good heart. He's just terribly confused."

"Well, whatever it may be, I couldn't live with it any more. Sara's much more patient than I am. I know she enjoys working with him, and in a way he's more gentle with her because she's more patient with him. And that's all right. I only hope Sara won't let him use up her life before she has a chance to live it herself."

"Is she still seeing that young man? What was his name? Mr. Hartford?"

"Yes, she's still seeing him. He's patient, too. I think the only way she'll ever marry him is if he consents to move into the house with her and Father. For me, I'm where I need to be. I really like it here, Ellie. I'm glad I came."

She smiled. "I'm glad you came, too. You're liking it here wouldn't have anything to do with Maddie Jo Hansen, would it?"

He chuckled. "It doesn't hurt, but I just like it here."

"Give it some time. You haven't experienced winter yet. Although I must admit, I do hope you'll decide to stay on. Having you around for a long time definitely appeals to me."

That evening Jon wrote Sara a long letter. He told her of his journey and how he was enjoying his stay with Ellie. He told her to tell their father he was safe and well and not to worry. He briefly mentioned Maddie Jo and sealed it up. Ellie said she'd have Fred mail it when he went into town the next morning.

Jon went to bed right after family prayer, and was up early to help Ellie prepare food for the picnic. They prepared enough for the entire family and then some, so it could be used for their evening meal. Jon certainly didn't have a problem with eating fried chicken twice.

The day was beautiful with a comfortable warmth and a hint of autumn in the air. He felt like a giddy schoolboy driving the buck-board toward Maddie's house. He arrived right on time and found Maddie sitting on the porch in a wheelchair—which answered a question he'd wondered over since he'd last seen her. He was glad to know that she had one. She wore a white dress and a white ribbon in her hair. He doubted he'd seen a woman so beautiful in his entire life.

"Good morning," he said, crossing the yard toward her.

"Good morning," she replied brightly.

He stepped in front of her and took her hand, first squeezing it, then kissing it. He felt warmed by the way she beamed, as if he'd just given her the moon. Was her life so dull? Had she been so secluded? Yes, he had to admit; it likely was, she likely had been.

"Are you ready to go?" he asked.

"More ready than you could possibly imagine," she said and they both laughed.

"Good morning, Mr. Brandt," Sylvia said, stepping onto the porch with a dishtowel in her hands.

"Mrs. Hansen," he nodded, "how are you today?"

"Well, thank you. And you?"

"Rarely better," he said, glancing toward Maddie. "I promise I'll keep her safe and have her home in two or three hours at most."

"I know you'll take good care of her," she said.

Maddie held her breath as Jon easily scooped her into his arms. She loved the way he lifted and carried her so effortlessly, and the perfect security she felt in his arms.

"Have a good time," Sylvia called as he carried her to the buckboard. They both waved to her after he'd set her down.

"Comfortable?" he asked, and she nodded firmly.

He climbed up beside her and took the reins. She laughed heartily as they started forward. "It's just a picnic, Maddie," he said.

"Oh, it's heavenly," she said with zeal.

"You don't even know if the food is good yet. What if I ended up cooking it myself? It could be horrible."

"Even if it was, it would still be a glorious picnic. But I'll bet Ellie had a lot to do with it."

"She did actually, although I helped considerably. I'm actually enjoying the way she's teaching me to get around in the kitchen a little. Maybe by the time I get on my own I'll be able to cook enough to keep from starving."

Maddie smiled at him. He put the reins in one hand and put the other around her shoulders. She smiled again.

When they got to the end of the lane he asked which direction they should go. Maddie pointed the opposite direction from town. Just around the bend they passed a small house set among some trees that looked quaint, but neglected and run-down.

"Who lives there?" Jon asked.

"I think that was the Caldwell home," she said.

"You think?" he asked. "It's only a hop, skip and a jump from your own home." He smiled at his own imitation of Ernest Mortensen, but it was apparently lost on Maddie.

"Well, I don't get out much," she said matter-of-factly. "But I'm pretty sure that's the house Ethan Caldwell owned. He worked in the mines. His wife died in childbirth; the baby died, too. He started drinking and lost the house to the bank. Last I heard he moved in with some relatives in Moroni. The house has been empty a few years."

"I see," he said, glancing back at the house a couple of times after they'd passed by. He was surprised at the idea that appeared in his mind, but he couldn't help wondering how much it would cost to buy the house and fix it up. He wondered if the money he'd brought with him would be enough.

Focusing on the road ahead, they quickly found a perfect picnic spot. Jon spread a blanket out between a couple of trees, not far from a tiny creek. He carried Maddie to the blanket, loving the way it felt to hold her, the way she draped her arms around his neck, her natural dependency on him. Once she was situated he went back for the food. They sat close together, talking and laughing, and finally eating. Maddie offered a brief, but sincere blessing on the food, and it made him realize how much he loved her simple faith—her deep convictions toward God.

Maddie noticed Jon's attentiveness as they talked, and she couldn't believe how happy she felt. She couldn't remember the last time she'd been away from the house, or outside for more than a few minutes. The glimmer in Jon's eyes helped her believe that this was not short lived, that this was the first of many opportunities to be out in the world, to live life fully, and to know the companionship of a good man.

While she was loading everything back into the hamper, Jon leaned onto one elbow and said, "So, would it be rude of me to ask why you can't walk? Were you born with the problem or—"

"No."

"No what?"

"It's not rude, and I wasn't born with the problem. I fell out of a tree when I was a child." She laughed softly. "I was always somewhat of a wild child, always getting bumped and bruised from being so rambunctious."

"And into mischief, I'd wager," he said, "like waking Ellie's rooster in the middle of the night."

"Precisely," she said with a little giggle, then her countenance sobered. "Father was always telling me I was *really* going to get hurt one day." She sighed. "It seems he was right."

Jon didn't like the way she'd said that, but he couldn't quite pinpoint what exactly was bothering him. She started talking of some of her childhood antics, making him laugh. He began longing to spend every day with her. He noticed how easily she sat with a straight back, just as she'd done at the piano and working at the kitchen table. He determined that her paralysis must have been in one of the lower vertebrae. No sooner did the thought cross his mind, when he saw her reach down and scratch her ankle. He actually felt startled.

"Is something wrong?" she asked.

"You felt that."

"What?"

"You felt your leg itch."

"Yes," she laughed, certain he was teasing her.

"Forgive me," he said. "I just assumed that you were paralyzed."

"I don't understand."

"Well, the most common cause I've seen for an inability to walk is paralysis, which means, well, it's when the spinal cord is damaged or severed, which makes everything below that point unable to function properly, but it also eliminates all feeling." She looked only mildly interested in what he was saying, while his many thoughts were churning so quickly that he could hardly get them straight.

"Maddie," he finally said, "when you had your accident, did you see a doctor?"

"Yes. My parents took me to see a doctor in Salt Lake City."

"Do you remember what he said?"

"He said there was nothing to be done. Maybe I would walk again, and maybe I wouldn't."

"And what did he tell you to do?"

"He said to stay flat down for . . . I don't remember . . . two or three months, and then see if I'd healed enough to walk. When I tried I couldn't."

"Did you ever have any tingling or numbness?"

"Not that I recall."

"Did you ever have one leg feel heavier than the other . . . or not work as well as the other?"

"No."

"Have you ever had any pain in your back after the first few weeks?"

"No." She laughed. "Is there a point to this, Dr. Brandt?"

He smiled. "Just curious. But as long as you mentioned it, pretend I *am* your doctor for a minute and don't get embarrassed when I ask you some personal questions."

"All right," she said, apparently unconcerned.

"Have you ever had any difficulty with your bodily functions? You know what I mean?"

"Yes, I know what you mean," she said. "And I never have. I can even get myself from the bed to the commode without any help at all."

Jon laughed. "Now you're embarrassing *me*. One more question. Have you had normal menstrual cycles?"

She narrowed her eyes on him, then blushed and turned away with a little giggle. "Yes, Doctor, my cycles have always been normal. There's only one thing wrong with me. I can't walk. It's as simple as that. So, what's the point to all the questions?"

"Well, you mustn't take what I say as absolute. There can be exceptions to the rules when it comes to the human body. But according to what you've told me, it sounds perfectly logical to me that you could have children."

Maddie's heart quickened before her mind fully comprehended what he'd said. She heard a noise erupt from her throat, something between shock and laughter. Fearing she'd heard him wrong or misunderstood, she forced herself to say, "Are you sure?"

"Well," he laughed softly, "I can never be completely sure. Some people are simply unable to have children for reasons we don't understand. What I'm telling you is that your inability to walk should in no way lessen your chances for having children. You're healthy and strong. Your body is functioning normally." He grinned. "You'll never know until you try."

Jon watched her press her hands over her mouth while tears leaked down her face. He was hard pressed to keep from blurting out: *And I want you to have my children!* He knew it was ludicrous to believe that he could know she was the one for him in so short a time. But he was willing to give it all the time it needed.

"Are you all right?" he asked when she continued to cry.

She nodded vehemently and cried some more. He chuckled and pushed his arms around her, urging her head to his shoulder.

"I'm sorry," she said, "I'm just so happy. I can't believe that it's even a possibility."

"You should never be sorry for being happy," he said.

"All I ever wanted was to be a mother . . . to raise a family."

"Well, now you can, and if it turns out you can't . . . we'll adopt."

She looked at him abruptly. "We?" she asked, wondering if she could tolerate any more happiness in one day. By the way his eyes sparkled she wondered if his thoughts were similar to hers. Did he feel the deepening bond between them? Did he feel this unexplainable affinity that somehow made everything better when they were together?

"Slip of the tongue," he said, but she knew it hadn't been.

While she was wondering how to question his feelings, to know if he felt any of the stirrings for her that she'd felt for him, he grinned and said, "So tell me, Maddie Jo, as long as we're on the subject, would you ever consider marrying someone like me, provided I became a Mormon, of course?"

Maddie's heart threatened to pound right out of her chest. But she managed to calmly say, "Oh, you mustn't do it for me, Jon. If you ever decide to join the Church, you have to do it because you know it's right. If it doesn't come from the heart, it just . . . well it just wouldn't be right."

"Okay, so let's say I did it from the heart, because I knew it was right. Let's say I adopted your beliefs and—"

"But it's not just beliefs, Jon. It's not just religion. It's a way of life, of living. It's a way of having peace no matter what life brings you. It's having a spectrum of eternity that's simply impossible to describe."

Jon became briefly mesmerized by her conviction. "Okay," he finally said, "if I truly came to understand all of that—for the right reasons—would you ever consider marrying me?"

She gave a delighted little laugh. "It's preposterous to answer such a question when I've only known you a few days."

"I'm not proposing, Maddie. I'm just asking if you'd consider it."

Jon's heart skipped a beat when she looked firmly into his eyes and said, "Yes, Jon, I most certainly would consider it. I doubt that anything could make me happier."

Jon heard himself laugh. Then what could he do but kiss her?

CHAPTER FOUR
The Chasm

Maddie felt the missing pieces of her life fall neatly into place with Jon's kiss. He eased back only far enough to look into her eyes. Then he kissed her again. She felt his arm go around her; and found her hand in his hair.

"Oh, Jon," she said, when his lips pressed to her cheek, her brow, her cheek again. "Where have you been all my life?"

"Boston," he said, and they both laughed.

He looked into her eyes and touched her face. "Maddie, I don't want to sound presumptuous, but there's something I want to say—just to be perfectly clear. What I said about your being able to have children; such a thing would have nothing to do one way or another with the reasons I would marry a woman. Do you understand?"

Maddie nodded and fresh tears appeared in her eyes.

"I should be taking you home," he said.

"I suppose," she said, not wanting to ever let go of this moment.

"Don't worry," he said, as if he'd read her mind, "you can't keep me away for long."

The drive home went far too quickly for Maddie. Jon carried her to the front door of her house, and she laughed at the way he could efficiently open the door while holding her with one arm, as long as she kept her arms around his neck. He set her on the sofa and sat down beside her.

"Do you want me to leave?" he asked.

"No."

"Do you *need* me to leave?"

"If you'll get my mother and give me a few minutes, I'll just—"

"Where in the name of heaven and earth have you been?" a harsh voice bellowed, and Jon sprung to his feet. The man standing in the doorway bore a striking resemblance to Maddie in coloring and features. He stood as tall as Jon, with a sturdier build.

"Papa!" Maddie said. "When did you get home?"

"About two hours ago," he answered, glaring at Jon as if he were the devil himself.

"I want you to meet my new friend, Papa. This is Ellie's nephew, Jonathon Brandt, and—"

"I know who he is," Glen Hansen growled. "When I came home and found you gone, your mother told me all about him. And Ellie filled in the rest."

Jon attempted to ignore this man's anger, as Maddie was obviously doing. He extended a hand and said, "It's a pleasure to finally meet you, Mr. Hansen. I—"

"It's no pleasure to meet a man who traipses off with my daughter without my permission." He kept his hands behind his back and Jon had no choice but to retract his. "What business do you have taking liberties with a girl who has no means of defending herself?"

"Defending myself?" Maddie echoed. "Jon has been a perfect gentleman."

"Forgive me, Mr. Hansen," Jon said. "If you had been here, I would certainly have notified you of my intentions." He purposely avoided saying that he would have asked permission, seeing that Maddie was plenty old enough to make her own decisions. "Mrs. Hansen was well aware of our plans, and Maddie is perfectly capable of letting me know whether or not she wants my company."

Jon could see Mr. Hansen's anger building, and he hated the way countless memories of his father's stubborn anger came to mind. He'd learned a long time ago that getting angry accomplished nothing. Still, he was shocked and appalled when Mr. Hansen said, "You are not welcome here, young man, and you will not see my daughter again."

"Papa!" Maddie cried. "How can you say something like that when you know absolutely nothing about him?"

"I know enough," he bellowed. "No daughter of mine is going to keep company with a man who smokes and drinks and does not share her beliefs."

"Glen," Mrs. Hansen said, appearing at his side, "you can't shun a man who hasn't had the opportunities we've been blessed with. The gospel would never go forth into the world if we closed ourselves off from good people who—"

"My daughter doesn't have to be the one to share those opportunities," he retorted unkindly. Sylvia's frustration was evident, but she said nothing more.

"Maddie is an adult, Mr. Hansen," Jon said. "She is capable of deciding such things without—"

"Maddie has special needs and concerns that you have no comprehension of, Mr. Brandt."

Jon couldn't believe it! And he couldn't keep himself from saying, "Her inability to walk does not make her a child."

"You have no idea what you're talking about," Mr. Hansen said, stepping toward Jon with so much anger that he almost wondered if the man would strike him. "Now get out! And don't come back!"

Jon turned to Maddie, but she wouldn't even look at him. He quickly left the house, feeling the happiness of an hour ago come crashing down around him.

* * * * *

Maddie winced at the closing of the door, and squeezed her eyes shut in an attempt to hold back her burning tears. She was startled to feel her father's gentle hand on her arm.

"Maddie, sweetheart," he said in a warm voice that was more like himself. He took her hand and wiped at her tears. "You must forgive me for getting so angry. It's just that . . . you have to understand . . . I couldn't bear to see you hurt again—not ever. You must trust me when I tell you that such a man isn't good for you."

"But when I'm with him, I feel so—"

"It doesn't matter how he makes you feel, Maddie," he interrupted gently. "We have to consider the facts here. You're not like other women, sweetheart. And no one knows what's best for you better than I do. Haven't I always taken good care of you?"

"Of course, Papa," she said earnestly. She knew her father was a good man; he'd always been good to her, always had her best interests at heart. "But I want more out of life than this. And Mr. Brandt is—"

"Not the man for you," he said abruptly, but without anger.

Maddie felt so thoroughly confused that she couldn't even respond. She looked to her mother for support, but Sylvia only gazed at the floor and said nothing. Maddie turned to look out the window, almost wishing that Jonathon Brandt had never come into her life. The pain she felt now was a sharp contrast to the joy she'd felt in his presence. And she doubted that her few hours with Jon would ever compensate for the heartache he had left in his wake.

* * * * *

The few minutes it took Jon to drive home were just enough for his building anger to explode. Ellie came out of the house to meet him when he pulled into the yard.

"Are you all right?" she asked.

"No, I'm not all right," he snarled as he jumped down. He forced himself to unharness the horse, if only to keep his hands busy. "I have never in my life seen such a ludicrous display of prejudice and absurdity."

"I was afraid of that," she said, following him as he led the horse to the barn.

"He was here, I take it," Jon growled.

"Yes, he was here. I did my best to help him see reason, and I told him all of your finer qualities, but he was angry before he got here, and he left even angrier." She sighed. "What did he say?"

"He told me I was not welcome there, and I would not see his daughter again."

"Good heavens!" she gasped. "How can he justify such drastic measures?"

"That's what I'd like to know."

With the horse cared for, Jon slumped onto a bale of straw and pressed his head into his hands. "I can't believe it, Ellie. Earlier today everything seemed so right, so perfect. It was like I knew exactly what I wanted, what I was going to do. And now I'm just so . . . confused."

"Well, I'm not certain exactly what you're talking about. But first of all, I think you need to know how Maddie feels about all of this, and what *she* wants. And then you can determine where to go from there."

Jon sighed. "All right, but I've been forbidden to see her, and it's not like she can sneak out of the house to see me."

"So write her a letter. It's something you're very good at. You can think about what you want to say, and let her know exactly where you stand. I'll see that she gets it."

Jon took a deep breath. "Okay. I will. Thank you."

Jon took the picnic hamper in the house and unloaded it while Ellie kneaded bread. He had trouble believing how something that seemed so right had gone wrong so quickly. He was grateful for his aunt's presence in the room, and he felt compelled to ask her, "Ellie, is it ridiculous to think that Maddie could be the woman for me, when it's been so short a time?"

Ellie stopped and looked at him firmly. "What do you think, Jon?"

"It feels right, but logically it's so . . ."

"Sit down, Jon," she said and left the bread dough as it was. She turned a chair and sat beside him. "You're a good man with a good heart. You have to listen to that heart and follow where it leads you. When I met Dave, it seemed that my life changed instantly. I recall having similar feelings. Could he be the one? Could I know so soon? Of course, I didn't know for certain right away. It took some time and I weighed my feelings carefully. But looking back, I know that I *did* feel something right away. I believe that God guides us through our feelings, Jon, or through our hearts. You simply have to trust your feelings. But you don't have to decide your whole life today, Jon. You only have to decide how to work with what you have *now*. So go write her a letter and see what she has to say. And then we'll talk some more later."

Jon put his arms around her and kissed her cheek. "Thank you," he said. "You have a way of helping me keep perspective. It's nice to get your advice firsthand instead of waiting for it to come through the mail."

"Well, at least it saves some time," she said, returning to her bread dough.

Jon sat at the table to write his letter, feeling the strength of Ellie's wisdom supporting him. He'd only written a few sentences when he asked, "Do you think it's wrong of me to be showing interest in Maddie when I'm not of her faith?"

"Some people have very strong views on that—like Glen Hansen, for instance. You know, of course, that I married Dave before I joined the Church. My father was furious over my intentions to run off with 'that Mormon heathen.' But I'm grateful I did. I don't think it's wrong for you and Maddie to consider marriage. You simply have to be very clear on how your beliefs are going to work in the relationship. Maddie's love of the gospel is a big part of her life. You'd have to respect that and be willing to completely support her in those beliefs."

"But her father won't even let me in the door if I'm not a Mormon. Is it wrong of me to consider adopting her beliefs—your beliefs—just so I can have a chance with her?"

"It's wrong if that's the only reason you're doing it. I would advise you to study and learn our beliefs, and then search your feelings. You should consider it based on your conscience as well. In my opinion, Glen Hansen's attitude is out of line. Of course, we would all prefer that our children marry members of the Church. It makes things less complicated, and it brings great blessings. But I'm not certain that your being a Mormon would make *that* much difference to him. You have to do what's right for *you,* and you have to do it for the right reasons. And, if I may express another opinion, Maddie is going to have to reach a point where she sticks up for herself and declares her adulthood and independence. I truly hope that your presence in her life will help her do that. But it might take some time."

"I hear what you're saying, Ellie, and it all makes sense. But how can I know if I'm making the right choices *now,* for me *and* for Maddie? I can't see into the future."

"I have an answer to that question, but I'll have to get the bread in the oven first. Just write your letter and—"

A knock sounded at the kitchen door just before Sylvia stuck her head in.

"Hello," Ellie said. "Come on in."

"Hello," she replied, her somber mood evident. She added toward

Jon, "I'm so sorry about that. Glen can be a hard man. I know it may be difficult for you to understand, but he's coming from a great deal of hurt and fear." She handed him a folded piece of paper. "Again I'm sorry," she said. She nodded toward Ellie. "We're doing plums tomorrow as planned?"

"Of course. I'll be there early."

Sylvia left and closed the door behind her. Jon unfolded the piece of paper in his hands. He took a deep breath and read:

> *Dear Jon,*
>
> *I appreciate everything you've done for me, and I meant everything I said. But I can't go against my father's wishes. Please try to understand.*
>
> *With love,*
>
> *Maddie*

Jon stared at it for several minutes, attempting to read between the lines, to digest what it meant. He was vaguely aware of Ellie putting the bread in the oven. He turned to see her by his side, wiping her hands on her apron.

"May I?" she asked.

Jon handed her the note and pressed his head into his hands. He felt Ellie's hand on his shoulder. "Well," he said, lifting his head, "at least I don't have to wonder what Maddie wants."

"I don't think you have to wonder how Maddie feels, either."

"What do you mean?" he asked.

"Read it again, Jon. Read it with your heart. And then write your letter. We'll talk later."

Jon sat staring at the page in front of him until Dave and the boys came in for supper. In the middle of the meal, Jon asked Dave, "I was wondering, do you know anything about the house just around the corner—the one that's been empty for a while?"

"Well, yes," Dave said. "What did you want to know exactly?"

"I was just wondering if it might be for sale, and how much it might be. I have some money that came from a trust fund my mother set aside for me; it was actually money she inherited from her father and never needed. And then, well, I've been saving most of what I've earned working at the hospital. I figure if I could afford to buy the house and get it fixed up, and still have some put away, then I might actually get by with learning how to be a farmer."

Dave chuckled. "You like it here that much, eh?"

"Yes, actually, well, I'm not saying I'd go out and buy a house tomorrow, but I was just wondering."

"Well," Dave said, "I can't say that I know who exactly owns it at the moment; I'm guessing the bank in Manti owns the deed. It seems no one's wanted to put the work into fixing it up. If you'd like I can check into it."

"Thank you. I'd appreciate it," Jon said.

"You know," Ellie said, "we'd love to have you settle permanently, but there's no hurry in making such decisions. You're welcome to stay with us as long as you need or want. You don't want to rush into buying something that you'd have trouble selling. Just give it some time."

Jon nodded, appreciating Ellie's sound wisdom, especially when his mind was in such a turmoil.

Dave told them all he did know about the house, which was exactly the same as what Maddie had told him earlier today. *He missed her so much.*

When the meal was finished Jon worked with the boys to clean up the kitchen, then they gathered for scripture time and prayer. Afterward, Jon was sitting on his bed staring at the note Maddie had written when Ellie knocked at his door.

"You didn't get that letter written, did you?" she asked, taking a chair near the bed.

"No," he admitted. "I don't know what to say if I don't know what to do. If Maddie really doesn't want to fight for me in her life, maybe I should just go on to California. Maybe I've done all I can do. On the other hand, I really like it here. I like the life you live here, Ellie. A part of me wants to stay here, but I don't know if it's right for me or not. Maybe it just feels so good to be away from Boston that I'm not looking at the situation realistically."

"Which brings me to a part of our conversation that didn't get finished earlier." He couldn't recall what she meant until she added, "You asked me how you could know if you're making the right choices now, for you and for Maddie. You were right when you said that we can't see into the future. But there is a way of knowing beyond any doubt that you're making the right choice. I've used the method countless times in my life, for many decisions, large and small. If you're interested, I'll share it with you."

"Of course I'm interested," he insisted.

Ellie handed him a book of scripture, opening to a particular page. He could see it wasn't the Book of Mormon, so keeping his finger in the page, he looked at the cover. *The Doctrine and Covenants.*

"What is it?" he asked.

"It's a book of modern-day revelations from the Lord, through the Prophet, to guide us."

"Modern-day revelations?"

"That's right," she said easily. "Do you think we're any less entitled to have God reveal His word to us than the people in Biblical times?" He shrugged, and she continued. "You don't have to answer that question. You just have to trust me when I tell you that this is the formula for making decisions—I've used it countless times, and it's never failed me. Read verse eight and nine, aloud."

Jon cleared his throat. "But, behold, I say unto you, that you must study it out in your mind; then you must ask me if it be right, and if it is right I will cause that your bosom shall burn within you; therefore, you shall feel that it is right. But if it be not right you shall have no such feelings, but you shall have a stupor of thought that shall cause you to forget the thing which is wrong . . ."

Jon thought about it a minute, and said, "I think I understand that, but . . ."

"Would you like me to explain how I interpret it?"

"Yes, I would."

"First of all, *you* have to make the decision. You can't expect God or anyone else to make it for you. He gave you a heart. He gave you a mind. Use them. Think it through. Listen to your feelings. Make a decision that feels right in your heart *and* your head. Then get on your knees and ask the Lord if the decision you've made is right. If it is, you'll feel peace. Simple as that. If it's not right, you'll feel confused and distressed. But you have to bear in mind that God's path for you might not necessarily be the easiest, but I know it's always the best."

Ellie left Jon with the book open on his lap. He read the verses over and over, contemplating what she'd said. It was somewhere in the middle of the night before he knew what he needed to do. The amazing thing was that he *knew*. As Ellie had said, it was as simple as that. He just knew. With the evidence close to his heart that God was guiding his decision, he prayed for guidance in expressing his thoughts appropriately to Maddie. He finished the letter just before four in the morning, and he was still awake when Ellie rose early; she had to put breakfast on before going to the Hansens' to do plums.

From his bedroom window, Jon watched her going up the lane, his letter tucked in her apron pocket. The distance he felt between him and Maddie left him aching. He marveled at how quickly she had brightened his life, like sunshine personified. Her smile, her eyes, her pale skin and blonde hair. He recalled how she had looked just yesterday, dressed in white and surrounded by sunshine that somehow paled in contrast to her presence. And now, in her absence, the whole world felt cloudy and a little colder.

Jon pressed his fingers to the glass as if he could will her thoughts to him, as his were on her. "One day, Maddie Jo. One day."

* * * * *

Maddie was seated at the table, ready to begin a mundane chore that couldn't help but make her think of Jon. She thought of him sitting across from her just a few days ago, talking and laughing with her as if they'd been friends forever. She forced back a fresh burning behind her eyes, wondering how she could have any more tears to cry. She had finally given up on her repeated attempts to discuss her feelings with her father when it became evident he wouldn't bend. She'd gone to bed without eating and cried half the night. Jon's absence made everything seem wrong, when she'd not even known him a week ago. She was tempted to curse fate for bringing him to her at all, but how could she question the hope he'd given her? The light he'd brought into her life?

Maddie started from her thoughts when Ellie came in. Their eyes met and she could almost feel that Ellie conveyed Jon's sorrow. She was wondering what to say when Ellie pulled a letter from her pocket and set it on the table.

"Where's your father?" Ellie asked, as if she'd read Maddie's mind.

"He's in the barn doing chores. He'll be quite some time yet."

"Then hurry and read it and I'll put it away for you."

"Thank you, Ellie," Maddie said, wishing she could fully express how deeply she meant it.

Maddie watched her hands tremble as she tore open the envelope, pulled out the page and unfolded it. The eloquent script was so like him. Her eyes misted over and she had to dab them with a handkerchief before she could read. She was warmed by the tender way he'd recorded their first meeting, and how strongly it had affected him. She marveled to know how completely he shared her feelings, and how well he'd been able to put them into words. He expressed respect for her religious beliefs, and made it clear that while he would not embrace them just to please her or her father, he had cause to be genuinely interested in their way of life—one that had touched him deeply in the brief time he'd known her. He told her of his desire to study and learn, and an equal desire to possibly settle in this community.

Jon concluded his letter by saying:

> . . . *It's impossible to know for certain at this point in time, if our futures will cross. But I want you to know how deeply you have touched me, and I cannot deny the hope I feel that we may yet have the opportunity to be together.*
>
> *Affectionately yours,*
> *Jonathon Phillip Brandt*

Maddie sighed and wiped away fresh tears. Ellie tucked the letter away in her dresser, and they quickly forced themselves to get to work. The hours dragged while she futilely wondered how she could ever find a future with Jon, and at the same time please her father. She hoped that if Jon joined the Church it would soften her father's heart. But deep inside she knew there was much more to the problem than that. The trouble was that she didn't know exactly what the problem was. If she knew how to define it, perhaps she could do better at fixing it. At the moment she simply felt confused. And once she'd weighed every aspect in her mind several times, she came to the conclusion that Jon was likely wasting his time. Somehow she just knew her father would never let go of her. *Never.*

* * * * *

Jon took advantage of being completely alone to immerse himself in study and prayer. Until now, he'd considered prayer something public and cursory to be said over meals or special occasions. But Ellie had taught him a lesson that he'd quickly applied and found strength in. His interest in the Book of Mormon grew as he read on, and he couldn't deny that there had to be something significant in what her people believed. He wished that he could know it all instantly. But he resigned himself to the fact that it would take time to learn all these people could teach him. Given the situation with Maddie, he reasoned that time was something he had plenty of.

The next day was Sunday, and Jon was eager to attend church with Ellie and her family. Not only was he thrilled by the prospect of seeing Maddie, if only from a distance, but he was hungry to learn more of this religion that had so piqued his interest. Ellie introduced him to many people; the majority were open and friendly, though some were standoffish. He couldn't help wondering if the hovering aroma of a recent cigarette was the cause for their subtle distance. Did the smell of smoke brand him as an outsider? He felt even more disconcerted recalling Sylvia Hansen's words to her husband: *You can't shun a man who hasn't had the opportunities we've been blessed with. The gospel would never go forth into the world if we closed ourselves off from good people.* Even so, it seemed evident that prejudice and derision were present only among the minority of these people; it was too bad that Glen Hansen belonged to that minority. Jon felt even better when he saw Ernest, who behaved as if they were old friends, and as he made the acquaintance of many who were equally friendly.

A few minutes after he sat down between Ellie and Joe, Jon saw Glen and Sylvia Hansen enter the chapel and sit down. He had to look down, consciously willing away the anger he felt at just seeing Mr. Hansen. His eyes darted to the couple again before he whispered to Ellie, "Where is Maddie?"

Ellie glanced at him briefly, pity and indignation flitting across her expression. In a toneless voice that didn't disguise the irritation in her eyes, she said quietly, "They don't bring Maddie to church, Jon. She hasn't come for years."

Jon couldn't believe it! He didn't even know how to respond without erupting into anger. He knew how deep Maddie's religious convictions were. He knew how much being a Mormon meant to her. Was her father not capable of bringing her to church? Jon slowed his thoughts down, and trying not to jump to conclusions, he whispered to Ellie, "Is there a reason for that? Please tell me there's a plausible reason for such . . . madness."

"No reason that I know of. Well, Glen believes he's protecting her from getting illnesses that might be going around, and I believe he's partly motivated by some teasing and cruelty that Maddie was prey to—children, you know. But that was years ago. I'm as appalled as you are, Jon. And truthfully, I think Sylvia is distressed over it as well. But she refuses to see anything but the best in her husband, and little is worth rocking the boat."

"Like my mother," he growled quietly, grateful for the organ prelude that drowned out their whispering.

"Yes, actually, I believe Sylvia is very much like your mother."

The meeting began and Jon willed himself to be calm. He suddenly felt haunted by his sister's statement: *You can't run from your problems.* Well, he *had* run, and he'd run right into a family so much like the one he'd come from that it was almost eery. Except, he suspected that Glen Hansen was far more removed from reality than his father had ever been. The thought was chilling.

Jon forced himself to be attentive to the meeting. He truly enjoyed it, but his mind was continually drawn to Maddie. He couldn't swallow the idea of her being home alone, now and every

Sunday. Every day. He recalled her enthusiasm for the picnic he'd taken her on, and wondered how long it had been since she'd been beyond her own home. The thought made him angry and heartsick. But there was absolutely nothing he could do about it—at least for now. But he was determined to bide his time.

The annual harvest ball was later that week. Jon went with Ellie's family, and he enjoyed the socializing. He danced with a few young ladies, but they held no interest for him. He found he preferred dancing with his aunt, liking the way he could make her laugh. But his heart was with Maddie, and seeing her parents there without her made him angry. He left the dance early, resisting the urge to sneak a quick visit to Maddie, when her parents were elsewhere. Instead he went home and went to bed early, glad that tomorrow was Sunday.

Jon quickly found Sundays to be very pleasant—beyond the startling evidence of Maddie's absence at church. He enjoyed the meetings, and how they provided concrete application of the principles he was learning and studying through the weeks. On Sundays only the absolute necessities were seen to. There was a lot of time to visit with Dave, Ellie and the boys, and he was continually surprised at all he learned from them. Their responses to his every question were as eager as his desire to learn.

During the weeks he did his best to make himself useful, balancing his time between the fields and the house, where he enjoyed working in the kitchen with Ellie as much as he enjoyed working the land with Dave and the boys. He figured it was good for him to learn the basics of cooking and cleaning, as well as the farming. If his visions of marrying Maddie came to pass, he would have to help around the house more than the average husband. But the very idea filled him with incomparable joy.

Jon was surprised when he was invited to Sunday dinner by a family in the ward—until he realized they had a daughter of marriageable age, one he often caught eying him coyly in church. Not wanting to be ungracious, he accepted the dinner invitation, but he admitted to Ellie while getting ready, "I really don't want to go. I know they're only trying to bring my attention to their daughter, whatever her name is."

"Luella," Ellie said, "and she's a very nice girl."

"I'm sure she is," Jon said. "But—"

"But she's not Maddie Jo," Ellie finished.

"That's right."

"No, she's not. But . . . well, I know your feelings for Maddie run deep, but it doesn't hurt to explore your opportunities a bit and know for certain. So go to dinner, be your gracious and charming self, and if Luella doesn't inspire you, then you'll have all the more reason to believe that Maddie is the right one for you."

Jon took Ellie's advice. He managed to enjoy the meal, and Luella's parents were fairly good company. But Luella hardly had an intelligent word to say. She was pretty enough, with auburn hair and freckled skin, but her apparent lack of depth left him decidedly uninterested, and all the more drawn to Maddie Jo Hansen.

Not long after his encounter with Luella, Jon came across a woman in the general store that he recognized from church. She was tall and strikingly beautiful, with dark green eyes and hair that was almost black. He knew she was a widow of a few years, and he guessed her to be near his own age. She had a young son he had teased good-naturedly a few times at church. But he had no idea of his name—or his mother's.

He was going into the store to get some things Dave needed, and he nearly ran right into her as she was leaving, her arms full and her boy whining over something. He could plainly see her difficulty in keeping her purchases from falling while holding her son close to her side. Jon helped carry her packages to her wagon, and learned that her name was Sister Hyde, and the boy's name was Jacob. At church the following Sunday they exchanged warm smiles and some conversation, but he felt more drawn to little Jacob than he did to the child's mother. Sister Hyde was obviously a fine woman, but she had a rigidity about her that made him mildly uncomfortable. And thankfully, he sensed that she was equally disinterested in him. Once again, he felt the evidence mounting that his heart was lost to Maddie Jo Hansen.

Time passed, and Jon took the opportunity to travel to Manti with the boys to pick up some supplies that weren't available any closer. Jon was able to get some clothes, shoes, and a hat that were more conducive to his new lifestyle. But the most memorable aspect of the trip had come when he noticed the huge white edifice on the hill at the northern end of town.

"What is that?" he'd asked Joe when he first noticed it in the distance only a mile or so outside of Sterling. He was taken back at such a massive, beautiful structure among people who were generally humble and conservative. It looked almost like some kind of castle.

"That's the temple," Fred answered with a trace of awe in his voice. "No matter how many times I see it, it still takes my breath away."

"Can we see inside?" Jon asked when it had come more clearly into view. He'd felt fascinated for a number of reasons.

"Only worthy members of the Church can go inside."

"Well then tell me about it," Jon said.

"Well, I haven't been there—yet," Joe answered. "The only time children go is to be sealed to parents who haven't previously been sealed."

Intermittently, Fred and Joe briefly explained the concept of eternal marriage and families, and how their people had worked to build the temple in spite of many hardships and challenges. He discovered there were also temples in Salt Lake City, Logan, and St. George.

The image of the temple, and all it represented, hovered in Jon's mind, which spurred a whole new string of questions for Dave and Ellie through the days that followed his visit to Manti. Then, as always, he greatly appreciated the opportunities to learn from Ellie and her family. He marveled at how he felt more a part of this family than he ever had his own. He wrote weekly to Sara, and enjoyed the letters she wrote in return, but he wasn't surprised to see that nothing had changed back home in Boston—except for his and his mother's absence.

As fall settled in deeply, with brilliant colors in the trees and cooler temperatures, Jon felt his desire to stay grow with each day. The hard work and humble lifestyle didn't scare him off. He loved it. And deep inside he felt something coming to life in him—it tempted him to believe this was the life he'd been meant to live.

"You know," he told Ellie one afternoon, while watching the first hints of snow fall outside, "I think I was meant to be your son. The stork just delivered me to the wrong family."

Ellie laughed soundly. "I don't believe the stork had anything to do with it, Jon. The good Lord put you where you needed to be—to learn what you needed to learn. If you had grown up in my family, you would never have had the opportunity to become a doctor."

"My thoughts exactly," he countered lightly. Ellie just smiled as if she knew some great secret he had yet to discover. Knowing her well, he suspected she probably did.

* * * * *

Jon mounted the saddled stallion; he circled around the house toward the west field where Dave and the boys were working. He'd barely cleared the trees when he saw Glen and Sylvia Hansen heading down the lane in the buckboard—toward town.

"Heaven help me," he murmured. *Maddie was alone.* How many times had he longed to be with her, to talk to her, just for a few minutes? Would she be angry with him for taking advantage of her parents' absence? Would there be negative repercussions?

Jon quickly explored his instincts and prayed for guidance, wondering if God would be with him as he willfully defied Maddie's father. His heart quickened, and he didn't bother to stop and analyze his motives, or Glen Hansen's. He heeled the stallion to a gallop and dismounted two minutes later in a cluster of trees near the Hansens' backyard. He took a deep breath and hurried to the back door. He knocked lightly but got no response; he doubted that she could hear him though, unless she was actually sitting in the kitchen. Pausing to study his thoughts, he faintly heard the piano playing. He closed his eyes, absorbing the evidence of her being near. He quietly opened the door and stepped inside. Her music became louder as he moved tentatively up the hall, hoping he wouldn't startle her, and praying she'd be glad to see him. He hesitated in the doorway of the parlor, attempting to soak in her presence. She was more beautiful than he could have ever remembered.

Unable to bear the distance another second, he blew out a long breath and forced himself to speak. "Hello, Maddie."

She let out a breathy gasp and turned toward him. Her eyes immediately told him that his being here was worth any risk. "Jon," she whispered, pressing a hand unconsciously to her heart.

"Forgive me," he said. "I didn't want to startle you, and I know I shouldn't be here, but . . . I saw them leave and . . ."

He stopped stammering when she reached a hand out toward him. "It's so good to see you, Jon," she said, and he stepped forward to take it. She squeezed so hard it almost hurt his hand, and then she laughed. That perfect, beautiful laugh! Jon felt the clouds that had surrounded him parting, and the light emitting from her filled every crack and crevice of his lonely, aching heart.

In one agile movement, Jon sat on the bench beside her and put his arm around her waist, holding her to him. He touched her face, her hair, her face again. She closed her eyes and sighed. "Oh, Jon," she murmured and took his face into her hands. He kissed her like he might never have the chance again. She moaned softly and pressed a hand into his hair.

"Maddie, Maddie," he muttered, "how can we live like this?" He kissed her again then looked into her eyes. "Let me take you away from here, Maddie," he whispered as if the walls might overhear. "I'll take good care of you. You'll never want for anything, I swear it. Maddie, please tell me you'll . . ."

He stopped when clouds filled her eyes. "I can't, Jon. This is my home. How can I leave here, everything I love, my parents? They've done so much for me."

"Yes, they have, Maddie. But eventually you're going to have to grow up and make a life of your own." She looked pointedly away. He softened his voice and took her hand. "I love you, Maddie Jo Hansen."

Maddie looked up again, searching his eyes for sincerity. She quickly found it, amazed at how it assuaged the emptiness inside of her. "You really mean that," she stated.

"I really do," he said. "I need you in my life, Maddie. My wish is not to defy your father. But his stipulations are unreasonable. You must be able to see that. I need you," he repeated, "and I believe you need me, too."

Maddie glanced away, not wanting to give him false hopes. But he touched her chin and lifted her face to his view. "Look at me, Maddie, and tell me that you don't love me. Just try and tell me that you don't feel this way, too."

Maddie heard her voice break as she admitted it, "I do love you, Jon. I do. I think about you every minute of every day."

Jon took hold of her shoulders. "Then marry me, Maddie. Pray about it if you must. *I* have. And I know in my heart we're meant to be together."

Maddie couldn't believe what she was hearing. Part of her longed to throw out her every hesitation and accept his proposal. But how could she?

"Maddie," he murmured, hating the desperation he could hear in his own voice, "you must know that your father's concerns are not valid. His prejudice against me is—"

"Some of his concerns are valid, Jon," she said firmly.

Jon paused to absorb what she was saying. He had to admit to her sincerity. "You're not a child, Maddie. His concerns are valid only if you agree with them; I mean *really* agree—from the heart."

Maddie took a deep breath and looked into his eyes. "I want to be married in the temple, Jon. It's all I've *ever* wanted; to marry in the temple, to raise a family, and to be loved for who and what I am."

Following a minute of strained silence, he asked, "Is there anything else?"

"What do you mean?"

"Is there anything else about me that would make you hesitate?"

"I want to live here, Jon. I don't want to be away from my parents."

Following *another* pause, he said, "Okay, Maddie. Now listen to what I have to say, and listen carefully. I have seriously considered settling here. Ellie taught me how to make decisions with the Lord's help, from the Doctrine and Covenants." Her eyes widened with pleasant surprise. "I can honestly say that I don't know yet if this is where I'm supposed to stay, but if this is where the Lord wants me to be, this is where I'll stay. I think it's good for a woman to be close to her parents; I do. I also believe that it's important when you marry to put such relationships in their proper perspective. I've been studying the scriptures a lot—all of them. In the New Testament it says that a man should leave his father and mother and cleave unto his wife. I think that works both ways. A marriage cannot succeed without two people being committed to each other first and foremost. In the Doctrine and Covenants it says: *Thou shalt love thy wife with all thy heart, and shalt cleave unto her and none else.* That's the way it should be, Maddie. I have no wish to take you away from here, I like it here. But one of the things I love about you is the way your beliefs run so deeply. Surely you know that where we decide to settle is a matter that should be taken up with the Lord. I will provide a home for you. If the good Lord wishes for us to be here, then we will be. If He wishes us to be elsewhere, then we should go where He wants us to go."

Maddie became mesmerized by the sincerity in his eyes. There was a blossoming glow about him that made him all the more admirable. "Of course," she said, and he nodded, seeming relieved.

"And as for that other, I—"

"What other?"

"Your wanting to marry in the temple," he said. "Just give me some time, Maddie. I already believe it's true. It's just a matter of time."

"But you can't just *believe* it, Jon. You have to *know*. Don't do it for me. Don't do it unless you know beyond any doubt that it's true and it's what God wants you to do."

Jon had to ask, "Do you know it's true, Maddie?"

"I do," she said firmly, with a conviction in her eyes that he'd come to recognize and admire.

"As I said, it's only a matter of time," he insisted. "Then I will court you properly, and I'll marry you the way you want to be married." He forced himself to his feet, knowing it wasn't wise to stay any longer. "In the meantime, don't you ever forget—not for a single minute—that my heart is yours."

Maddie sighed and silently thanked God for sending Jon Brandt into her life. "As mine is yours," she said firmly.

"I love you, Maddie."

"And I love you," she said.

He bent to kiss her, caressing her face as he did. Then he hurried away before he was tempted to scoop her into his arms and carry her away then and there.

Maddie sat with her eyes closed long after she heard the door shut. She just wanted to absorb the aura Jonathon Brandt had left in the room. Oh, how she loved him! And how grateful she was to know that he loved her, too! "Thank you, dear Lord," she murmured and sighed, pressing a hand over her quickened heart.

* * * * *

Jon was filled with gratitude as he rode quickly from Maddie's home. He felt a tangible hope he'd not felt since he'd last seen her and touched her—the day he'd taken her on a picnic several weeks ago. The chasm that had opened between them that day felt somehow lessened with the conviction he'd absorbed from her. He felt determined to increase his efforts in study and prayer, knowing beyond any doubt that he was on the path intended for his life, and that he would share that path with Maddie. He *would!*

CHAPTER FIVE
The Reluctant Doctor Brandt

In spite of Jon's continual efforts to help on the farm and around the house, he often felt that he wasn't earning his keep. He was amazed with the family's generosity in seeing that he was well fed and comfortable, especially with the evidence that money was tight. He offered only once to pay for his room and board. Their adamant refusal hinted at insult, and he never brought it up again. So, he just did his best to help where he was needed, and kept his eyes open for opportunities to appropriately contribute to the running of the household.

On a particularly cold day, past the middle of November, Ellie expressed her reluctance at going into town against such temperatures.

"Why don't you let me go for you?" he asked. "Just give me a list of what you need, and I'll take care of it."

"Really?" she said, as if he'd suggested that he could provide the moon for her.

"Sure," he insisted. "I can take a little cold."

Ellie quickly wrote a list with specific instructions. She fussed over Jon to make certain he was bundled up adequately before he set out with the wagon toward town. He picked up the mail, took a basket of food to an elderly widow, and stopped at the general store to procure a number of items on the list. Jon felt a secret delight at the opportunity to pay for the purchases with his own money, since Ellie had told him to have the amount put on their account at the store. She might never know the difference.

He had no trouble finding everything he needed. While the amounts were being added up, an idea occurred to him that increased his delight.

"Would you have that put on the account?" Mr. Larson asked.

"No, I'll pay for it now, and if you'll tell me the balance due, I'll take care of that, too."

Mr. Larson looked a little surprised, but Jon caught the faint sparkle in his eyes. The amount due increased the evidence that Ellie's family was struggling. Of course, she'd said when they sold that last hay cutting they would get everything paid up. But now they could use that money for other things.

Jon left the store feeling warm and secure. He knew Mr. Larson would keep his little secret, and when—or if—Dave and Ellie figured it out, Jon would just have to let them know that the Lord worked in mysterious ways. He laughed at the thought and headed back home with his wagon-load of supplies.

As winter set in fully, Jon's feeling of uselessness increased. With no work to be done in the fields, Dave and the boys worked on repairing fence lines, as well as did maintenance on the house and barn. There were still sheep to be fed, and the horses, cows, goats, and chickens to care for. But there was a slowing down of life that replaced the bustle of the harvest season. More time was spent gathered around the fire, and Jon enjoyed the opportunity to continue his exploration of Mormonism. The more he discovered, the more sense it made. He had little doubt that it was all true, the problem being in that little bit of doubt. He simply couldn't say that he knew beyond any misgiving that it was true. He'd heard many people at church bear testimony to knowing the truth of the gospel. He'd heard Maddie do the same. And Ellie and Dave, and even their sons. Having completely read the Book of Mormon and the Doctrine and Covenants, there was only one point that caused him any concern or hesitation. He wondered if that might be his reason for holding back, or more likely, the reason he was being denied his answer. Determined to find the truth, one way or another, Jon talked with Ellie about his concerns.

"Everything makes sense to me, Ellie. It all feels right and good, except . . ."

"Except?" she pressed.

"I just have a hard time swallowing this story about Joseph Smith. How can a fourteen-year-old farm boy be the means for all of this," he motioned toward the Book of Mormon and Doctrine and Covenants, "to come about? It just seems so illogical."

"The parting of the Red Sea was illogical, Jon, but that doesn't mean it's a myth. For me, I know beyond any doubt that it's true. I can't explain how I know, I just do. If you know the Book of Mormon is true, then you know that the means it came to us is also true—specifically, that Joseph Smith was given the record and translated it. Consequently, he couldn't have possibly done such a thing without divine intervention, which means the first vision is true as well. It all fits together. Either it's all true, or it's all false."

"And you believe all of that is true," Jon asked, "without any doubt."

"I do," she said firmly.

"How?"

"I just . . . feel it, Jon. The Holy Ghost manifests the truth of such things to those who earnestly seek the answers."

Jon sighed. Hearing the conversation come back to the issue that troubled him most, he had to ask, "What's the feeling like, Ellie? How do I know if I've felt it, if I don't know how it feels?"

"Well," she said, "it's impossible to explain, mostly because it seems to affect people differently. I can only say that it's, well, it's like seeing a beautiful sunrise. You look at it and can't believe how incredible it is. You wish there was a way to capture it and keep it, but you can't. You try to tell somebody about it but it's just not the same. They can't fully understand how beautiful the sunrise was until they see such a sunrise for themselves. You want so badly to share it, especially with those you love, but they just have to be there when the sun comes up, with their heart and mind open to fully absorb the experience, not just to look at it."

Jon was briefly mesmerized by her description, then she chuckled and startled herself from some kind of reverie. "Read Moroni chapter ten once more, Jon. It's the very last chapter. Notice verse four especially. Then be diligent and patient. You'll see your sunrise in time."

Jon did as she asked, and he took Moroni's challenge very seriously. He made up his mind to do just that, but life suddenly became very busy with the arrival of Thanksgiving. Ellie's oldest son, Dave Jr., came home from college in Provo to spend the holiday. He took the tiny guest room, even though Jon insisted he could take the guest bed while Dave Jr. was home. But they all insisted that for the time being it was Jon's room.

Jon really liked Dave Jr. He was very much like his father, with an added sense of humor that brought a great deal of laughter into the home. The holiday was pleasant, captured in a glow of simple abundance that shone through their humble circumstances.

On the day that Dave Jr. returned to Provo, his father suddenly became ill. Jon determined that it was some type of influenza. He knew well how to care for Dave, keeping him as comfortable as possible while the symptoms ran their course. And he also instructed the family on things they could do to lessen the likelihood of having it spread. By frequently washing their hands, and keeping Dave secluded, no one else in the family got it. But Dave was down in bed for several days, and terribly weak beyond that. Jon became busier as he helped Fred and Joe with the animals and chores. He learned how to milk the cows, gather eggs, and feed sheep. And he spent a fair amount of time chopping wood to keep the fires going against the deepening winter cold. He'd never imagined such cold. Ellie often teased him about changing his mind on staying once he'd spent a winter in Sanpete valley, but he always countered with, "A little cold isn't going to scare me off. I love it here."

And he did. Time only made it more evident to him that this was where he wanted to be—whether Maddie Hansen ever decided to *cleave unto him* or not. But oh, how he prayed that she would! His deepest wish was to make her his wife, and he often occupied his thoughts with dreams of sharing their lives in the house down the lane. An hour didn't pass without his thoughts straying to her. And he'd not so much as had a glimpse of her since the day he'd sneaked into her house to make his intentions known.

Dave was finally managing to come to the supper table without getting out of breath when Joe ran panicked into the house. "Fred's hurt bad," he declared. "Come quick."

"You stay here, Dave," Jon said, reaching for his coat. "I can take care of it."

"I'm coming with you," Ellie insisted, putting on her own as she ran for the door.

Dave's frustration at being left behind was evident, but so was his weakness.

"Just pray," Jon said on his way out the door.

"I don't know what happened," Joe said breathlessly, leading the way to the barn. "He was trying to get the old shoe off that horse. You know Madge. That horse can be so temperamental. Next thing I know, he's laying on the ground, bleeding and groaning."

"Good heavens!" Ellie said when she saw the blood on Fred's face. The handkerchief he was holding to it with one hand had stopped doing any good long ago. And Jon noticed him cradling the other hand against his chest.

"What happened?" Jon asked, kneeling beside Fred in the straw. He took out his own handkerchief and dabbed at the boy's forehead, attempting to find the source of the bleeding.

"I don't know," Fred said. "Something must have spooked her. She kicked me in the head then stepped on my hand."

"Is anything else hurt?" Jon asked, finding a long, deep cut through Fred's eyebrow.

"I don't think so."

Jon pressed the handkerchief over the wound, and then guided Fred's good hand to hold it there. "Put some pressure on it to slow the bleeding and let's get you inside. You're going to need some stitches I think."

"You can do that?" Fred asked.

"I can," Jon said, and he and Joe helped Fred to his feet.

Once inside the house, Jon ordered, "Ellie, get a pillow and lay him down on the kitchen table. Joe, go to my room and get the black bag on the floor of the closet." In response to Dave's helpless expression he added, "Dave, I need some clean rags and a basin."

Jon first pulled a bottle out of his bag and gave Fred a spoonful of the bitter tasting liquid.

"What is that?" Fred grimaced after he'd swallowed.

"It'll take the edge off the pain and help you relax. Getting this stitched up isn't going to be pleasant. Then I'll take a look at your hand."

An hour later Jon had efficiently put fourteen stitches in Fred's forehead, and he'd set and splinted two broken fingers. With Fred sleeping up in his room, Jon helped Ellie clean up the mess while Dave rested and Joe finished the chores in the barn.

"That was incredible," Ellie said.

"What?"

"You were so efficient."

"It wasn't a big deal," Jon said, hoping to divert the conversation.

"It would have been a big deal if you hadn't been here. We would have had to drive him to Manti to have done what you did, and even then your confidence and expertise far outweigh what's available. That's evident." Jon tried not to scowl at her. He tried to be indifferent. But he hated the expectations associated with what she was saying. "In my opinion," she added, "cutting hay and milking cows is a waste of your training and talent."

Jon said nothing. Beyond seeing that Fred's stitches remained free of infection, he quickly put the whole matter out of his head. He was kept busy helping Joe with the chores, since neither Dave nor Fred could help. More than once Ellie said she didn't know what they would have done without him. "You're an answer to our prayers, Jon. And you came along even before we knew we were going to need you."

"It's nice to feel needed," he admitted, and left it at that.

On Sunday Fred got a lot of attention at church with his splinted fingers and stitched forehead. Jon overhead him telling more than one person that his cousin had fixed him up, along with the explanation that Jon was a doctor with years of experience working in a Boston hospital. Jon tried not to be angry with him. Fred had no idea of Jon's feelings on the matter, and now he wished that he'd taken a minute to explain. He knew now that it was only a matter of time before word got out. He recalled that Ernest Mortensen had known the day Jon arrived, but nothing had been said until now. He made a mental note to thank Ernest for not being a gossip.

Two days later, the family had just sat down for scripture time when an urgent knock sounded at the door. Ellie rose to answer it. Jon heard a woman's voice frantically asking, "Your nephew's a doctor? He's here?"

Ellie answered with a nod and showed the woman in. Jon stood and turned, his eyes first drawn to the immense amount of blood on her dress. Close behind her came her husband, carrying a young girl in his arms. She was whimpering in a way that Jon recognized as a combination of shock and pain. Her hand was wrapped in a blood-soaked towel. He knew these people from church, but he couldn't recall their names.

"Take her to the kitchen," Jon ordered, and Ellie led the way. "Joe, get my bag," he added, thinking he needed to thank Sara in his next letter.

"What happened?" Jon asked, carefully unwrapping the towel.

"We were visiting the Nielsens," the mother explained. "Carrie took a liking to their dog, but it . . ." She broke off into tears as the towel came off.

"Mercy," Jon muttered, wishing for the hospital he'd become accustomed to working in, where sterile instruments and assistance were readily available. He quickly washed his hands while Ellie gave the child a spoonful of laudanum to ease the pain.

He set to work while the father continued the explanation. "Bo's not a bad dog, but Carrie set to teasin' him when he was eatin'; I think Carrie just got a little too close and he took hold and . . ." The father's words faded with emotion as well.

"How old is she?" Jon asked, his attention focused on his frantic efforts to stitch an open artery in the wrist that wouldn't stop bleeding.

"She just turned five," the mother reported.

"It hurts, Mama," the child's voice was slurred, evidence that the medicine was taking effect.

"I know it hurts, Carrie," Jon said gently while he kept working. "But you're being such a brave girl, and everything's going to be all right. You just rest." He took a moment to look at her face and smile. She smiled in return and closed her eyes.

Jon spent nearly four hours repairing the child's mangled hand. While Ellie stayed by his side, proving an efficient assistant, Joe made certain they had everything they needed, and Dave and Fred kept the parents occupied and calm.

When there was nothing more to be done, Jon washed the blood from his hands and sat to talk with the parents. "She's lost a lot of blood, which will make her weak and tired for quite a while. Rest, good nutrition, and time will eventually put that right. The biggest concern with something like this is infection. Keep it clean and dry, and apply disinfectant to the stitched areas regularly. And also—you must know—it's difficult to tell how much nerve and tendon damage there is. Once the wounds heal she'll need to work at getting the strength and mobility back in her hand. I can show you how to do that. But there may be some level of permanent damage."

Both parents nodded gravely.

"I'll check on her tomorrow," Jon added.

"Thank you, Doctor," the woman said. Jon just nodded.

The man shook Jon's hand, saying in a cracked voice, "We're so grateful you were here." Again, Jon simply nodded.

The father wrapped Carrie in the blanket they'd brought her in, and scooped her into his arms. Just before they opened the door, he turned back and said, "You let us know how much we owe you, Doctor Brandt. We'll find a way to pay you."

Jon was briefly startled, but said quickly, "You don't owe me anything. I'm glad I could help."

"But surely," Carrie's mother said, "you can't afford to give medical care for nothing. You must have—"

"You don't owe me anything," Jon repeated and walked away.

Jon was sitting at the kitchen table, staring at a basin filled with bloody rags when Ellie set her hand on his shoulder.

"I'm proud of you, Jon," she said and sat beside him. He looked toward her and she added, "Do you have any idea what your gift must mean to them?"

"Gift?"

"Medical care is a valuable commodity, Jon. And the Christensens have practically nothing."

"Yes, that was evident," he said, recalling their humble dress and manner. Then his mind wandered back to thoughts that had been churning all during the delicate surgery.

"What is it, Jon?" Ellie asked gently.

"I never wanted to be a doctor, Ellie. I fought it every step of the way."

"I know."

"And in the hospital where I worked, well, I did a lot of good, but there were many doctors. I certainly wasn't indispensable. It was easy to leave and know they'd likely not miss me for long. And now . . . it's just that . . ." He couldn't put words together to express something that he'd never in his life expected to feel.

"What is it, Jon?" Ellie repeated.

Jon forced his voice past a growing lump in his throat. "I'm just glad I was here . . . glad I knew what to do."

"So am I," she said emphatically. "And I'm certain Brother and Sister Christensen feel the same way. I don't know what they would have done. By the time they'd gotten her to Manti, it would have been so much worse and—"

"She never would have made it to Manti, Ellie. If I hadn't been here, the Christensens would have been planning the funeral by now." He sighed and came to his feet. "I guess that's what bothers me." He set to work cleaning up the mess, not knowing what else to say.

"Bothers you?" Ellie rose to help him. "Jon, you just saved a life."

"I know, but I don't want to be a doctor, Ellie. I want to stay here, but I don't want to be a godsend to these people. I just want to live a simple life in a quiet town."

"Don't you think it's possible to be a doctor and live a simple life in a quiet town?"

Jon scowled at her and closed the conversation with a firm repetition of his words: "I don't want to be a doctor, Ellie."

Jon appreciated the way Ellie didn't push the conversation or attempt to convince him of the error of his ways—something his father would have done. The following day she went with him to the Christensen home to check on little Carrie. They found her weak and complaining of the pain in her hand, but in fairly good spirits. Jon examined the wounds and said he'd check back again. At the door Sister Christensen gave him a basket with a loaf of bread, some cookies, and three jars of preserves. He hesitated to accept it, knowing how hard it must have been to come by. But Ellie nudged him with her elbow. He met the silent prompting in her eyes and graciously accepted the offering.

"Isn't that sweet," she said, as he helped her into the buckboard.

"I hate to take anything from them."

"But Jon, they will be blessed for their willingness to share, just as you will be."

Jon said nothing. He felt so humbled that he could hardly speak.

They returned home to find a box on the porch with a ham, two jars of jelly, some eggs, and another loaf of bread. The note attached read:

> *Thank you for being here for little Carrie. We felt respon-*
> *sible for what our dog had done, and wanted to help*
> *with the payment. God bless you.*
>
> *Brother and Sister Nielsen*

Jon couldn't help but be touched, but he felt somehow unworthy of their offering.

"Isn't that sweet," Ellie said again, reading the note.

Jon set the box on the table and said, "Well, at least this way I can make some contribution to the household."

"You've contributed more than enough, Jon."

When the food was put away, Jon slipped outside. He needed a cigarette. With time he passed off the incident, refusing to give it much thought beyond checking occasionally on Carrie Christensen. He found her to be improving, but still felt concerned about possible infection.

For days Jon stayed busy with the chores, and he continued his avid study and prayer. He was mindful of his desire to know the truth for himself, but that undeniable witness continued to elude him. He believed it was all true, in spite of certain aspects that seemed too incredible to believe, but he wanted to feel that burning he'd heard so many speak of. He began to wonder what might be wrong with him that he would be denied something so many others had been blessed with. Added to that frustration was the constant emptiness he felt in being forced to stay away from Maddie. The entire situation seemed so ludicrous that there were times he found it difficult not to be consumed with anger. Knowing that anger would only hold him back, he prayed especially hard one night as he lay in bed staring at the ceiling. He slept little and rose late. He'd barely finished his breakfast when Brother Christensen came to the door, insisting that Jon come with him. Dave and Ellie rode along.

Jon arrived at the Christensen home to find Carrie hot with fever, and definite redness and swelling in her hand. The severity of her illness was evident in the way she writhed and moaned, lost in a kind of delirium. Jon felt helpless and frustrated as he repeated to such good people what little they could do beyond attempting to keep the fever down.

"We must give her a blessing," Dave said to the distraught father, who nodded firmly.

It wasn't the first time Jon had heard reference to *a blessing*. Some men had come and given Dave a blessing during his bout with the flu, but Jon hadn't been present; he'd wondered if it was inappropriate for him to be around for whatever it might entail.

"Perhaps I should go," Jon offered.

"No, please stay," Sister Christensen said. There was a pleading in her eyes that he knew well from his years at the hospital. There was only so much even the best physicians could accomplish, and he recalled many times having to tell loved ones that it was out of their hands. He'd always felt that he was somehow letting people down—the patients, their families, *his father*. And now he was letting the Christensens down. He almost resented the way people looked to him as some kind of miracle worker. He just simply didn't know how to respond.

Ellie urged Jon to sit beside her, and he watched as Carrie's head was anointed with some kind of oil. Dave and Brother Christensen both put their hands on her head, and then gave her a blessing. Their words appealed to the power of the priesthood and the authority of Jesus Christ. Carrie was told that it was God's will for her to recover completely from the ordeal; that she would live a full and complete life. The infection was commanded to leave her body, and she was told that with time she would regain full use of her hand. She was also told that God was mindful of her; that she had great things to accomplish in her life; and that she had been blessed with loving parents and the help of a good doctor to get her through the illness.

The prayer ended and casual conversation began. But to Jon every sound became distant and obscure. He felt suddenly a million miles away, carried off in some incomprehensible state of elation. Instantly everything had changed. *Everything!* And the tangible heat he felt in his chest was the least of it. Warm chills filtered throughout his every nerve. Hot tears froze in his eyes. His hungry soul was filled, his aches were soothed, and his doubts had vanished. His fears lost their power. He *knew* the source of what he was feeling. It was the light of Christ, illuminating its way into every dark crevice of his heart and soul. And everything made sense, perfect, wonderful sense. He knew the Book of Mormon was true, and the Doctrine and Covenants. He knew that Joseph Smith had seen what he said he had seen. He knew that life was eternal and that the power he felt in the room was real. He felt invincible and completely humble all at once.

The intensity of the experience melted into a burst of emotion that refused to be held back. Jon erupted to his feet, barely managing to mutter, "Excuse me." He hurried outside and around the house, dropping to his knees in the snow beside the winter skeleton of a huge oak tree.

"Oh, God," Jon uttered. "My dear God." He turned his face heavenward and marveled. Tears coursed down his face in torrents.

When the emotion finally settled, Jon realized his knees were cold. He felt as if he'd somehow been returned to the earth from some higher plane. He turned and looked around: the tree, the house, the snow, the sky overcast with heavy clouds. It was still the same world. But he was different. He knew that the struggles of this world lay before him just as they always had. But the gift he'd been given would carry him through as long as he chose to hold onto the light he'd been given and never forget.

Recalling the circumstances that had brought him here, he wondered how long he'd been outside, leaving the others to wonder what madness had overtaken him. But oh, such incredible madness! He came to his feet and brushed the snow from his pants. Walking toward the door, he felt drained of strength and full of energy at the same time. He knocked lightly and heard a voice call for him to come in. He entered tentatively to find everyone exactly as he'd left them, except that Carrie was now sleeping peacefully.

"Sorry," he said, closing the door behind him. In response to the expectant expressions before him, he added, "I just . . . needed to be alone. I didn't mean to be so long."

"It was only a few minutes," Ellie said.

"Really," he laughed, "seemed like an hour."

"Are you all right?" Ellie asked.

"Me? Oh, yeah, I'm fine. And I think little Carrie here is going to be just fine, too."

"Yes, I believe she is," her father said.

Dave and Ellie prepared to leave. Jon felt hesitant to go with them, but he promised to return in the morning and check on Carrie.

The minute they got home Jon dug through his every drawer and pocket, then he hurried to the back door with his stash.

"What are you doing?" Ellie demanded when he hurried past her.

"I'm throwing my cigarettes in the trash. What does it look like I'm doing?"

"But . . ."

He looked up at his aunt. She was obviously struggling to come up with the right words to inquire about his actions. He took her by the shoulders and looked into her eyes. "After what happened to me a while ago, Ellie, I could never smoke again if my life depended on it."

He saw tears brimming in her eyes, as if she could feel what he felt without him even saying a word. She touched his face and smiled. There was something in her eyes he finally understood. "Oh, Jon," she murmured, "do you know what it's like to see the sunrise?"

"I do," he said, in awe of the fresh emotion that overtook him just recalling the experience. Ellie embraced him, holding him tightly, and he wished he could begin to tell her of all he was feeling, and how grateful he was for all she had taught him, all she had given him that had guided him to this moment. He eased back and looked in her eyes, and somehow he knew that she understood. She understood perfectly.

"Oh, Ellie," he said with urgency, "will you be seeing Maddie today?"

"I see Maddie every day," she said. "Why is today different?" Her smile told him she already knew the answer; she just wanted to hear it.

"Everything's different today, Ellie. *Everything!*" He laughed and hurried upstairs to write Maddie a letter.

* * * * *

Maddie toyed idly with the piano keys, unable to find even a degree of the joy she'd once found in playing the piano. She silently cursed Jonathon Brandt for ever showing up in her life, and in the same moment she ached just to see him and feel some evidence of his love for her. He had given her light and hope, and shown her a glimpse of the world outside this mundane existence. And in his absence the darkness had closed in more tightly than she'd ever imagined.

Maddie heard Ellie in the kitchen and willed herself to be cheerful. She didn't want Ellie reporting to her nephew that anything here wasn't as it should be.

"Hello, Maddie Jo," Ellie said brightly. "How are you?"

"Fine," she insisted. "And you?"

"Very well, thank you," Ellie said, and laughed as if she couldn't contain her happiness.

"What?" Maddie laughed as well.

"We've had a miracle at our house," Ellie said, then she held out an envelope.

Maddie heard herself gasp before she even consciously realized what she was looking at. "Thank you," she said, and took it with trembling fingers. Ellie left her alone as she hurried to remove the lengthy letter from the envelope. She thought of the countless times she had secretly reread the letter he'd written to her before. The very idea of having another letter, even longer, filled her with unspeakable joy.

Maddie had to stop often and wipe her tears as she read of his continued devotion to her, and his hope that they would be together soon. He told her in detail of his ongoing efforts in studying the scriptures, gospel discussion with Ellie's family, and earnest prayer. She was amazed at his recent experience, and felt her joy magnified at the news. He told her that he would be baptized at the first opportunity, and then he would be speaking to her father. He concluded by saying:

> *I did it, Maddie. I did it for the right reasons, and I got the answer I was seeking. I love you dearly, Maddie Jo, and my new convictions only make me love you more. My love for you has grown deeper each day, and my*

greatest hope is that you feel the same for me. With any luck, and God's blessings, I will be seeing you soon. Pray that we can be together, as I will be.

All my love,

Jonathon Phillip Brandt

Maddie was grateful for her father's extended trip into town; it gave her the opportunity to reread the letter three times before she had her mother help her to the kitchen table where she wrote Jon a note in return. She sent it with Ellie, and prayed, as Jon had suggested, that they would soon be together.

* * * * *

Jon's spirits soared further when Ellie finally returned from her lengthy visit with Sylvia and handed him a note. He opened it to read:

Never in my life have I felt such joy! My heart is with you and my hopes are as yours. You are in my every prayer.

Forever yours,

Madeline Josephine Hansen

He tucked the note away with the other she had written him, somehow knowing that everything would be all right.

Checking in on Carrie Christensen the next morning, he found her free of fever and no sign of infection. And he marveled at the miracle.

In the following days Jon felt the reality of life—with his separation from Maddie—dim the light he'd been given. But Ellie had told him that's how it would be. "It's holding onto that light you've felt that will get you through the dark times, Jon. As long as you never let go of that light, you'll be fine."

Jon felt certain she was right. He felt impatient to be baptized, and the bishop had told him that he was ready. But he wanted Dave to be the one to do it, and Dave needed to build up his strength a little more.

In the meantime, Jon was occupied with what Ellie had called "an unusual outbreak of little problems." He set a broken arm, stitched a number of cuts, treated an earache and a toddler with croup, and he even delivered a baby. "Now that last one wasn't a problem," she said when he returned home to tell her it was a healthy boy.

Jon couldn't begrudge the opportunity to help those in need, but it didn't change the way he felt about being a doctor. It simply wasn't for him and he knew it; and he hoped with time that people would accept that.

He felt humbled by the payments he was offered in exchange for his services. A small envelope of money showed up anonymously on the doorstep after he'd refused payment. But since he'd seen three different people, he honestly didn't know who it had come from. And that was fine. He was also given jars of jam and preserved fruit, eggs, a ham, home-baked goods, and even a freshly plucked chicken—ready to roast. As always, he turned the food over to Ellie in an effort to contribute to his support. On such occasions she commented more than once, "Well, if you had a house that was paid for, you could work as a doctor and never go hungry."

Jon said nothing, but he couldn't deny that she had a point. At least he could fall back on it if his farming efforts failed.

Jon was baptized the week before Christmas. It was an incredible moment, and could have only been better if Maddie had seen for herself that his life was starting over.

Christmas was one of the best he'd ever known. The absence of the usual tension between him and his father contributed to his appreciation of the humble celebration. Jon missed his mother, and Sara as well, but he received a package from his sister that included gifts for the whole family. She wrote that she'd received the package he'd sent for her and his father, and he concluded that one day he was going to go back there and visit.

A new year brought the hope of living a new life. Jon prayed fervently for guidance, and decided that he would buy the house he'd had his eye on. The asking price was even less than he'd anticipated, and he was pleased to know that he had plenty of money to buy it free and clear, fix it up, and then some. He was disappointed to learn that the house didn't come with any land beyond the yard, corral, and a barn that was in fairly good condition. But he knew that when his father died he would receive a significant inheritance—provided he hadn't been disowned. If the money came through, he would use it to buy his own land and equipment.

"Just as well for now," Dave said. "Having land can be a big responsibility—even a burden. I can keep you busy helping me. And I might even be able to afford to pay you now and then."

"We can at least keep you fed," Ellie said.

"Which is no small thing," Jon declared with jovial affection.

"Besides," Dave said, "I think you could use a little more training before you take on land of your own. Maybe when you're ready for that you'll be able to get some."

"Maybe by then you'll admit what everybody else already knows," Ellie said.

"What's that?" Jon asked.

"That you're a doctor, not a farmer."

Jon just grunted and changed the subject.

CHAPTER SIX
Hope

Jon made up his mind that it was time to approach Glen Hansen about courting his daughter. He missed Maddie so desperately that at times her absence was a tangible ache inside him. He prayed earnestly for guidance in being able to approach the situation to his best advantage. Knowing that Glen Hansen was a difficult man, at the very least, he was counting on some divine guidance to get past him in order to be with Maddie.

On a particularly cold morning, just after breakfast, Jon hovered at the table lost in thought while Ellie cleared the dishes away.

"You all right?" she asked.

"Yes, of course, I just need to think."

Ellie said nothing more. Jon sat there for several minutes, thinking that he should go out to the barn and help with the chores, but he felt somehow frozen to his seat while thoughts hurled themselves about in his mind. Then an idea appeared there suddenly, as if a hundred random, meaningless thoughts had immediately come together to make perfect sense.

"Merciful heaven," he muttered, and pressed both hands over his chest, willing himself to breathe.

"Jon?" Ellie said, but he held up a hand to indicate that she give him a minute. He methodically recounted what had led him to the idea, then he laughed. "What?" she demanded. "It's like you're having a conversation with yourself and leaving me out."

"Not with myself, Ellie. It's as if . . . an idea was just put into my mind with such clarity that . . ." He chuckled. "I can't believe it."

"What?" she demanded again, sitting across from him.

"Well," he said, "I was thinking through all of the things Maddie and I had talked about those few days we had time together. There was a lot of spiritual stuff. I know her conviction planted some of the seeds that helped me come to where I am."

"Yes, of course."

"And we talked about a lot of trivial things. What's-your-favorite-pie kind of stuff. But that day, on our picnic, I asked her about the reasons she couldn't walk, and then I realized she wasn't paralyzed—like I had thought—because she has complete feeling in her legs." Ellie looked surprised, but he pressed forward, certain she wasn't as surprised as she was going to be. "I asked her all kinds of questions out of curiosity, and it quickly became apparent, from a medical perspective, that she could likely have children and—"

"Are you serious?"

"Yes, of course."

"Did you tell her?"

"Yes, actually. That day. She was so happy she cried." He smiled at the memory. "I resisted the urge to propose to her then and there, but . . ."

"Jon, if she can have children, then . . ." She looked at him as if she didn't know how to say what she was thinking.

"Listen, Ellie, I'll tell you what I told her. Some people just can't have children. What I believe is that her inability to walk has nothing to do with her ability to bear children. And whether or not she can has nothing to do with whether or not I would marry her." He noticed that Ellie looked somehow distressed, so he asked, "What?"

"It's just that . . . from what Sylvia's told me, I think Glen is convinced that Maddie shouldn't even consider marrying because she couldn't be a mother—or even a good wife."

Jon sighed and tried not to be angry. "I would like to know such a man's definition of a wife." As he said it he recalled things Maddie had told him; "Does she have no value if she can't work beside him in the fields and produce babies?" he finished sarcastically.

"Calm down, Jon. You can't change Glen Hansen's views on his daughter."

"Maybe not. But eventually I'm going to get her away from

there—one way or another."

"You still haven't told me what you were going to tell me. What's this idea that just came to you?"

"Well," he said, feeling the anger relent behind this new epiphany, "the thing is, I was recalling what Maddie said about the symptoms of her accident, and now it's just occurred to me out of nowhere that . . ." He laughed. "You're going to think I'm crazy."

"No, I'm not. Tell me."

"Ellie," he said with the severity he felt, "I think she can walk." Ellie gasped and pressed a hand over her mouth. "I think the only reason she couldn't walk once she'd healed from the accident was the fact that her legs hadn't been used for a few months. Her legs should have been exercised and put back to work. But she was just put back to bed and the muscle atrophy has just gotten worse over time. It would take time and a lot of work, and someone who knew what they were doing would have to help her, but . . . I really think she is capable of walking."

With tears in her eyes, Ellie said, "Someone like you."

He shook his head and chuckled tensely. "No, Ellie, not me."

"But—"

"Under the circumstances, it would be completely inappropriate. If I were only her physician, perhaps. As it is, I could only help her if we were married. You could help her. Sylvia could help her. It's mostly a matter of massaging and exercising the legs. I could teach you what to do. But . . ."

Ellie's eyes told him she knew what he was thinking even before she said it, "But only if Glen had the sense God gave a cow—to look past his own nose and see the reality of what he's doing to his daughter."

Jon was surprised by her apparent anger. He was beginning to understand more fully her hope that he could make a difference in Maddie's life. Her support encouraged him to admit what he'd been feeling for days. "I need to talk to him." And he knew now that it was important to tell Maddie's parents what he believed. He didn't know how he knew. He just knew.

That evening Jon walked toward the Hansen home, willing his heart to be calm. He felt confident in what he needed to say to these people, and he had to believe that, as inspired as he felt over the matter, his words would have the desired effect.

Jon held his breath and knocked at the Hansens' front door. Sister Hansen answered, her expression betraying that she wasn't surprised to see him there. She and Ellie had been talking. He could see that she was pleased. He could also sense her concern. Did she fear that her husband would kick him out again?

"Hello," she said eagerly, as if she had the same hopes he did.

"Hello," he replied. "I wonder if I might speak with you and Brother Hansen. If now's not a good time, I could come back when—"

"Now is fine," she interrupted, opening the door wider. He stepped inside and she closed it, motioning him to the parlor. "Have a seat. I'll get Glen."

"Thank you," Jon said, but he couldn't bring himself to sit down. He slowly paced back and forth, his eye often drawn to the piano and the memories it held for him. He wondered where Maddie was exactly. Could she hear what was taking place? Would she be brought into the room and included in the conversation? Not likely.

"Yes?" Glen Hansen bellowed, startling Jon. He resisted the urge to extend his hand, not wanting to have the effort rejected as it had been last time.

"Brother Hansen," Jon said, "I wonder if I might have a word with you and your good wife."

"Sit down, please," Sylvia said, taking a seat on the sofa. Jon took a chair near the piano. Glen sat near his wife, his reluctance readily evident.

Jon considered the man's scowl a bad sign, but he forged ahead anyway. "Well," he said, and loudly cleared his throat, "the last time we spoke you made it very clear that you would not allow your daughter to associate with a man who didn't share your religious beliefs. I want you to know that I have diligently studied and prayed, and I have gained a testimony for myself. I was baptized recently by my uncle. I've given up my bad habits, and I've even been given the priesthood."

Jon wanted—even expected—to hear some kind of positive response to his statement. He'd been welcomed into the fold with gracious enthusiasm by every member who knew of his conversion.

He'd shared many conversations with people in the community on the wonders and blessings of the gospel and of the priesthood. He felt it would be natural to hear some degree of that same response now. But only silence answered. Glen's expression was even more skeptical than when Jon had entered. Jon could almost imagine that Glen was trying to find some reason to kick him out, but was having trouble coming up with one. Sylvia was watching her husband, unmasked hope in her expression. Jon wished he could express his appreciation to her somehow; and he wished she could convince her husband of what a fool he was being.

Glen finally cleared his throat and said, "And what exactly did you plan to do, young man? I know your kind; big city folk who get the city in their blood. Would you be thinking you can cart my daughter off to some faraway place and we'd never see her again?"

"No, sir. Of course not. I've quickly grown to love it here. I've bought a house that I'll be working on fixing up. I have enough money to put it in proper order. I'm here to ask permission to court your daughter, Brother Hansen. And perhaps . . . when the house is ready, and if she's willing, I would like to take her to the temple to be married."

"And how would you be intending to provide a living?" Glen growled.

"Well, I'm learning to work the land, and . . ." He hesitated at Glen's deepening frown.

"Mr. Brandt is a doctor," Sylvia said firmly. "He's helped a good many people since he's been here. Why, they say that little Carrie Christensen would have bled to death from that dog bite if it hadn't been for Dr. Brandt."

When Glen's expression showed a little less distress, Jon had to admit he was glad for being a doctor if it helped him win this man's approval.

Again there was silence. A deafening, aggravating silence. Just when Jon thought the anticipation would make him scream, he recalled the idea that had come into his head earlier. In fact, it had come to him again now with some matter of force. He had to believe he was being prompted, and he prayed it would make a positive difference.

"There is," he began, hating how coarse his voice sounded in contrast to the ongoing silence, "another matter I wished to discuss with you." Sylvia looked hopeful. Glen looked angry.

Jon took a deep breath. "What I want to say regards Maddie's physical condition." He paused to gauge their reactions, but knowing he had to go on regardless, he forced himself to finish; he felt almost compelled against his will.

"The thing is, I've been thinking about the things Maddie told me about her accident, and the symptoms that followed, and the situation now, and . . . well, being a doctor, with the experience I've had, I really believe there's a good possibility that Maddie can walk."

They both gasped, but their expressions differed drastically.

"How can that be possible?" Sylvia asked.

Jon almost felt comfortable as he ventured to speak in familiar territory. "Maddie doesn't have any of the symptoms of paralysis, which is generally the cause for such a disability. According to what she's told me, I—"

"Have you been talking with my daughter against my wishes?" Glen growled.

"No, sir," Jon said crisply. "I was speaking of a conversation that occurred the week I met her. With my medical background, naturally I was curious over the cause of her difficulty. And what I believe is, well, whenever a serious injury occurs with a long period of healing after, muscle atrophy ensues." They looked confused, so he clarified, "The muscles lose their strength when they're not used. Maddie was down in bed long enough that when she initially tried to walk again, her legs simply weren't strong enough. At that point, if she had been helped through some simple exercises to build up her strength and flexibility, she would have been able to walk. But by continuing not to use her legs, they've continued to decrease in strength. It could take time and patience, but I really believe there's a good chance that she would walk."

"That's incredible!" Sylvia said breathlessly. "To think that such a thing is possible. If only we had known then that . . ." She didn't seem to know how to finish.

"Apparently the doctor you saw in Salt Lake City overlooked mentioning the need for rehabilitation therapy following such an injury. If he was like most doctors, he was likely just too overworked to think of everything."

Sylvia inhaled deeply. "Oh, Jon, do you really think that—"

"You have some nerve, young man," Glen's voice was loud and angry, surprising Sylvia every bit as much as Jon. "Do you really believe that coming in here with some outlandish tale will buffalo us into believing you're out for Maddie Jo's good?"

"Glen!" Sylvia scolded, but he ignored her.

"How dare you insinuate that we've done something wrong by our daughter."

Jon attempted a rebuttal. "I don't recall any such insinuation or—"

"Maddie Jo cannot walk. It's as simple as that. And you have a lot of nerve thinking you could get her hopes up over something that will never be. If you so much as step into the same room with her, I will hunt you down and—"

"Glen!" Sylvia said again. "Calm down and be reasonable. You cannot expect to—"

"Get out of here!" Glen growled at Jon, once again ignoring his wife.

"Glen!" she repeated. "You cannot—"

"You be still!" he shouted at his wife, and Jon wanted to take him by the throat, if only for the way he treated her. He turned again to Jon and repeated, "Get out of here. And don't you ever come near my daughter—*Not ever!*"

Jon found himself standing on the front porch, willing himself not to force his way back into the house and break something—most specifically Glen Hansen's nose. He closed his eyes and prayed with everything he had, knowing nothing short of divine intervention could keep him calm. Within a few minutes he felt some composure seeping into him, and he blew out a long, slow breath.

Jon walked home slowly, confused and discouraged beyond his ability to define. He walked through the kitchen door to Ellie's hopeful expression. But it faded quickly when she saw him.

"How did it go?" she asked.

"It was an absolute disaster," he said, slumping into a chair. "I cannot believe how absolutely stubborn and difficult that man is."

"I recall hearing those exact words in your letters, in reference to your father."

"Yes, well Glen Hansen has a way of making my father look like a pussycat."

"Not necessarily," Ellie said, sitting beside him. "It's just that you've only seen Glen when he's angry, and you're the one threatening to take away something he's worked very hard to protect. His methods may be appalling, his reasoning may be way out of line, but at heart he's really not such a bad person. I've felt angry and frustrated with him a number of times myself, but I've also seen a very good and tender side to him—which is more typical, actually. We mustn't judge, and we have to keep perspective."

"I'm sure you're right," Jon admitted, taking a deep breath. "What I don't understand is that I prayed for guidance in handling this, Ellie. I felt so sure that I said what I'd been inspired to say. Until I brought up this thing about her being able to walk, I sensed he didn't like what I was saying, but he didn't have an argument. Then when that came up, he just flew through the roof. Why would I be inspired to say something that turned out so disastrous? Or maybe I don't know how to hear the answers as well as I thought I did."

"Now you listen to me," Ellie said firmly, "you know how to get answers just fine. You've learned how to discern the whisperings of the Spirit; that's apparent enough. What you need to understand is, well, it's been my experience that God's answers for us are not some guarantee to the easiest route. His answers are for the best good. And we must remember that He has a perspective that we can't possibly comprehend."

Jon accepted his aunt's wisdom, and disappointment settled in to coat his anger. He had no trouble admitting his feelings, "I can't believe how much I love her, Ellie. We shouldn't have to live this way."

"I know, Jon. But I really believe that if you bide your time, everything will work out. This is not just about Glen Hansen being willing to let you see her; I'm not certain he ever will. As I see it, this is about Maddie reaching a point where she's willing to fight for the right to her own happiness. And from what little I know about human nature, I think she's going to have to get much lower in her *unhappiness* before she can reach that point."

Two days later, Jon was still attempting to digest everything Ellie had said when Sylvia came by to visit. From his bedroom he heard her voice in the kitchen, and he went down to say hello, if only to be in the same room with her, knowing how close she had been to Maddie only minutes ago.

"Hello, Jon," she said warmly.

"Sister Hansen," he said with a cordial nod.

"I'm glad you're here," she said and motioned him toward her. He sat down in the chair beside her and she went on. "Once again I'm sorry for Glen's behavior. I can't justify it. I can only hope that with time he'll see reason. I have trouble understanding Glen myself sometimes. But I love him and I must stand by him. You understand?"

"Of course," Jon said, even though he didn't. He didn't understand why his mother had meekly stood by and conformed to her husband's often ludicrous behavior. And he didn't understand how Sylvia Hansen could stand by and watch her husband's behavior stifling their daughter's happiness, even her very existence.

"Jon," she said gravely, and he wondered if she would ask about Maddie's ability to walk. But she smiled slightly and said, "I'm going to be here visiting with Ellie for quite some time." He narrowed his eyes, attempting to perceive her meaning. "And since Glen left for Provo yesterday to deliver a load of furniture, no one would ever know if you sneaked over to visit Maddie. No one—not even me."

Jon erupted to his feet, heart pounding. He wanted to fall down on his knees and praise Sister Hansen for her insight and good heart. He wondered if God understood the reasons a good woman would feel pressed to some level of dishonesty for the sake of her daughter. Somehow Jon knew that He did.

Jon pressed a quick kiss to Sylvia's cheek, then he turned to Ellie and said breathlessly, "I think I'll go for a long walk, Ellie. I'm feeling the need to get out."

"That sounds like a wonderful idea," Ellie said. "If you're not back in an hour, I'll send Dave out looking for you." She winked and turned her back as he grabbed his coat and hurried out the door.

* * * * *

Maddie worked vigorously at the crocheting in her hands, forcing her mind from the dismal thoughts that were becoming increasingly difficult to ignore. She felt as if a tangible darkness would swallow her if she didn't get out of the house, or at least have conversation with someone besides her parents and Ellie. She had prayed and prayed for her father's heart to soften; for her to be able to find any degree of the light and hope that Jonathon Brandt had brought into her life. But the more that time passed, the more her hope dwindled. She'd not so much as heard of his existence since she'd received the letter telling her that he'd made the decision to be baptized. She kept expecting him to approach her father about courting her, as he'd promised. But she was beginning to believe his feelings toward her had changed. And if Jon Brandt had given up on her, what hope was there of ever seeing a life beyond this?

Maddie forced her mind to her work, counting stitches until she felt certain she was going mad. A knock at the door startled her. Visitors were rare, but she hated the way a knock at the door reminded her of the day Jon had showed up searching for his aunt. Once she forced her mind to the present, she decided that any company would be a pleasant diversion.

"Come in," she called, grateful she had a strong voice to compensate for her inability to get up and answer the door.

She heard the door close while she attempted to finish the row she was on, absently saying, "Mother's over at Jensens and—"

"I know," Jon said.

Maddie squeezed her eyes shut, fearing she'd truly gone mad. Did she want it to be him so badly that she'd imagined his distinct Boston clip?

"Hello, Maddie," he said, and she looked up to see him standing there, hat in hands, eyes glowing with the love and adoration that had always been there.

"Hello, Jon," she said with a voice that cracked in spite of her effort to keep it steady. She set her handwork aside without taking her eyes from him.

He seemed tense and hesitant as he said, "I happened to hear your mother say that your father had gone to Provo and I . . . couldn't pass up the opportunity."

The blatant yearning in his eyes answered her every doubt, and she quickly told him, "If I could run into your arms I would, but . . ."

Jon tossed his coat and hat into a chair and rushed to sit beside her, pulling her into his arms with a feverish sigh, as if he'd been holding his breath since the last time he'd seen her. He touched her face as frantically as she touched his. It was a feeble attempt to reacquaint themselves with each other, to grasp some tangible evidence of the affection they had both craved through their separation. He pressed his lips to hers, kissing her in a way that didn't begin to express the ache and longing he'd felt. But oh, how it felt to be with her! To touch her! To hold her! *He loved her so much!*

She drew back to look at him and laughed with tears in her eyes. "Oh, Jon," she murmured. "You're here. You're really here. You haven't given up on me."

"No, of course not," he said and kissed her again.

Maddie relished the feel of his kiss, noting how thoroughly familiar it was to her memory. She paused to absorb him more fully, and said to him, "You look different. There's a definite glow about you that wasn't there before." She laughed softly. "It only makes you all the more handsome. And you don't smell like smoke."

"No, I don't," he said proudly. "I threw out every cigarette the day I discovered it was all true. I haven't even missed them . . . well, I haven't given in to missing them," he admitted sheepishly.

Maddie laughed and touched his face again, hoping his presence wasn't too good to be true. She felt compelled to ask him, "Is it really true, Jon?"

"What?"

"That it's possible for me to walk again?"

"You overheard me talking to your parents?"

She looked completely dumbfounded.

"No! When were you talking to my parents?"

"A couple of days ago. I came to ask your father if I could court you."

Maddie gasped. While his presence had soothed her doubts, knowing that he had followed through on his promise meant more than words could say. "I didn't even know you were there. I wasn't feeling well for a few days and went to sleep early. Oh, Jon. I was afraid you'd forgotten about me."

"Never," he murmured. "So, how do you know what I said about your being able to walk?"

"Mother mentioned that she'd talked to you, but she didn't say you'd come over."

Jon felt angry, wondering why Maddie's parents felt it was necessary to keep their daughter in some kind of cold storage. Though the problem mostly lay with Maddie Jo's father, Sylvia, for all her good intentions, compounded the problem by her lack of backbone. Even now, as much as he appreciated the opportunity to be with Maddie, he didn't understand why Sylvia felt she had to sneak around behind her husband's back, as opposed to being Maddie's advocate straight up front. He forced his mind from things he didn't understand and couldn't judge. He didn't want these precious moments to pass in anger.

"Well, yes it's true, Maddie." He repeated what he'd told her parents, and she cried as much as when he'd told her of the possibility of having children. He also told her that nothing could be done about it if her father adamantly refused to believe it was a possibility.

"What are you saying?" she asked.

"I'm saying that someone would have to help you diligently massage and exercise your legs. I could teach your mother and Ellie what to do, but Ellie told me that when she suggested it to your mother, she refused because your father would never approve."

"Then why would mother have told me if . . ." She couldn't find the words to define her own confusion.

"I believe your mother is hoping that I will rescue you somehow, and that she won't be put into a position where she has to go against your father. The truth is, Maddie, I can only rescue you when you're ready to be rescued." She looked so thoroughly distressed that Jon forced himself back to the subject. "When we're married, Maddie, we'll work on building the strength up in your legs, and we'll just have to see what happens. It's only a theory, but I believe there's a very good possibility."

Maddie sighed. "The thought seems too incredible to believe."

"Well, your father told me I would be wrong to get your hopes up when it would come to nothing. What do you think, Maddie?"

"I think that without hope, we have nothing."

Jon smiled. "Well, as I said, when we're married, we're going to give it all we've got. We'll just have to see what happens."

"And what if I can't walk, Jon? After everything we can do, what if I still can't?"

"Then I shall be honored and privileged to carry you wherever you need to go. And we'll start making some good use of that wheelchair you have. Because you're going to go shopping, and to church, and to the temple, and anywhere you want to go. Are you hearing me?"

Maddie nodded, too emotional to speak. The picture he painted of her possible future just seemed too good to be true. But she reminded herself of what she'd just told him: without hope, she had nothing. She had to believe in the possibility of what he was telling her. She just *had to!*

Sensing Maddie's emotion, Jon pressed a kiss to her brow and just held her. "Oh, Maddie," he said, already feeling the end of their time together looming before him. "We shouldn't have to live this way."

She sighed and laid her head on his shoulder. He eased her closer just as she said, "I keep praying that my father's heart will be softened."

"I fear it will never soften toward me, Maddie."

She looked up into his face. "But surely with time he will be able to see what a fine man you are and—"

"How can he see anything when he won't even let me in the door, Maddie? This is not about *me*. This is about *you*. He's become so accustomed to being completely in control of your life, that he can't tolerate the idea of your ever being anything but his little helpless girl. It's time for you to take a stand, Maddie. You have to follow your heart, in spite of what he says."

"But how can I ever go against my father? He's always wanted what was best for me."

"Maddie, listen to me. I'm certain your father believes he's doing what's best for you. I'm certain his motive is to keep you from getting hurt. But you're a woman now. He's hurting you by keeping you from living the life any normal woman should live. He will never relent, Maddie, because somewhere along the way his reasons stopped being to protect you, and started being fear and pride. He's afraid of losing you; that's understandable. But if he loves you he would want you to be happy, to live a full life. And he's too proud to admit that his protection and concern have gotten way out of hand. He won't even take you to church, Maddie. You have the right to go to church. And he needs to understand that I'm not taking you away, I'm offering you a good life—a life where you can continue to be close to your parents and enrich their lives as well. Do you hear what I'm saying?"

"I'm hearing that you sound angry."

"And why shouldn't I be angry? He's keeping me from the woman I love for reasons that are too ridiculous to understand."

Maddie took his hand in an attempt to calm him down. In a gentle voice she said, "Just be patient, Jon. I'm certain that with time he'll come around." She smiled and touched his face. "Be patient," she repeated, and what could he do but nod his agreement? He knew in his heart that Glen Hansen would never come around. He recalled Ellie telling him: *this is about Maddie reaching a point where she's willing to fight for the right to her own happiness.*

Jon touched her face in return and said, "I'll be patient, Maddie, but I want you to think about . . ." He paused to gather his words. Recalling once that Ellie had said the situation with Maddie and her father was similar to his sister's, he felt certain it was relevant to give Maddie the advice he'd given Sara many times. "You're a woman, Maddie, not a child. You're strong and beautiful. You have a mind and heart that are yours and only yours; don't let anyone take away the power of that mind and heart. It's up to you to decide your own future."

Maddie nodded, but he sensed her doubt and confusion. He resigned himself to giving her time and being patient, just as she'd asked him to be. He also concluded that until he had the house ready, it wasn't feasible for them to be married, anyway.

Jon changed the subject, knowing there was nothing more to say on the presently fruitless matter. He told her of all the changes that had occurred in his life. He told her how word had gotten out of his medical experience, and that he'd been called upon as a doctor, although he made his feelings clear on the matter. He shared his experience with little Carrie Christensen in more detail and found her crying. When he asked what had been going on in her life, she simply had nothing to tell him. Nothing at all. Though he shouldn't have been surprised, he had trouble not being angry. She showed him her crocheting, and told him that she'd made more blankets and scarves than she could count. Sometimes her mother sold them, sometimes they were given to people in need. She had some put away with the hope of having a home to use them in one day.

Jon carried her to the piano bench and she played for him. He left her there with a kiss, and a reluctant promise to heed her father's word and not visit again without his permission, even though he would be gone for several more days. While Jon didn't *want* to heed such a ridiculous edict, he had to admire Maddie's integrity, especially in the face of a difficult situation. Through the following days he concentrated on his gratitude over the opportunity he'd been given to see her at all, and he constantly kept a prayer in his heart that their waiting would come to an end before they both went mad.

Jon found it increasingly difficult to keep his promise to keep his distance, especially knowing that Glen was gone. Three days before he was expected to return, Sylvia came to visit Ellie, saying to Jon, "You can't believe the difference in Maddie since she saw you last week. You've made her so happy, Jon, but . . ."

"But?" he pressed when she hesitated.

"I wish there was a way for her to have some tangible hope. I mean . . . I really believe you love her, Jon."

"I do," he said firmly.

"Then . . . forgive me if I'm being presumptuous, but knowing my daughter as I do, I know that it could take some time, but . . . if there was some way for you to . . . I don't know, Jon. It's just as I said. She needs to have some tangible hope."

"I'll think about that," he said. "And thank you."

"For what?"

"For believing in me, for liking me, and for trusting me."

Sylvia smiled warmly. "She needs you, Jon. Don't ever let her down."

"Never," he said firmly, and went up to his room. He only had to think about it for five minutes before he knew exactly what Maddie needed. He dug into a drawer in search of something he'd tucked away there soon after his arrival. Then he hurried to Maddie's house.

He knocked and got no response. He opened the door and hollered, "Maddie? Where are you?"

"I'm in my bedroom," she called back.

"Are you decent?" he asked, moving closer to her voice.

"Of course," she said with a little laugh. "Second door on the left."

"Hello," he said, coming into the doorway. She looked so beautiful, even before she smiled. Then she laughed. "What's funny?" he asked.

"Not funny," she said. "Just happy. I'm so glad you broke your promise."

He laughed with her, then returned to his purpose. "We're going out."

"Out?" she echoed. "But it's freezing outside."

"So, where's your coat?"

"I don't have one," she said almost lightly, but the reality tore at him. Was there no need because she was never taken out? The thought annoyed him, but he kept to the point.

"Very well," he said, and picked up a blanket from the foot of the bed. He wrapped her securely in it and lifted her into his arms. She laughed as he headed toward the door.

When he had her seated in the buckboard, she asked, "Where are we going?"

"Just down the lane and around the corner," he said. He couldn't help staring at the way she lifted her face toward the sun and inhaled deeply. *She was so beautiful!*

"I love you, Maddie Jo Hansen," he said. She turned toward him and smiled.

"And I love you, Jonathon Brandt."

He counted on the horse to keep going up the lane as he bent to quickly kiss her. Then they laughed together.

"What are we doing?" she asked when he went up the drive of the house that was now his.

"We're just going to have a quick look around and then I'll take you home."

"But . . . why?" she asked, looking puzzled.

Jon reached into his pocket and pulled out a piece of paper. Since her hands were holding the blanket around her, he opened it and held it in front of her face. She still looked puzzled. "What is it?" she asked.

"It's the deed to this house and the property it sits on. You'll notice it has my name on it."

"You bought it?" she squealed.

"I did," he said, and laughed at her delighted laughter. "I nearly brought it up when I saw you last week, but it just didn't seem like the right moment."

Jon put the deed back in his pocket and carried her into the house. It was sorely neglected and the dust was thick, but he carried her through each room, telling her his vision of how it would look and feel when he was done. The last room they entered was a small bedroom just off the main bedroom. Jon sat on a dusty chair and encircled her with his arms once she was situated on his lap.

"And this," he said, "will be the nursery. In that corner will be the crib, where our baby will sleep, and right there will be a beautiful rocker where you will sit and sing our baby to sleep."

Maddie looked into his eyes, her tears brimming. She buried her face against his shoulder and wept. He just held her closer and let her cry. When she had calmed down, he said, "I know you need some time, Maddie. I'm going to fix up the house, and I'm going to take you to the temple." He reached into his pocket, took something out, and held out his hand. "This was my mother's. She gave it to me when she was dying, and told me to give it to the woman I married on our wedding day. Well, I want you to have it now. Wear it next to your heart, beneath your clothes where your father won't see it if you have to. And each time you feel it there, think of me and know that I'm counting the hours until you'll be my wife."

"It's so beautiful, Jon," she said, admiring the gold, heart-shaped pendant. "Thank you."

He fastened it around her neck and she tucked it inside her blouse.

"I'll treasure it always," she added, and kissed him.

He kissed her back, and he enjoyed it so much that he kissed her again. And again. When he began to enjoy it a little too much, given the circumstances, he cleared his throat and chuckled. "I'd better take you home," he said. She looked both confused at his embarrassment and disappointed, but he figured that one day she would know the full extent of what he felt for her.

Jon left Maddie sitting on her bed, exactly as he'd found her. No, he thought, not exactly. With any luck he'd given her what he'd set out to give her, according to Sylvia's suggestion. *Hope.* And just as Maddie had said, without hope they had nothing.

CHAPTER SEVEN
Refiner's Fire

Maddie found her mind wandering, as it often did, to those precious moments she had spent with Jon. She imagined his vision of how their home would be, and the life they would share together. She felt herself smile, and rubbed her arms to soothe their tingling.

"Hello there, honey," her father said, bringing her back to the present.

"You're home," she said, putting more enthusiasm into her voice than she felt.

"I am," Glen Hansen laughed and sat beside her, hugging her tightly, "and I sure missed you."

"I missed you, too," Maddie said, feeling as if she were lying. She would never have had those wonderful encounters with Jon if her father had been home.

"I brought you some presents," he said. "I'll be right back."

He returned with an armload of packages. Sylvia followed, beaming with happiness as she watched Maddie open them. There were several books, some scented soap, some sheet music, and several beautiful colors of yarn for crocheting.

"Why so much?" Maddie asked, feeling overwhelmed.

"I got a good price for the furniture, and there's nothing I'd rather do than spend it on you."

"Thank you," Maddie said, not realizing how evident her emotions were until her father touched her chin and looked into her eyes.

"Why so sad?" She shook her head, not wanting to talk about it, and he added, "We have so much to be grateful for, honey. There's no reason to be sad."

Maddie recalled the things Jon had told her. She truly believed her father's heart would soften with time, but it would never happen if she didn't tell him how she felt. "Yes, we have much to be grateful for," she repeated, "but I must confess that sometimes I feel like I'll go mad if I don't get out of this house and go somewhere."

"The world out there isn't so great," he said. "Take my word for it. You have everything you need here."

"No, Papa," she said, forcing herself to be firm, "I don't."

He looked so shocked that she was tempted to take it back. "What is it you want that I haven't gotten for you?"

"I want what every young woman would want, Papa. I want to have friends. I want to be courted and . . ." She glanced at her mother and caught a subtle nod of encouragement. "I want to marry, Papa, but it will never happen if I don't—"

"Maddie Jo . . . honey," he said gently, but she recognized the tone of voice. He was going to compassionately tell her that she was not like other girls and she couldn't expect such things out of life. She listened as he gave the same old speech, and she realized that at one time she had actually believed what he said was true. But Jonathon Brandt had given her the hope that more existed for her than what she had within these walls.

Maddie's heart pounded, and her palms began to sweat as she contemplated telling her father how she really felt. Again she felt her mother's silent support, and took a deep breath. "Papa, I . . . I believe that I can be a good wife and mother and . . . I don't see any reason why I can't live a full and complete life—just like other women, and . . ."

"Maddie Jo . . . honey," he said again. "You know you're not like other women. You can't expect to—"

"But I am!" she insisted. "I have a heart and a mind. I'm strong and beautiful. And I am perfectly capable of having children of my own and—"

"Who told you that?" Glen demanded, although his voice remained gentle. Before she could answer he said with a scowl, "It was that Mr. Brandt, wasn't it. And what other nonsense will you believe from that young upstart with his city ways? You never had a moment's discontent until he showed up."

"That's not true," she insisted. "I just didn't realize how empty my life was until he showed up."

While her father was apparently trying to come up with some response, she added, "Papa, I love Jonathon Brandt. He's a good man, and it's right for two good people to be married and—"

"Forgive me, honey," he said with no trace of anger, but she could feel the condescension in his manner, "I know it's hard for you, but you're just going to have to accept that you're not like other women, and the picture he's painted for you is simply not possible. I know what's best for you. And I'll hear no more about it."

Maddie watched her father leave the room. She felt like throwing his gifts and screaming that he had no idea what he was talking about.

As she lay in bed that night, doubts began to creep in and she wondered if her father was right. She'd always looked up to him, always trusted him. He'd always been gentle and loving and good to her. So why did she suddenly feel that he was wrong? What if he wasn't wrong? What if she was setting her hopes on something that would simply never be? What if Jon's visions of their future were unrealistic? What if Jon really didn't know how difficult it would be to care for her? And if she couldn't have children, and never walked . . . would he continue to love her as he did now?

Maddie cried into her pillow until she finally slept. She had horrible dreams wherein she felt as if she were being torn in half, and she woke up feeling just that way—torn in half. She didn't know how she could go on. But she didn't know what could possibly be done. So she started crocheting a new blanket and tried not to think about it.

* * * * *

With spring coming, Jon got busy working on the house in between helping Dave on the farm. Dave offered to pay Jon for his help, even though Jon knew he couldn't afford it. Jon insisted that he didn't need to be paid, that he had plenty set aside to fall back on.

"I just appreciate the opportunity to learn a new trade," Jon said.

"It's kind of like I'm a college student."

Dave laughed. "And me the professor?"

"You are the expert in the field," Jon laughed. "No pun intended."

Jon also found a great blessing when he discovered that a young father in the area by the name of Peter Carter was skilled with carpentry and building, and was presently out of work. He gave Jon an estimate which Jon gladly agreed to, and Peter quickly set to work on remodeling the house and putting it in good repair. Jon helped Peter some everyday, patching and painting with images in his mind of the future he would share there with Maddie.

With Ellie's help, Jon ordered some furniture and other necessities for the house. He made arrangements for whatever could be made or acquired locally, wanting to support the community. Everything else he ordered from a catalog. He also determined that he needed to order some medical supplies. People had continued coming to him for help, and he couldn't very well turn them away when there was no one else qualified to help them for miles around. Ellie set aside a cupboard in her kitchen for the supplies, since most of his 'patients' were treated there.

With the arrival of summer's heat, and the pressure of the first hay cutting, Jon was glad to see that the house had become almost livable. Most of what it lacked were the little extras that hadn't yet arrived, and of course, the presence of the woman who would make it home. Patience, he reminded himself.

Jon knew, from Ellie's reports, that Maddie was aware that the house was nearly ready, but she still seemed determined that her father's heart would soften and she could somehow break her ties without upsetting him. Reminding himself to be patient became an hourly occurrence.

Ellie suggested that Jon write Maddie a letter with an official proposal of marriage, now that he was in a position to give her a home and marry her in the temple. Jon liked the idea, but he wanted to take some time, be prayerful, and make certain he was going about it in the best possible way.

On a particularly hot day Jon was sitting in church and found his mind wandering, as it often did, to Maddie. Although he loved being in church for the way it replenished and filled him, Maddie's absence, and all it represented, hovered in his thoughts like a dark cloud. Suddenly, he felt an unexplainable urgency to check on her, and he wondered if she was all right. The urging was strong, but to get up and walk out of church would bring attention to himself—most specifically from Maddie's parents. Just what he needed, to go check on her and have Glen Hansen follow him. He'd probably bust Jon in the jaw if he found him anywhere near her. Jon forced the thought out of his mind, only to have it appear again with more strength. He focused on the thought, trying to determine if it was a prompting and not his imagination. Then he knew that he needed to stand up and leave. He was almost standing when Sylvia Hansen erupted from her seat and practically ran out of the chapel, her expression frantic. Jon's heart pounded. Had she received the same prompting?

Jon didn't bother taking note of what Glen Hansen or anyone else was doing. He got up and followed her outside, only to see her driving away in their buckboard, as fast as the horse would go. He quickly surmised that the wagon he'd come in with the family would not go anywhere near that fast. He unharnessed the horse and mounted bareback, galloping in the direction Sylvia had gone.

Jon's pounding heart threatened to beat right out of his chest when he saw smoke rising into the sky—the source could only be the Hansen home. He arrived to see the smoke pouring from behind the house, with no visible flames. The front door was open and he considered it a fair guess that Sylvia had just gone in. He went inside and was confronted with thickening smoke.

"Sylvia!" he called. "Maddie! Where are you?"

"We're here," Sylvia called. He took a few steps and found her attempting to drag Maddie toward the door. Maddie was coughing and gasping for breath. He scooped Maddie into his arms and hurried back out the door with Sylvia right behind him. He laid her on the lawn and quickly determined that she'd not been harmed, although her clothes and hair were dark with smoke, and she was obviously upset.

"Are you all right?" he asked.

She nodded and coughed.

"Talk to me, Maddie," he insisted, fearing she'd inhaled more smoke than her lungs could handle.

"I'm fine," she said, and coughed again though her tears, but it was enough that he felt confident she would be all right.

"Stay with her," he ordered Sylvia, and ran around the house to see how bad the situation might be. There were no visible flames from this side either, but smoke was pouring out of the kitchen windows. He held his breath and went inside to find a portion of the kitchen in flames, but the water pump was easily accessible. He found a towel and tied it over his mouth and nose, then worked quickly to get water on the fire with a bucket. Sylvia appeared at his side, saying firmly, "She's fine. Let me help you."

Sylvia kept the pump going while he threw bucket after bucket on the flames. Within a few minutes they had it out, and threw some more water on it for good measure.

"How do you suppose that happened?" Jon asked, leaning against the wall to catch his breath.

"It seems something wasn't right with the stove," Sylvia said breathlessly, "but we'll probably never know for certain."

Jon hurried back to the front lawn to find Maddie where they'd left her, still coughing occasionally. And still upset.

"It's all right," he insisted, kneeling beside her. "You're going to be fine."

"I thought I was going to die in there," she cried. "I've never been so afraid in my life."

Her confession put Sylvia in tears, but Jon reminded both of them, "We're here, aren't we. God wasn't going to let you die."

Jon looked up to see Ernest Mortensen pulling up in his wagon, and seated next to him was Glen Hansen. Glen jumped down and started toward Jon with that angry, determined expression Jon knew so well. He could see no trace of concern for his home or his daughter as he marched toward Jon, apparently oblivious that Maddie was sitting on the lawn coughing.

"What do you think you're doing?" he growled at Jon.

Jon stepped toward him and retorted, "I was saving your daughter's life."

Glen's eyes only hardened and Jon didn't even think before he drew back and busted Glen Hansen in the jaw. Glen lost his balance and nearly went down. Jon took hold of his collar to steady him and hissed in his face, "Do you see what your *protection* has done now? She could have died in there! If you would have let her mother help her a long time ago, she would have had the strength to at least *crawl* out of the house. But she should have been in church with the rest of us!" He threw Glen out of his grasp, leaving him too stunned to respond. He added firmly, "Your wife and I got the fire out, so you still have a home. As the only physician around, I'm taking Maddie to Ellie's house to keep an eye on her and make certain the smoke inhalation doesn't cause her any problems. You can come and get her when the house is livable."

Jon briefly caught Ernest's stunned expression, although he didn't miss the subtle sparkle of support in his eyes. Sylvia rushed to her husband's side without looking at Jon. And he ignored the disappointment in Maddie's eyes as he scooped her into his arms and carried her toward Ellie's house. Ernest offered them a ride. He said nothing as they drove, besides offering to take back the horse Jon had ridden so that the family could get home.

"Thank you," Jon said when Ernest pulled up in front of Ellie's house.

"My pleasure," Ernest said with a subtle smile, and he drove away.

Jon kicked the door open and laid Maddie on the sofa.

"I can't believe you just did that," she said with an edge of disdain.

"Did what?" he retorted. "Was it the saving your life or putting out the fire you can't believe? Or is it the fact that I finally did what I've kept myself from doing for nearly a year now? What exactly can't you believe, Maddie?"

"You hit my father!"

"Yes, I did," he said. "And if the life he's sentenced you to ever puts you in danger again, I'll hit him a lot harder."

"I can't believe it," she said.

"I can't believe it either, Maddie. I can't believe that any man would be so stubborn and closed-minded. And I can't believe that in spite of everything that's happened, you can't see what's really going on here. You know all those boys who never came around? They weren't afraid of the fact that you can't walk, Maddie. They were afraid of your father. He'll let you shrivel up inside, Maddie, before he'll ever allow you to be happy. Because his control over you is far more important to him than your happiness. That's why his first concern five minutes ago was not your welfare, it was the fact that I was there. You think about that. Think about it long and hard, because my patience is wearing thin, Madeline Josephine. I've said it before and I'm saying it again. He will *never* soften his heart toward me, any more than *my* father would ever find reason to believe that I was good enough. This is not about *him,* Maddie. It's about *you!* You're not a child. When are you going to grow up enough to realize that you're entitled to be happy?"

She turned away and squeezed her eyes shut. "I need to be alone," she said, sounding angry herself.

Jon resisted the urge to shout. "Not to worry, Maddie," he said. "I'm going upstairs to pack my things. I'll be moving out so that you and your mother can stay here until your home is habitable. We wouldn't want to upset your father any further by having me under the same roof as his daughter. She is, after all, his most precious possession—emphasis on the word possession. It's becoming more and more evident that the only way to get you away from him is to steal you, but I can't do that. Not as long as you believe that the road to happiness is found only through your father. He doesn't want your happiness, Maddie. He wants you locked in some cage like a prize bird to sing for him and only him. But you can't hide in that cage any more without feeling the repercussions. The minute I walked through your door last summer this stopped being just about your happiness. It's not just you this is affecting, Maddie. But you're the only one who can fix it." He sighed and added, "You know where I'll be, Maddie. Ellie can bring me word if you decide you need me."

Jon hurried upstairs and quickly unloaded his belongings from the drawers and closet. By the time Ellie and the family arrived, he was packed and ready to leave.

"Where are you going?" Ellie asked him.

"Maddie can tell you all about it," Jon said. "She's got everything figured out."

By the time Jon had put his things away in the new house, the anger had chilled into raw fear. He knew the biggest source of his anger was his fear in seeing Maddie come so close to dying. But just as he'd told her, it had to be up to her to change the situation, which left him feeling helpless. And afraid. He had to admit now that his deepest fear was that—after all he had invested in his hope of their future—she might never loose the tether that held her to her father.

Jon curled up on the bed that had recently been delivered, but he realized he'd overlooked the fact that the bedding hadn't arrived yet. He'd be sleeping on a bare mattress tonight. But it seemed to suit his mood. While his mind was caught up in a turmoil he couldn't solve, he drifted into a fitful sleep.

"You all right?" Ellie's voice startled him awake.

He moaned and looked over his shoulder to see her standing in the doorway. The angle of the sun told him it was early evening.

"I'm fine," he lied, and sat up.

"I brought you a plate of supper. I know you don't have so much as a grain of wheat in this place yet."

"Thank you," he said, and his stomach growled in echo of his appreciation.

"Come and eat before it gets cold," she said, and he followed her to the kitchen.

While Jon was eating, Ellie went out to the buckboard and brought in a large basket.

"What is that?" he asked, standing to help her with it.

"Just a few things to get you by," she said, and he peered in at a loaf of bread, some biscuits, butter, a jar of jam, and a few bottles of fruit.

"Thank you," he said, and kissed her cheek. "You're an angel. I'll make it up to you."

"You already have, Jon. Besides, you're family."

When she started back toward the door he said, "What else? Why don't you let me get it and—"

"Just eat your supper before it gets cold," she insisted. "I'm perfectly capable of bringing a few things into the house."

A few minutes later she hurried past him before he could get a good look at what she was carrying. Once he'd finished eating, he found Ellie in his bedroom, smoothing a blanket over the sheets she'd just put on the bed. He sighed and said again, "You *are* an angel."

"Nonsense. If you're done eating, now you can help me get the rest."

"The rest of what?"

"Just help me."

Jon helped her carry in a pillow, a box of dishes and linens, and a crocheted blanket.

"I need the dishes back when the ones you ordered get here. The rest is a house warming gift. I've had it in mind all along." She set the blanket into his hands and added, "Maddie made this. She gave it to me a few years back, and I always thought it was too pretty to use. I want you to have it."

Jon was momentarily too touched to speak. He found his voice enough to say, "Ellie, if she gave it to you then—"

"I'm certain she'll make me another one eventually. I want you to have this. Simple as that. Consider it a tangible reminder of what this is all about."

"And what is that?" he had to ask, hearing the disheartening tone in his voice.

"You and Maddie are meant to be together, Jon. I know it with all my heart. And you know it, too. But it's easy to lose perspective when you're in the middle of that refining process God sees fit to put us through. It's for our own good, of course. But you mustn't lose sight of what you're doing and why."

"Thank you, Ellie," he said, and pressed his fingers over the blanket, imagining Maddie's beautiful hands creating it.

"So, what else is wrong?" she asked.

Jon looked at her and chuckled. "You're practically a mind reader."

"No," she said. "I just know you well."

"And you have a great deal of discernment."

"So, what is it?"

"What if she can never see it, Ellie? What if she can never get beyond whatever it is she's afraid of? Will everything I've worked for be a waste?"

"Jon," she urged him to sit beside her on the edge of the bed, "you joined the Church because you knew it was true. You bought the house because you like it here and you want to stay. I really believe she'll come around, but you have to remember that you've done what you've done for the right reasons. You must have the faith that everything will work out according to God's will."

"And what if God's will is not for Maddie and me to be together?"

She answered, "What if it is, Jon? When you put your life in God's hands, you have to know there's a path that leads to peace and happiness."

Just as countless times in the past, Jon inhaled Ellie's humble wisdom. "Thank you, Ellie. I'd be lost without you."

"I'll always be here, Jon. Like I said, we're family."

"Ellie," he said as she walked toward the door, "tell Maddie that I'm sorry I got so angry. And tell her I love her."

Ellie nodded and smiled. "I'll tell her."

The next morning Peter arrived to do some finishing touches on the house. Jon interrupted his work and handed him a significant amount of money.

"What's this for?" Peter asked. "You already paid me in full."

"I want you to get the materials for the repairs on the Hansen home, and if Brother Hansen asks where the money came from, you tell him it was an anonymous donor."

Peter smiled. "That's real nice of you, Jon, but I don't think it will cost this much for—"

"You'll see that the repairs are made, won't you? And see that you do as good a job as you've done for me."

"Word's already going around that everybody's pitching in to help put the house in order. I had every intention of helping. I don't need to be paid for that."

"I'm not paying you for that," Jon said. "I'm giving you a bonus for the beautiful job you've done in making my house so fine. Enough said."

Jon knew, from the time he spent helping Dave in the fields, and an occasional visit from Ellie, that the Hansens were staying with them, and the work on the house was coming along. The Relief Society had gone in to clean away the smoke damage as much as possible. Ladies had taken curtains, bedding, and clothing to their homes to clean them. Other ladies had scrubbed the floors, walls and furniture.

Learning when the main part of the building project would take place, Jon stopped by to help the work along. He blended easily into the group working on rebuilding the kitchen, and he didn't even bother to glance at Glen Hansen. He felt good about the money he'd given Peter, who winked at him as he lifted another piece of lumber from the stack, recently delivered from the mill. It had depleted his savings significantly, but he doubted the money could have been spent any better. It might not make up for his anger toward Maddie or her father, but at least it would help the family.

In the midst of the building project, Jon heard that Sister Hyde and her young son had moved to Salt Lake City. She would be marrying a man she'd met while visiting relatives there some months ago. He was happy for her, happy to know that she'd found someone, but the news increased his ache to be with Maddie.

When the repairs were done, Jon was relieved to hear that the Hansens had moved back into their home. He'd missed spending time at Ellie's house and feeling like a part of the family. Now that he didn't have to worry about being under the same roof as Maddie, he shared meals and scripture time with the family, and continued working each day in the fields with Dave and the boys. People continued to seek him out for medical help, and they quickly learned that if they couldn't find him at Ellie's, they could find him at his new house. He left a few supplies at Ellie's, but moved most of them into a freshly painted cupboard in his new kitchen.

With life settling back into a comfortable pattern, Jon's mind was drawn to Ellie's suggestion, weeks ago, to write Maddie a letter with an official proposal of marriage. Jon put a great deal of time and thought into the letter, praying continually for guidance in saying what needed to be said in an appropriate way. He discussed his ideas with Ellie, and gave them a few days to settle before he finally put the full spectrum of his thoughts to paper, praying with all his heart and soul that Maddie would be able to reach past her fears and concerns and be willing to commit her life to him. After he'd put in writing everything he'd ever told her about finding her own happiness and making her own choices, he expressed his love and commitment, and his desire to do what was right and best. He told her that the bishop had weeks ago told him he was ready to go to the temple, and he wanted to take her with him. Knowing that in a few weeks time her father would be making his semiannual trip to Provo, he suggested that they marry then. They could move all of her belongings to their new home, and be married and on a honeymoon before he returned. He poured his heart out to her of how he'd prayed and mulled this decision over, and he knew it was right. He challenged her to take it to the Lord herself and then to let him know if she would accept his proposal.

Ellie delivered the letter to Maddie at a time when she knew Glen would be out in the fields for a few hours. Ellie returned with a note, reporting that Maddie had sat in her room and cried most of the time Ellie had been there. Jon opened the note to read:

> *My dearest Jon,*
>
> *You must know how I love you with all my heart, and my deepest wish is to be with you as you have proposed. But I simply cannot under the circumstances. It would break my father's heart; and I cannot hurt him after all he's done for me. I pray that his heart will be softened and can only wait for that. Thank you for all you've done for me, and I pray that one day you will forgive me.*
>
> *All my love,*
>
> *Maddie*

Jon sucked in his breath and gripped the back of a chair, fearing his knees would buckle.

"What?" Ellie asked. He handed it to her and slumped into the chair.

"I can't believe it," Ellie said and sat weakly next to him. "I just can't believe it."

Jon wanted to echo her words. He wanted to scream and cry and throw something. But all he could do was lumber out of the house. He dropped to his knees in a cluster of trees near the barn and cried himself into a numb state of shock. Then he laid back on the ground and stared up through the leaves, willing away the desire he felt to curse God and deny everything he'd come to believe in. In agony, he even considered going to California.

It was hours later before he could make himself stand up and go through the motions of living. Three days later he was still just going through the motions. He couldn't bring himself to get on his knees and pray, yet his mind was tormented with senseless pleadings to God for some measure of hope and peace. When he felt certain he could go no lower, Ellie returned from visiting Sylvia to report that Maddie hadn't gotten out of bed for three days.

"There are no apparent signs of illness. She simply says she doesn't feel well. She stares at the wall as if she's completely lost her will to live."

Jon squeezed his eyes shut and swallowed hard. "Don't expect me to respond to that without breaking something." He groaned and kicked a chair across the kitchen floor. Ellie didn't seem affected. "What has he done to her to make her believe so completely that she cannot live without him—or at least his approval?"

"I don't know, Jon, but you've got to find a way to undo it—and soon."

"And what am I supposed to do? I could carry her away and force her to marry me, but what does that accomplish beyond transferring her sentence from one cell to another? If she doesn't want the life I'm offering her badly enough to just reach out and take it . . . what can I do?"

"There's no easy answer, Jon. But God knows what can be done. And we're going to fast and pray for her. If the answers don't come, we'll do it again."

Once again Jon was struck with wonder at Ellie's humble faith and wisdom. She determined a day when she and Dave would fast, and informed Jon that Sylvia would be doing the same. At least he didn't have to feel like he was in this alone. For Jon, going without food seemed an insignificant sacrifice when he considered what he was up against. The answer seemed so simple, but apparently to Maddie it wasn't simple at all. It occurred to him somewhere in the middle of the day that Maddie had inherited her father's stubbornness. She was rigidly clinging to the idea that this decision had to be up to her father, and the only answer was for his heart to be softened. Jon prayed that *Maddie's* heart would be softened, that she would be enlightened with the understanding of her own accountability in making choices. And if there was anything—anything at all—that he could say or do to make a difference, he asked for divine help in knowing what it might be.

When a few days passed and nothing changed, they all fasted again. And while no immediate answers came, Jon couldn't deny the peace and hope he felt in bringing himself closer to the Spirit. Somehow he knew that everything would be all right.

Following their third fast, Jon was surprised early one morning to answer his door and find Sylvia there.

"What is it?" he asked in response to her alarmed expression. He didn't want to admit it, but he had prayed many times that Maddie would not sink so low as to consider taking her own life.

"She's getting worse, Jon," Sylvia said. "Will you come—as a doctor—and make certain there isn't something really wrong with her?"

"Where is—"

"He's gone out to the fields. Please come."

Jon nodded. "Of course. Go on home. I'll be there shortly."

Jon arrived at the house filled with anticipation and dread. He ached for any opportunity to see Maddie at all, but he'd heard Ellie's reports of how badly she was doing, and he wasn't certain he could face it. Sylvia opened the door before he stepped onto the porch. She silently led the way into Maddie's room. She was curled up in bed, facing the other direction. He could see nothing but her blonde hair laying against the bedding. He'd never seen it down before. His heart quickened.

"Maddie, honey," Sylvia said, touching her shoulder, "I asked Dr. Brandt to come and see if everything's all right."

She didn't respond, and Sylvia motioned Jon to the other side of the bed where Maddie could see him. He slid a chair close to the bed and sat down. Her face was mostly buried beneath the sheet.

"Maddie," he said gently and touched her brow. He knew it would be impossible to treat her like any other patient. At the sound of his voice she lifted her face to his view, and he quickly sucked in his breath. Her eyes looked sunken, almost glazed. Her countenance was completely void of the light and natural glow that had always been there.

When she said nothing he asked, "Are you hurting anywhere, Maddie?" She looked confused, so he said, "Do you have any pain, anything that's causing you discomfort?" She digested the question as if her brain were working slowly. In concern, he looked carefully into her eyes, then he pressed his fingers to her throat to check for swelling and to measure the rate of her pulse. "Maddie?" he urged when she remained silent.

"No," she said, her voice raspy, "I'm fine."

"Then why won't you get out of bed?" he asked. "Why are you only eating barely enough to survive? Why won't you talk to anybody?"

She looked briefly saddened just before huge tears brimmed in her eyes. Then with a seeming burst of energy, she sat up and reached her arms around him, holding to him as if he could save her from the very powers of hell. Jon returned her embrace, glancing at Sylvia over her shoulder. She had a hand pressed over her mouth and tears were trickling down her face.

Jon eased back to look into Maddie's eyes. He took her face into his hands and said firmly, "Tell me what you want me to do, Maddie. Anything. I'll do it. You can't allow yourself to lay here in bed and waste away. Are you hearing me?" She nodded but didn't speak. "Just give me the word, Maddie, and I'll give you the world. If you—"

The back door closed loudly. Maddie glanced quickly over her shoulder as if to verify that her mother was still in the room. Then, like a frightened rabbit with a wolf on the prowl, she ducked beneath the covers just before Glen's voice boomed through the house, "Who's here, Sylvia?"

He appeared in the doorway of the bedroom and Jon could see him turn visibly red.

"What in the name of heaven and earth are you doing here?" Glen demanded, glaring at Jon.

"*I* asked him to come," Sylvia said firmly, and Jon felt proud of her. He knew how difficult it was for her to stand up to him. "There's something terribly wrong with Maddie, and he's the only doctor for miles around."

"And what might your conclusion be, Doctor?" The remote evidence of concern in Glen Hansen's eyes was quickly squelched by the ring of sarcasm in his voice.

"There's nothing wrong with Maddie that some exposure to the world wouldn't cure. Physically she's fine. She's depressed, Mr. Hansen. She has no purpose or meaning to her life. And she seems to believe she has no control or power over who she is and what she does. Imagine that," Jon continued, imitating Glen's sarcasm. "Maddie will be just fine when she figures out that she has a right to be happy."

Glen's scowl tightened as he said angrily, "You have no idea what you're talking about, young man. Now get out of my house."

Jon moved toward the door, saying almost lightly, "I knew you were going to say that."

CHAPTER EIGHT
Light

Maddie winced when she heard the front door slam, knowing that Jon had once again come and gone. He seemed her only link to happiness, but there was this horrible, invisible wall that stood between them, and she simply didn't know how to break past it. She recalled what Jon had just told her father, and she knew he was right. She had no purpose or meaning to her life. She simply couldn't find any reason to get out of bed.

Maddie was surprised to hear her parents' voices raised in heated tones. While she knew that her mother and father often disagreed, she'd rarely heard them argue or become angry. She wondered what had happened to bring this on—this horrible side of her father she'd never even realized existed. She cried silent tears as she listened to her father angrily disparaging every aspect of Jonathon Brandt's character, and it was evident the greatest source of his anger was the fact that her mother had invited him into the house.

Maddie fully expected her mother to apologize profusely and promise that it would never happen again, but she distinctly heard her say, "She's not a little girl anymore, Glen. You can't hold her here like some kind of prisoner."

"Is that how you see it?" he growled.

"I see it how it is."

"I'm protecting her," Glen defended hotly. "I will not allow anything or anyone to ever hurt my little girl again."

"You're a good man, Glen, and I love you dearly. But you must open your heart and understand that she's not a little girl. She's a grown woman. And you're trying so hard to keep her from being hurt that you're hurting her worse than she's ever been hurt in her life. And eventually you're either going to force her completely away from you forever, or she will shrivel up and die. She needs to live, Glen. She needs to experience life and—"

"Now you listen to me," Glen interrupted in a voice more angry than Maddie had ever heard. "I will not tolerate such an attitude from my wife and you will not—"

"No, you listen to me," Sylvia's voice came with strength and power that Maddie had never believed her mother possessed. She could almost imagine her like a mother cat, hair standing straight up, and hissing at a stray dog that was threatening her young. "I've stood by and done my best to support you, even when I didn't agree. But it's gone too far. It's way out of hand. She's my daughter too, and she's dying in there." Sylvia's voice became tainted with emotion. "If you have any grain of genuine love for her, you will go in there and tell her that she has the right to be happy, and to choose her own future."

Through the silence that followed, Maddie prayed with every fiber of her being that her father would do just that. But he finally said, "He's got the wool pulled over your eyes, too. And I'm not going to stand here and listen to such nonsense. You'd do well to pay your husband a little more respect."

Once again, Maddie expected her mother to apologize and back down. But Sylvia said firmly, "You'd do well to pay attention to the counsel of your wife, and take a good long look at what's really going on here."

The back door slammed, and Maddie winced again, just as she'd done when Jon had gone out the front door. That was the sum of the matter, she thought. Jon was going one direction, and her father the other, leaving her and her mother caught in the middle of something that didn't seem to have any answers. No matter what Maddie chose to do, she would leave one of these men terribly unhappy.

Maddie was startled to hear her mother's voice in the room, and even more startled to hear the firm tone she was using—a tone she'd not heard since she was a child getting into mischief. And she'd not been able to get into mischief since she'd fallen out of that tree.

"Maddie, there's something I need to say to you. Turn around and look at me so I know you're paying attention."

Maddie hurried to wipe her tears and turned toward her mother. "Now you listen very carefully. I don't agree with your father's attitude about this situation. I have prayed that his heart would be softened. I believed that if I had enough faith he would change his way of thinking. But I've come to realize that no amount of faith will take away someone else's free agency. Are you understanding what I'm saying?"

Maddie nodded and Sylvia went on, "I have fasted and prayed over this matter more than I have ever done in my life. Now I'm going to tell you the conclusion I've come to. I'm not getting the answers because it's not my problem. It's *your* problem, Maddie girl. You need to pray about this. You need to open your heart to be receptive to whatever God tells you through the promptings of the Spirit. You're going to get past all of your own fears and worries and really listen. Are you understanding me?"

"Yes," Maddie said, wondering when this incredible transformation had taken place in her mother.

"And beyond that, I only have this much to say on the matter: I must stand beside my husband. I love him, and I know that at the heart of the problem is mostly a lot of fear and pain. But he's got them all covered over in pride so thick that it's become impossible to reach him. At the same time, you're my daughter. You're my flesh and blood. And my mother's heart is telling me that it's time for you to break free. You need to make some decisions, because I'm not going to tolerate this lying around all the time and wallowing in the mire. So you think about it. You pray about it. And you decide what's best for *you.* Not what's best for me, or your father, or even Jon Brandt. You only have control over you, and you're the only one beyond the good Lord who knows what's right for you. God wants you to be happy, Maddie, just as I do. He did not put you on this earth to waste away. He told us not to put our candle under a bushel, but to put it on a candlestick to give light. What are you going to do with the light that God gave you, Maddie? That's all I have to say. You let me know when you want to talk. You tell me what I can do to help, and I'll do all I can."

Sylvia turned and left the room. Maddie stared after her for endless minutes, while her words whirled around in a mind that had been recently void of any thought at all. When the thoughts were no longer original, she did as her mother suggested, and prayed. She prayed constantly through the remainder of that day and into the night. She finally slept and woke up praying. While her mind went through silent conversations with her Father in Heaven, she began to feel some measure of understanding, a glimmer of hope.

Maddie got out of bed for breakfast. Her father smiled at her across the table, then in a condescending tone he said to her mother, "I told you she was just fine."

Maddie continued to pray and ponder, intermittently reading from the Book of Mormon. She did little else that day and again late into the night. The following morning after breakfast her father left for Provo with a load of furniture. Maddie hugged him tightly and told him that she loved him. She cried after he left, instinctively knowing that it would be a long time, if ever, before they would be close again.

Maddie continued her study and prayer. She reread several times the letter Jon had written her most recently. When certain aspects of doubt hovered, she took out a piece of paper and wrote down a list of all the positive points of accepting Jon's proposal, as well as a list of the possible negative. She did the same thing regarding staying as she was. While she had a few specific questions she wanted to pose to Jon, the evidence before her was startlingly clear. It was evident which choice she had to make if she ever hoped to be completely happy. She asked the Lord specifically if the choice before her was the right one, and the peace that filled her was undeniable—which prompted her to ask: *Then why am I so afraid?*

"Mother!" she called, suddenly feeling the need to talk.

"What is it, darling?" she asked, appearing in the parlor doorway.

"Do you have a few minutes?"

"Yes, of course," Sylvia said, and sat down beside her on the sofa.

Maddie told her mother of all she'd been feeling and what she believed she should do. Sylvia smiled with tears in her eyes when Maddie said, "I really believe that I should marry Jon, no matter how difficult it might be. I believe that for all of Father's well meaning, he simply doesn't understand that this is right for *me.*"

"That's wonderful, darling. So what's wrong?"

"Why am I so afraid, Mother? Have I become so accustomed to Father making all my decisions that I don't believe I can make a decision without failing somehow? I almost feel going against him will leave me cursed or something."

"This is a big step for you, honey. But I believe it's simply habit making you afraid. Most children gradually come to terms with making their own choices a little bit at a time. But you didn't have those opportunities. I'm not sure we always did what was best for you, Maddie Jo. All I know is that we always loved you. Every parent makes mistakes; we're not perfect. It's up to you, as an adult, to determine what you're going to do with what life has given you. I believe that if you know this is the path God wants you to take, you need to put your trust in Him and know that He *is* perfect. He will see that you're protected, and I think He knows, just as I do, and just as you do, that Jonathon Brandt is a good man and he'll take very good care of you."

Maddie took a deep breath, feeling as if she could fully breathe for the first time in . . . she couldn't even think how long. "Mother," she said, "are you going to visit Ellie today?"

"Of course."

"Would you have her tell Jon that I'd like to see him? And could you get that dress out for me, the one you made last year, the red one?"

Sylvia beamed. "The one you've only worn once?"

"I've hardly had cause to wear it, now have I." Sylvia laughed and embraced Maddie tightly. "I love you, Mother," she finished.

"And I love you," Sylvia said, erupting to her feet. "I'd best hurry along."

Maddie laughed as she watched her mother bustle from the room and heard her rooting in the closet down the hall. She lifted her face heavenward and closed her eyes, willing the light she felt to come closer and fully penetrate her. She laughed and cried at the same time as it seemed to chase away her every doubt and fear. "Thank you, Lord," she murmured and laughed again.

* * * * *

Jon faintly heard the ringing of the triangle bell that Ellie had on her back porch. She had used it for years as a signal to let Dave know she needed him. More recently it had become the means to let Jon know that he had a patient needing attention.

Jon wiped the sweat from his brow with his sleeve, and waved toward Dave some distance up the field. Dave returned the wave, indicating that he understood, and Jon hurried to the house. He went in the kitchen to wash up, expecting to find a hurt or sick child there. When he only found Sylvia and Ellie, he asked frantically, "What's wrong? Is Maddie—"

"She's fine, Jon," Sylvia said, just before breaking into a smile. "But she wants to see you."

The quickening of Jon's heart turned instantly from fear to anticipation. He told himself not to get his hopes up as he said, "I should hurry home and change." He glanced down at himself. "I need to wash up and—"

"You have a clean shirt right here," Ellie said, as if she'd predicted his concerns. "There are advantages to having me help with your laundry."

"Thank you, Ellie," he said and kissed her cheek. Then he kissed Sylvia's for good measure. Within five minutes he was on his way to Maddie's house. He tethered the horse by the porch and took a deep breath before he knocked. It had been almost exactly a year since he'd come here for the first time. And his life had never been the same since. It was nice to know that Glen Hansen was miles away.

"Come in," he heard her call.

Jon stepped into the parlor and caught his breath. She was sitting in the center of the sofa, dressed in red taffeta, giving her pale skin and blonde hair an almost unearthly glow. Or perhaps the glow came from within, he reasoned, marveling at the stark contrast to the last time he'd seen her, only a few days ago. Her eyes were as bright as her smile. Her countenance radiated with the light that had initially drawn him to her. And he noticed she was wearing the heart-shaped pendant he'd given her.

"Hello, Jon," she said with a little laugh. Oh, to hear her laugh!

"Hello, Maddie," he replied, fidgeting with the hat in his hands.

While he sensed her purpose, he was determined to let her make the first move. Still, he offered, "It's good to see you, and to see you looking so well."

"It's good to see you too, Jon. Won't you sit down?" He moved toward a chair and she added, "No, over here." She patted the sofa beside her. He put his hat aside and sat down. She took his hands in hers and said, "That's better. There's something I need to ask you, because I don't want to ever have any reason to doubt. I want to know exactly where we stand."

"Of course," Jon said. "Ask me anything."

"You must understand, of course, that I may not ever be able to walk."

"I understand."

"And that means there is a great deal that I can't do for myself. I would need help from you that my mother wouldn't be there to give."

Jon's heart threatened to explode with hope and joy, something he hadn't dared indulge in for months now.

"I understand that, Maddie. I'm a doctor. I've cared for people in much worse condition. I will see that your every need is met, and I won't even get embarrassed, no matter what you might need me to do."

Maddie smiled. "It's not as bad as all that." She sobered and went on, "You must also understand that if I can't have children . . ."

"Maddie," he said when she hesitated, "I would love to have children, and I know you would, too. But that's not why I want to marry you. Who knows? Maybe I won't be able to father children. That issue is irrelevant."

She looked searchingly into his eyes, then she smiled, as if she'd found what she was looking for. Without moving her gaze she said, "Then I believe there's a question you need to ask me."

"I'm sorry?" he said, suddenly disoriented.

"You've asked me before, but it was on paper. I want to hear you say it, Jon. And then I can give you my answer."

Jon felt briefly dazed. He hoped she meant what he thought she meant. But he didn't want to be presumptuous and make a fool of himself. His remaining doubts vanished when she said, "I believe it's customary for you to get down on one knee."

Jon immediately did just that, taking both her hands into his. It was easy for him to speak with strength and passion. "I love you, Maddie Jo Hansen. I'm willing to pledge my heart, my life, my soul to you. Will you do the same for me, Maddie? Will you marry me?"

She touched his face and tears brimmed in her eyes. "Yes, Jon. Oh, yes!"

Jon watched her blur before the mist in his eyes. He felt her arms come around him and he pulled her close, moving to sit beside her as he did.

"Forgive me, Jon," she murmured tearfully, and close to his ear, "for being so stubborn and so blind. I promise to never be so stubborn again."

Jon laughed and looked into her eyes. "Now, what excitement would we have if you were never stubborn?"

She laughed as well. "I do believe you've got a stubborn streak yourself." Her smile sobered, and her eyes filled with fresh tears. "Where would I be if you hadn't stubbornly insisted that we should be together? What if you had given up on me? Being stubborn's not so bad, as long as you're stubborn about the right things. And looking at it that way, I intend to be stubborn too, Jon. I intend to give you all that I have, and never stop giving, because I know you will do the same for me."

Jon nodded, too moved to speak. He embraced her again, and then he kissed her. He kissed her as he never had before, attempting to express all of the hope and perfect happiness he was feeling in that one kiss.

"Oh, Jon," she said dreamily and looked into his eyes, "I have a feeling we're going to be very happy." She laughed. "At least I know *I* am."

"Oh, you won't be the only one happy, Maddie," he said and kissed her again.

"So," she said when he drew back, fearing he might get carried away, "how long do you think it will take us to put a wedding together? Five hours? Six?"

Jon laughed. "It might take just a *little* longer than that. I think I'd have to consult my dear aunt on such matters. I've never done this before."

"Well, go get her. And get my mother while you're at it."

"I've got an even better idea," he said as he stood and put on his hat.

He scooped her into his arms and she laughed. "What are you doing?"

"How long has it been since you got out of this house?" he asked as he kicked open the front door.

"Too long," she laughed as fresh air struck her face. When she noticed the horse tethered to the porch she said with urgency, "Wait a minute! What are you doing?"

Jon stopped walking and looked at her severely. "Do you think I would ever let you get hurt, Maddie?"

"No, but . . ."

"But?"

"I've never even been on a horse."

"Well, it's about time you had the pleasure." He set her sideways on the saddle. "Now just hang on to the saddle horn there until I . . ." He was almost immediately in the saddle behind her, with her situated partly on his lap. With one arm securely around her and the other holding the reins, he eased the horse into an easy walk. Maddie laughed and snuggled closer to him.

"That's not so bad, is it?"

"No," she laughed again, "it's wonderful, actually."

"Yes, it is," he said and pressed a kiss into her hair.

Jon and Maddie both laughed as he carried her into Ellie's kitchen before the astonished faces of his aunt and her mother. He sat on a chair and situated Maddie on his lap before he said, "Maddie wants to know how long it would take to pull a wedding together. She was guessing five or six hours. What do you say?"

Maddie laughed again with perfect happiness, and Jon noticed a hint of moisture in both Ellie and Sylvia's eyes. He knew exactly how they felt.

They spent the remainder of the day together, talking and laughing, and making plans. And Jon marveled at the miracle. Just to be sitting at the same table with her and share a meal was like a dream come true. That evening, after he had delivered Maddie home and reluctantly said good night, he knelt and poured out the gratitude in his heart. He'd never been so happy in his life.

The following morning Jon and Dave left early for Manti to see that all of the arrangements were made. They returned to hear that the bishop had paid Maddie a visit and she was ready to go to the temple. Over the next few days Sylvia and Ellie helped pack all of Maddie's belongings. Dave and the boys helped Jon move everything to his house, including a dresser, a cedar chest, and a rocking chair that belonged specifically to her. Sylvia and Ellie helped Jon make certain the house had everything it needed, and they put Maddie's things in order.

Sylvia spoke frankly with Jon concerning Maddie's care and needs, and he assured her that he would see she was cared for and comfortable. In truth, he was pleased to learn that she was actually quite independent with her personal care. She mostly needed help moving from one place to another, and to have all she needed put within her reach.

"And she's a fine cook, Jon," Sylvia insisted. "I've taught her all I know. You just put her on a chair between the stove and the table—scoot the table close enough for her to reach—and make sure she has what she needs, and she can handle it just fine. She can do the same with the laundry. Don't be waiting on her and doing everything for her, now. She's strong and capable."

"I know," Jon said. "And thank you."

"For what?"

"For raising her to be strong and capable, in spite of . . . the circumstances."

She smiled faintly. They both knew he meant her father's attitude of coddling her and being overprotective.

Sylvia touched his face briefly. "You're a good man, Jon. I thank God you came into our lives. No matter what happens, I want you to know that."

"Thank you . . . Mother." He chuckled. "May I call you Mother?"

"Yes, of course," she said, and he pressed a kiss to her cheek.

* * * * *

In the midst of all the preparations Sylvia took Jon to the attic and asked him to carry a trunk down to the kitchen where Maddie was sitting. Then she told him to make himself useful elsewhere. Sylvia lifted the lid and folded back some tissue before she pulled out a shimmery white dress.

"Oh, Mother!" Maddie said. "Wherever did you get it?"

"This is the dress I was married in," she said, pressing her fingers nostalgically over the fabric. "I know you have a white dress that would be suitable; it's practically new. But I don't think it would take much altering to make this fit you . . . if you want to wear it."

"Oh, I would love to!" she said. "It's beautiful." They embraced. "Thank you, Mother, for everything."

"It's a pleasure, Maddie, truly."

Maddie sighed. She didn't want to bring dismal thoughts into her plans, but she had to say, "I fear you will feel the repercussions of this far more than I."

"I'm prepared to meet those repercussions, Maddie, because I know in my heart that it's right. I don't want you to worry about that. I just want you to enjoy every minute of your special day—and your new life."

Maddie looked down. "I fear he will never speak to me again."

"I suspect that will be his attitude at first," Sylvia said. "But I believe with time he will soften. Perhaps missing you will lessen his pride. Perhaps seeing your happiness will help. All that really matters is that *you* continue to follow your heart, wherever it leads. And you can never go wrong."

Sylvia set the dress over Maddie's lap and dug further into the trunk. She brought out a set of temple robes and a veil that she had made specifically for Maddie years earlier.

"I dreamed of this day for you with every stitch. Nothing could make me happier than to see you married in the house of the Lord."

Maddie was too moved to speak, and too happy to believe that it was real. But Jon came back in the house a while later. His smile, his kiss, the light in his eyes were all evidence that it *was* real. And she thanked God, once again, for sending him to her front door, and subsequently into her heart.

* * * * *

The sky was still completely dark when they set out for Manti.

Dave drove the wagon with Ellie sitting next to him. Jon, Maddie, and Sylvia sat comfortably in the back against some pillows and blankets they'd brought along. At first Maddie felt sleepy and rested her head against Jon's shoulder, feeling perfectly secure. As the sun began to peek over the east horizon, she became enthralled with her surroundings. Never had the world looked so beautiful! Never had she felt so happy, so filled with hope.

"You know," Jon said, "we didn't do it on purpose, but it was exactly one year ago today that we met."

"Really?" Maddie said and laughed. "And when did you first know you were in love with me?"

"The first time I heard you laugh—like you did just now." She laughed again. "Yes, like that," he said, and laughed with her.

"I looked at you standing there in the parlor and wondered what I had ever done to deserve such a man coming into my life. But I never dreamed . . ."

"I'll tell you what you did," Sylvia said. "You were always a good girl with a good heart. It's evident God had the two of you picked out for each other."

"Amen to that," Ellie said.

A while later Dave said, "I can see the temple up ahead in the distance."

Maddie squealed with delight and Jon helped her to a position where she could see it.

"Oh, it's beautiful, Jon. It's a dream come true."

"Yes, it is," he said firmly, marveling at how deeply his life had changed in a year. He felt compelled to turn to Ellie, saying, "Ellie, have I ever told you how glad I am that you married a Mormon, came out west and joined the Church?"

"I don't believe you have," she said with a little laugh.

"Well, thank you. Now that I've done the same—thanks to you—I'm eternally grateful."

"Not quite," Dave said.

"Not quite what?" Jon asked.

"You haven't quite married a Mormon. Give it a few more hours."

Once inside the temple, Maddie marveled at the beauty. She'd heard countless times of its magnificence, but she never could have conjured up such splendor in her mind. The workers were all so kind and gracious, not seeming the least bit ruffled over her inability to stand and walk. They treated her like a queen and saw to her every need. Through the endowment presentation she often found herself looking at Jon, and him looking at her. She wished that her father could have been with them, but she knew in her heart this was the way it had to be. She prayed that he would forgive her, and she concentrated on all that she was learning and being given.

As Jon carried her up the stairs from the World Room into the Terrestrial Room, she caught her breath and whispered, "Oh, Jon, it's magnificent!"

"Yes, it is," he whispered back. "And being here with you is as close to heaven as I can imagine being in this world."

She drew her attention away from the beauty of the room to look into his eyes. "I couldn't agree more," she said and he set her down on one of the white benches, according to the temple worker's direction. Jon crossed the room and sat facing Maddie, feeling close to heaven, and as if the heat of his heart would melt through his chest.

Maddie stared once again at the beauty surrounding her as Jon carried her into the Celestial Room, and they sat close together on one of the many sofas. She admired the lofty ceiling, rich carpet, and sparkling chandeliers. But she still preferred the blue and white decor of the Terrestrial Room. She would never forget the perfect joy she'd felt to look over at Jon, and she could almost believe that their relationship had begun before this world had ever been created, and she knew it would go on long after death ended their time on earth. The crowning moment of the experience was the exchange of vows over the altar, sealing their marriage eternally in the presence of God and angels. And Maddie knew that she would have suffered any trial just to be here at this moment, knowing that what she felt for Jon—and he for her—would last forever.

They left the temple to find the sun high in the sky. After sharing a fine meal in town, Dave drove them to the train station, where they only waited a short while before the train arrived that would take Jon and Maddie to Salt Lake City. Farewells were exchanged on the platform where Maddie sat on a bench, wearing her red taffeta dress and the pendant Jon had given her.

"We can never thank you enough," Jon said to Dave, Ellie and Sylvia. "All of you . . . thank you for everything."

Sylvia embraced him, saying, "I know you'll take good care of my little girl."

"I will," he promised, and then smiled, "Mother. And you take care of yourself. Don't let him treat you badly."

"I promise," she said. "He's really a good man, Jon. I believe he'll come around . . . someday." Jon nodded and Sylvia sat beside Maddie to embrace her.

Dave shook Jon's hand firmly. "We're sure glad you decided to stick around, boy."

"So am I," Jon said. "I'll send a telegram to let you know when to expect us. Don't work too hard while I'm gone."

"I'll save some for you."

Jon laughed and turned to Ellie, hugging her tightly. "You've given me so much," he said. "I could never thank you enough."

"We're family," she said, and kissed his cheek. "Now, don't get all mushy on me. It's just a honeymoon, Jon. You'll be back in a couple of weeks."

"Yes, I will. And we'll be counting on an invitation to Sunday dinner."

"You know you're both welcome any time."

With their luggage and Maddie's wheelchair loaded, Jon carried Maddie aboard and she sat by the window to wave at the others as the train pulled away.

"Oh, Jon," she said when they were no longer in sight, "I just don't know how much happiness I can handle in one day."

"Don't worry, Mrs. Brandt, I'm certain you'll catch up with it."

She laughed and he put his arm around her. "I love to hear you call me that."

"No more than I love saying it."

"Tell me what we're going to do," she said, thinking that she'd not been to Salt Lake since she'd gone to see a doctor there following her back injury. And then she'd been utterly miserable.

"Whatever we feel like doing at any given moment. We're going to stay at a fine hotel, and we'll discover the city together. I hear they have concerts at the Tabernacle on Temple Square, and we can go through the temple and, well, we'll just unwind and let all the happiness catch up with us."

"It sounds delightful," she said and relaxed her head on his shoulder. She lifted her hand to admire the gold band shining there and laughed.

"What's funny?" he asked.

"Not funny, just happy," she said. "I'm Mrs. Jonathon Phillip Brandt."

"Yes, you are," he said, and pressed a kiss into her hair, amazed that such happiness existed.

CHAPTER NINE
Home Is Where the Heart Leads

Dave and Ellie were waiting at the station when the train pulled in. Carrying Maddie out to meet them, Jon couldn't help thinking of the day, little more than a year ago, when he'd first arrived here by train. He felt so grateful for the changes in his life. Being Maddie's husband had left him every bit as happy as he'd ever dreamed. And it had been readily evident that Maddie was equally happy. Her continual laughter and glowing eyes put a distinct light in his life.

Ellie squealed with delight when she saw them. He set Maddie on the bench and they all laughed and embraced.

"It's so good to see you," Ellie said. "Did you have a good time?"

"The most *wonderful* time," Maddie insisted. Ellie sat beside her to hear all about it while Jon and Dave collected the luggage and Maddie's wheelchair.

On the ride home, the conversation finally ran to the inevitable question. "So . . . how are my parents?" Maddie asked Ellie.

"Well . . ." Ellie drawled, "in a manner of speaking, everything's fine."

"Dare I ask what you mean by that?" Jon said.

"Well . . ." Ellie continued again, "when it was getting time for Glen to come home, Sylvia purposely stuck close to our house. Glen came looking for her, and of course he'd figured out that Maddie was gone and so were all of her things. His reaction wasn't a surprise. He raged and yelled, but Sylvia just listened, didn't argue, didn't get upset. I was real proud of her. Finally Dave told Glen that he had to calm down or leave. Glen told Sylvia to come home with him. She said she wasn't going anywhere with him until he calmed down and treated her decent. You know as well as I do, Maddie, that he's never been so prone to getting angry as he has over this."

"I just bring out the best in him," Jon said with sarcasm.

Ellie chuckled. "Well, he's always had a difficult streak, but I think this problem just hits close to something we don't understand. Anyway, Sylvia told him she'd done her best to stand by him, even though she hadn't agreed with him, that she'd been a good wife and worked hard for him and she would not tolerate him talking to her that way."

"Tell them the best part," Dave said eagerly.

"Well," Ellie laughed slightly, "Glen listened for a minute then he started getting angry again. But Sylvia just stopped him cold. She said that we had a bed for her, and she wasn't going to live under the same roof with him if he was going to act like that. She told him that Maddie was a grown woman and she had made the choice, and as her mother, she had chosen to help her and be with her when she was married. Then she asked if he wanted her to come home or not. He said he did, and she said that was fine, but the first time he raised his voice to her, she would be staying elsewhere and he'd be awfully hungry because he couldn't boil water without help. Since then, Sylvia tells me he's been rather quiet and moody, but he's gotten over the angry part."

"That's good then," Maddie said eagerly and squeezed Jon's hand. He knew how hard they'd both been praying that her father's heart would be softened, now that this step had been taken.

When Ellie and Dave exchanged a cautious glance, he knew there was more. Maddie's countenance fell and he feared what else Ellie had to tell them.

"Well, it is good. But your mother's had to make a concession in order to keep peace and make your father feel that there's some compromise. It's hard, but I have to say I understand why she stands by him as long as he behaves himself."

"So, what's this concession?" Jon asked warily.

"Well . . ." Ellie's tone suggested that something akin to a death had occurred. When she finally said it, Jon felt the tone was appropriate. "Glen said that Maddie had made her bed, and she was going to have to sleep in it. He said she'd made her choice, she'd severed her ties, and he no longer considered her his daughter."

Maddie gasped, and huge tears spilled down her cheeks. She pressed a hand to her heart and her face to Jon's shoulder. He held her close and told her how he loved her and everything would be all right, while inwardly he seethed with anger toward Glen Hansen. He was amazed that one man's pride and stubbornness could cause so much grief.

"But don't you worry, Maddie honey," Ellie said. "Your mother and I have already got a plan worked up. You and your mother can exchange letters and leave them with me. Sylvia's going to read your letters at my house and keep them there, then your father won't be the wiser. And of course, you'll see each other at church."

"Church?" Maddie said. "You mean . . ."

"What?" Jon asked when she hesitated.

"I just hadn't thought about being able to go to church. It's so wonderful."

"Yes, it is," Ellie said.

"Amen," Dave added.

"We went to church in Salt Lake City," Maddie told them eagerly. Jon smiled seeing her sorrow over her father's attitude quickly disappear in her happiness. He'd enjoyed every minute of sharing a world with her that she'd been completely sheltered from. And now that they'd come home, she would have the opportunity to immerse herself in the community she had always lived in but never been a part of.

Dave pulled the wagon up in front of the house and Maddie just beamed in delight. Jon laughed as he carried her toward the door, glad he'd chosen to wait to show her the house until now.

"I guess carrying you over the threshold isn't a surprise, is it," he said as they stepped inside. She laughed spontaneously as he carried her from room to room, giving her a quick tour. He left her sitting in the kitchen while he helped Dave bring in the luggage. He returned to find the women together in the kitchen, Ellie pointing out how the kitchen had been well stocked, and how most of the things Maddie would need for cooking had been put down low enough for her to reach. After Dave and Ellie left, with an invitation for Sunday dinner, Jon pointed out to Maddie how the furniture had been arranged for easy maneuvering with the wheelchair. Then, when the moment was right, he went out to the barn and came in with the new wheelchair he'd ordered.

"It came while we were gone," he said when she was too emotional to speak. "Not only is your other chair getting old and worn, but this one is easier to maneuver, and it's built so that you can push the wheels yourself with your hands, which means . . ." he couldn't help laughing, "you can move around most of the house all by yourself."

Maddie laughed through her tears. "I never dreamed that such a thing could be possible," she said. "It's wonderful."

"Well," he said, pulling her onto his lap, "I should only need to leave for a few hours at a time to work in the fields, but I didn't like the idea of your being stuck and unable to move if you had a problem."

"You're so good to me," she said, hugging him tightly. "I don't understand how you can love me so much."

Jon looked into her eyes and touched her face. "You're so easy to love, Maddie. Loving you is the easiest, greatest thing I've ever done in my life. You're the best thing that ever happened to me."

"You can only say that because I introduced you to the gospel," she said.

"Yes, well . . ."

"And you're the best thing that ever happened to *me.*"

He took her out to the barn to show her the cows, horses, and chickens that Dave had been caring for in their absence. They sat in the used buckboard he'd purchased, and he told her his plans for getting some pigs next spring, since he was rather fond of pork.

They returned to the house to unpack, and then together they prepared supper, ate, and cleaned the dishes. Jon felt at peace with her presence, and the light that surrounded her. Finally this house had become a home. Finally, he'd found his place. His heart had led him to Maddie, and she had already given him more happiness than he had ever dreamed possible.

"Thank you," he said before he extinguished the lamp to go to sleep.

"For what?" she asked, settling onto her pillow.

"For making my house a home," he said, touching her face. "For making my life worth living. For making me feel like I've truly come home—in all respects."

Maddie touched his face in return. "The feeling is mutual, Jon. As long as we're together, I'll always be home." She laughed softly. "It's like my grandmother used to say: *'Home is where the heart leads.'*"

"Amen," Jon said and kissed her.

She snuggled close to him and relaxed. Jon was nearly asleep when he realized she was crying. He leaned up on one elbow and demanded quietly, "What is this?"

"I thought you were asleep," she said and sniffled.

"So, you're trying to hide something from me? Is that how you think it should be?"

"No, but . . ." She sniffled again. "I didn't want anything to mar our happiness. And I am happy, Jon. I don't want you to think otherwise. I'm glad I made the choice I did. I know it's right, but . . ." She became too emotional to speak and he drew her head to his shoulder.

"Tell me," he urged once she'd calmed down somewhat. He had a pretty good idea what the problem was, but he knew it would be better for her to say it.

"I just don't understand why I had to make a choice. Other girls have their fathers at their weddings. Why can't I have a father and a husband both? Why does it have to be this way?"

"I can't answer that, Maddie," he said gently. "I know it's hard for you, but what else can you do?"

"Nothing, I know. That's the problem. I feel so helpless. It's all so . . . stupid."

"Well, if you need to cry, Maddie, go ahead and cry. But don't be trying to hide your grief from me. You have a right to grieve. You've lost something. I know that."

Her voice brightened, "But I've gained so much more, Jon. And I'm grateful. Truly I am."

"As long as we always stop to count our blessings, I'm sure we'll make it through."

"I'm sure we will," she said and drifted to sleep.

The following morning as they were finishing breakfast, Jon said, "There are a few things we need in town, so—"

"Oh, don't you worry about me," she said. "I'll be fine. You take as long as you need and—"

"I have no intention of leaving you here," he said, his indignation mingled with humor. "If you think you're going to pin all of the shopping on me, you're quite mistaken. Now hurry up and eat."

"You mean . . ." She couldn't seem to put the words together.

"Yes, Maddie," he said. "We're going into town—both of us."

Maddie let out a spurt of the delightful laughter he loved so dearly, then she hurried to get ready to go. She kept smiling as they drove toward town in the wagon Jon had recently purchased. The barest hint of autumn hung in the air. The sun was as warm and pleasant as the happiness in Maddie's eyes.

They felt curious glances as Jon stopped the wagon, took out the new wheelchair and put Maddie in it. They went together into the general store, and Jon felt a bittersweet joy at the evidence of Maddie's innocent excitement. She observed the shelf items like a starving child in a candy store. He reminded himself not to feel angry over the past, but to enjoy all that was good in the present. They looked around and discussed what they needed while Sister Larson, the storekeeper, helped a customer with some lengths of fabric. When Sister Larson finally turned to help them, her eyes nearly popped out of her head. She squealed as if she'd seen a mouse, then laughed with obvious embarrassment at her reaction.

"Would this be Maddie Jo Hansen I see out shopping?" she asked, extending a hand to Maddie. "I haven't seen you since over a year ago when I was out to visit your mother."

"Actually," Maddie began, "I'm—"

"And how are you, Brother Brandt?" she asked Jon. "Haven't seen you at church the last couple of weeks. We were speculatin' over whether or not you'd gone inactive." He wondered who exactly she meant by *we*. Probably the entire town, and then some. But he was pleasantly surprised to realize that the few people who had known about their marriage hadn't provided any fodder for idle chatter. He'd have to thank Ellie and Dave for not being gossips, and for teaching their children the same.

"No," he said with a little chuckle, "I haven't gone inactive. We went to church in Salt Lake City the last two Sundays. And now we're—"

"We?" she echoed, looking speculatively at Maddie, then him again.

"My wife and I," Jon said, putting a hand on Maddie's shoulder. "This is now Mrs. Brandt."

"Well, I'll be," Sister Larson said with obvious pleasure. "I do believe that's the best news I've heard all year."

"I could agree with that," Jon said.

Mrs. Larson helped them gather all they needed. They lingered and took their time, while Maddie obviously enjoyed the experience. Other people Jon knew from church came and went, some who hadn't even known that the Hansens had a daughter, others who hadn't seen her in a long while. The news of their marriage was received with genuine pleasure and Jon felt certain it would travel far before nightfall. More than one person expressed their appreciation to him for medical services rendered in the past. He noticed Maddie giving him a sly smile each time it came up.

As people lingered to speak with Maddie, the store became a little more crowded, with several people wanting to talk with her at once. He noticed her becoming visibly agitated. He could hardly imagine how it might feel for her to be in such a situation after so much seclusion. Their time in Salt Lake City hadn't brought such personal attention; this was an entirely new experience for her.

Jon hurriedly pushed her wheelchair through the small crowd, saying lightly, "We're finished here, and we've got lots to do at home. It's been good seeing all of you."

Once they were outside, Jon discreetly asked, "Are you all right?"

"I think so," she said breathlessly. "I just . . . panicked all of a sudden. I don't know why."

"You haven't been around too many people at once. I think it will take some getting used to. And naturally people will be curious and excited."

"I'm sure you're right," she said, but she sounded doubtful.

Jon got her situated in the wagon and went back in to get their purchases. "I'll just be two minutes, I promise."

She nodded, but he sensed her anxiety. He returned quickly, sitting beside her and starting the horses toward home. Within a few minutes he could see her relaxing.

"Feeling better?" he asked.

"Yes, thank you."

"Are you wishing you hadn't gone?"

"No, of course not," she insisted. "I had a good time. I think it's just like you said: people are naturally curious and excited. It will just take some getting used to."

"Do you think you'll be up to going to church?" he asked. "Practically everyone there will be happy to see you."

"I'll be fine," she insisted. "As long as you stay close to me, I'll be fine." A few minutes later she smiled thoughtfully and said, "I really did have a good time."

Jon laughed, "If an outing to the general store is that exciting, you're not going to be too difficult to please."

"Just as long as I have you," she said, taking his hand, "I couldn't ask for anything more."

Jon smiled at her, appreciating her sincerity, but he couldn't miss the glimmer of sadness in her eyes. There was only one deterrent to their happiness, but neither of them were capable of changing Glen Hansen's heart. Jon squeezed her hand and said firmly, "I love you, Mrs. Brandt."

Maddie met his intense gaze and it was easy to forget about her father's disdain. "And I love you . . . Dr. Brandt."

"I hate it when you call me that," he said. His voice was light, but there was a hint of hardness in his eyes.

Maddie was well aware of the difficult feelings Jon had toward his father, and why Jon had become a doctor. He'd done it to please his mother, and leaving Boston had been partly with the intention of leaving behind his medical profession. But Maddie had come to know Jon well enough to realize that he was stubbornly clinging to an idea that made little sense. She knew better than to try and talk him out of his feelings, but she hoped that eventually he would come to see what was obvious to everyone else—that he had a talent for the field.

"And why shouldn't I call you that?" she asked. "You are, after all, a doctor."

"Technically, yes," he said. "And I'm glad to be able to help people when they need it, but it's just not what I want to be."

"Okay, but whether you farm or mine or keep a shop, Jon, you're still a doctor. You have the education and the experience; you've earned the title. Isn't it appropriate to be called *Dr. Brandt?*"

He scowled at her and she laughed.

"What's so funny?"

"You are," she said. "You're absolutely adorable when you get frustrated."

"Well, I am frustrated," he said, ignoring her compliment. "Why don't they put a title in front of everyone's name? Farmer Jensen? Shopkeeper Smith? Miner Christensen?"

"I don't know, Jon. I can't say why society functions the way it does. Perhaps because those professions didn't require years of education to be qualified."

"Not officially, perhaps. But Dave, for example, knows the land like the back of his hand. The fact that he didn't have the opportunity for a formal education is irrelevant. He's very good at what he does."

"Yes, he is. But that's just my point. You *did* have the opportunity for an education—an education that many would greatly envy. Your knowledge and skill are valuable, especially in a community where medical help isn't readily available. But, well, at the risk of making you angry, my dear husband, I must say, you treat this gift you've been given very flippantly. Perhaps you should consider how very blessed you are and simply admit that you're a doctor."

Jon's scowl deepened, but he said nothing. Maddie wondered if his silence was the only way he could avoid showing that he was angry. She questioned her own judgment when she added, "I think this has a lot more to do with your feelings toward your father than it does your preference in profession."

Now he looked angry.

"It would seem I've hit a sore point," she said.

"It would seem you have," he admitted, his voice low and gruff.

When he said nothing more she added, "I will always love you no matter what your profession may be. And I know you would do whatever you have to in seeing that our needs are met. I just think that maybe you should give the matter some thought. If you want to be a farmer—or anything else, for that matter—it's entirely up to you. But do it for the right reasons. Don't throw away your education and experience because you have difficult feelings for your father."

Jon glared at her, but he said nothing. When it became evident she wasn't going to be intimidated by his scowl, he quietly turned away and concentrated on the drive home, all the while telling himself that, in spite of her advice, he had no intention of giving the matter some thought. He didn't want to think about it *at all.*

But late that night, while Maddie slept beside him, Jon stared toward the ceiling; echoes of unpleasant conversations with his father paraded through his mind. He couldn't count the arguments they'd had through the years—and most of them had been centered around one particular issue: Phillip Brandt's wish to see his son follow in his footsteps. Privately, his mother had pleaded with him time and again to trust his father in spite of his brash ways and lack of sensitivity. She had wanted only to please her husband and keep peace. However, Jon couldn't resent her for that; Carol Brandt had been so completely without guile and full of love that Jon never found reason to do anything that would make her unhappy. He'd hated every minute of medical school, but he'd worked hard to get good grades in order to please his mother. His years of work at the hospital had been for the same reason. His father had always wanted for them to work together, to pass his practice on to his son. But that would have been more than Jon could stand.

Jon knew that his biggest reason for leaving Boston had been to get away from his father. But his leaving had brought him to a life he loved—in spite of still being a doctor. He couldn't deny that he enjoyed helping people in need, but that didn't change the way he felt about being trapped in the profession. He didn't want to be a doctor. He wanted to be a farmer, a miller, a miner—anything but a doctor. He just didn't want to! *Did he?*

Maddie's words refused to leave his conscience in peace. Did he truly not want to be a doctor, as he'd always tried to convince himself? Or did his feelings have more to do with his relationship with his father—or rather the lack thereof?

Jon finally slept, and he woke with barely enough time to care for the animals and get to church. He was pleased to see that Maddie was excited about going to church, but he hoped the situation wouldn't cause her any anxiety.

"I've missed it so much," she said when they arrived.

"There's no reason why he couldn't have brought you to church, Maddie," Jon said.

"Oh, he had his reasons," Maddie said. "I just found them difficult to understand."

"As do I," he added. "Now, let's not talk about that. Just enjoy the moment."

Maddie's heart quickened as Jon carried her into the chapel; they didn't want to bother with the wheelchair since she wouldn't be needing to move around. They entered in the middle of the opening song, and were only noticed by a few people as they settled on the back row. Maddie felt people staring and whispering, but she sensed that their surprise was positive, just as it had been in town yesterday. She was glad to have arrived late so that she could avoid any personal attention until she had a chance to get her bearings. With a quick scan of the room she located her parents on the other side of the chapel. Her father was focused straight ahead with a stern, harsh expression that chilled her. But she exchanged a longing glance and a smile with her mother that brought back the warmth she'd been feeling.

That warmth deepened as the meeting progressed. Maddie was close to tears through most of it, so filled with gratitude for all that her mother and Jon had done for her. Little could make her happier than to actively participate in the gospel that meant so much to her, and to have Jon at her side. As the meeting ended, they became surrounded by ward members with questions and well wishes. She kept Jon's hand in hers and willed herself to not get panicked as she had in town. Many people asked if she was feeling better, or commented on her improved health, making it evident that they had been led to believe she was absent due to poor health. She appreciated the way Jon steered around such comments. There were so many that she wondered if her father would be confronted with the same. She also wondered how he might answer questions concerning her long confinement.

After answering the same question what seemed like dozens of times, Maddie began to feel nervous despite the well-meaning faces of the members. She felt her heart rate increase and her palms sweat. She forced a smile and squeezed Jon's hand tightly. He immediately responded, graciously moving her out to the buckboard. She took a deep breath once she was seated.

"I'm fine, thank you," she said before he had a chance to ask. "It wasn't as bad as yesterday. I'll get used to it."

Jon smiled and sat beside her. About halfway home, she said, "That was wonderful. Thank you."

"It's my pleasure. Before long church will just be an ordinary occurrence."

"After being away for so long, I don't know if I could ever feel that it's ordinary."

"Well," he said, "the reasons we go to church should never be *ordinary*. Let's just say that eventually you'll wonder how you ever survived without going."

Maddie looked down at her hands and had to admit, "I already do."

"What?"

"I wonder how I ever survived." She knew he'd caught the emotion in her voice when he shifted the reins to his right hand and put his arm around her. "I love my father, Jon, but . . ."

"But?"

"This is difficult to admit, but . . . I have to ask myself why he would keep me so thoroughly secluded? Why was I not allowed to participate in simple things like going to the store? Or going to church? Does he have any idea how *horrible* that feels? And do you know how horrible I feel for even thinking of such things?"

Jon sighed and searched for the right words. He'd never heard her speak about her father this way, but he reasoned that it was a good step. "Maddie," he said, "it's good for you to honestly admit to your feelings. Now that you're away from the situation you have a broader perspective. It's okay to admit that you're angry; you have cause to be. But being angry with him won't do any good. The best way your father can understand what he's done is for him to observe how happy you are."

"How can he observe anything if he won't even see me?"

Jon tried to smile. "Give it time. Just enjoy your life and live it the way you choose. You musn't let your feelings toward him keep you from living the life you were meant to."

Jon saw her countenance soften and knew she would be all right. But he wasn't prepared for the way she turned to him with severe eyes and said, "Maybe you should take your own advice, Jon."

It took him a minute to recall what he'd said and how it applied to him. And then *he* felt angry; angry with Maddie for confronting him on feelings he didn't want to look at, and with himself for feeling this way at all. Surprisingly enough, he wasn't angry with his father. It seemed that the time and distance had lessened the tension he felt concerning his father.

In response to Maddie's expectant gaze he said, "Maybe I should." And then he changed the subject.

They went to Dave and Ellie's house for dinner and had a wonderful visit. It was one more reminder of how dearly he loved the turn his life had taken. He'd always loved being in Ellie's home and feeling like a part of the family, but being with them was only made better by having Maddie there, and knowing they had a home of their own.

Maddie loved being in Ellie's home. The closeness she shared with her mother's best friend deepened with the blessing of being able to spend time in her home; and the distance she felt from her mother was eased by Ellie's presence.

When dinner was over and the boys were washing the dishes, Ellie gave Maddie a letter from Sylvia. Maddie shed a few tears as she read it, but her mother's assurance that all was well, and her joy over Maddie's happiness, soothed the ache of the ridiculous separation. That evening, while Jon wrote his weekly letter to his sister in Boston, Maddie wrote a long letter to her mother, telling her all they'd done, and how happy she was. Jon delivered it to Ellie's the following morning after the chores were done, and he returned to tell her that Dave wouldn't be needing his help that day.

"Which makes it a perfect day for a picnic," he said eagerly.

Maddie almost squealed with delight just recalling the picnic they'd shared over a year ago.

"It was one of the best days of my life," Maddie said while they worked together filling a hamper with food.

"What was?" he asked.

"The picnic you took me on right after we met."

Jon smiled. "It's pretty high on my list, too."

They didn't have to go far from the house to find the perfect spot under a cluster of trees. Jon spread out a blanket, then made certain Maddie was comfortable there. She watched him retrieve the hamper from the buckboard and silently thanked God for blessing her life so completely.

"Jon," she said after they'd eaten and cleared the blanket so they could lay back and look up through the trees. "Do you remember when you said that . . . it might be possible for me to walk again?"

"I remember," he said.

"I know I asked you this before, but do you really think it's possible?"

"I do," he said firmly, and leaned on his elbow to look into her eyes. Now that he'd become more familiar with what she was physically capable of, he was even more convinced that it was possible. He'd given the matter a great deal of thought, but he didn't want her thinking that whether or not she could walk made any difference to him, so he'd decided to say nothing until she brought it up.

"Tell me what you think," she said, and he repeated his theory on the situation, going into more detail from a medical perspective. He explained the process of exercising her legs, and felt certain that within a reasonable length of time they could determine whether it would be worthwhile to continue.

"I want to try," Maddie said eagerly.

"It won't be easy," Jon cautioned. "It's going to take a lot of hard work and determination."

"From you as well," she said.

"Yes, but . . . I'll gladly do anything I can to help you, Maddie, if it's what you want."

"Oh, I do, Jon."

"Your father told me I shouldn't get your hopes up. If it doesn't work out, will you—"

"At least I'll know I tried. You've already taught me that good things come from reaching beyond what's comfortable. And what about you, Jon? If it turns out I can't walk . . ."

"As I told you before, Maddie, it's an honor to be your husband, and to take care of you, no matter what." He smiled and kissed her. "And either way, you have to take care of me too."

"I'll do my best," she said.

He touched her face. "You already take such good care of me, Maddie. I never dreamed I could be so happy."

"Amen," she said and kissed him as if the sun could rise and set on a single kiss.

"Ooh," he teased, "we didn't kiss like that on our *last* picnic."

"That's because it would have been scandalous, Dr. Brandt."

"And now?" he laughed, almost getting used to having her call him that.

"Now, I'm yours. And your mine. And everything is perfect."

"So it is," he said and kissed her again.

* * * * *

The following day it rained off and on. Maddie sat near the window and watched the weather while she crocheted. She felt anxious for Jon to return from working with Dave, and had to remind herself that she needed to get used to having time without him every day. They'd been together almost constantly since the day they'd married. She forced herself to stay busy and keep her thoughts elsewhere and was actually surprised to hear him come in the back door.

"Hello," she said eagerly when he entered the room in his stocking feet.

"Hello," he replied, and bent to kiss her before he sat down close by. "So, what have you been doing?"

"Mostly daydreaming," she said.

"Tell me."

Maddie looked out the window and mused, "I couldn't help thinking about all the times as a child when I used to sit and watch it rain, and how I longed to go out and play in it. Of course, my father wouldn't let me. He was certain I would get terribly ill or something."

She sighed and Jon said, "A little rain never hurt anybody."

With no warning he lifted her into his arms and carried her toward the door.

"What are you doing?" she laughed.

He pushed the door open with his foot. "Like I said, a little rain never hurt anybody."

Maddie laughed and lifted her face heavenward as the rain bathed over her. Jon laughed too, and he turned with her in his arms until they were both dizzy, then he sat on the porch step with her draped over his lap.

"Oh, it's wonderful," she said, holding out her arms as if she could catch every drop and hold it. "I wish I could just dance in the rain like some kind of wild wood nymph."

Jon laughed, but his voice was intense as he said, "Maybe you can."

Maddie looked into his eyes, recalling the hope he'd given her that she might be able to walk again. With firm determination she repeated his words, "Maybe I can."

That very day Jon began helping Maddie exercise her legs. It made her feel that he was working very hard, and that she was incapable of doing anything at all. But he assured her that would change with time. She didn't bother verbalizing the grain of doubt she had—that all his effort would be for nothing, and she would end up a burden to him for the rest of his life. As she struggled he smiled at her and told her he loved her, and it didn't take much effort to remind herself that he'd made it clear—both by his words and actions—that he would always love her no matter what. She felt truly blessed.

When Sunday came again, Maddie felt no change in her inability to move her legs, but Jon assured her it would take much longer than that. She enjoyed church even more than she had the previous week. Now that people had become accustomed to seeing her, and she'd become more comfortable being in public, she was able to relax and felt very little anxiety. However, she was saddened when she discovered that her father was absent. She couldn't help wondering if it had something to do with her being there, and all the fuss everyone had made over her appearance in society after so many years. A letter from her mother later affirmed that her assumptions had been correct. Maddie shed a few tears, but made up her mind not to allow this one sadness to mar the joy she was finding in her new life. She prayed for her father's heart to be softened, and did everything she could to be a good wife to Jon.

Later that week was the annual harvest ball. Maddie was surprised when Jon announced they would be going.

"But I can't dance," she said, as if it might not have occurred to him.

"It's not just about dancing, Maddie. It's a social. You can visit with people, and they have great punch and cookies. I went to this thing last year and missed you dreadfully. We're going, and we'll love it."

Maddie couldn't deny her excitement at the prospect, and she wore her red dress at Jon's insistence. "It has great sentimental value," he said. "Not to mention you look stunning in it."

In spite of Maddie longing to be able to dance, she had a wonderful time, and she felt absolutely no anxiety at being with so many people. On the way home Jon said, "You seemed to enjoy yourself."

"Oh, I did," she said. "I remember my parents taking me to the harvest ball a couple of times as a child. I dreamed for days afterward of being all grown up and dancing the way I'd seen the ladies dance." She sighed deeply. "Maybe next year I will be able to dance."

Jon smiled and kissed her hand. "Maybe you will," he said. "Either way, we'll go and have a marvelous time."

Through the remaining weeks of autumn Jon worked helping Dave in the fields, and in the garden with the final stages of harvest. Maddie worked with Ellie in preserving the bounty, except for the times that Ellie went to her mother's house to work. Maddie ached over not being allowed to participate in something she'd done for years. She had to consciously control feelings of anger and resentment toward her father, knowing they would accomplish nothing.

Each morning and evening Jon diligently exercised and massaged her legs. She found the ritual tiring and not necessarily enjoyable, except for the way Jon talked and teased her. She concluded that almost anything was endurable as long as she had Jon.

Maddie loved the mobility of her new chair; and Jon gradually helped arrange the furniture and household items in a manner easily workable for her. She felt an independence that added to her contentment, and with it she almost believed she could be content to never walk again. Almost.

On a particularly gray day, Jon went out to help Dave soon after breakfast. Maddie finished cleaning the dirty dishes and proceeded to wipe them dry. She was nearly finished with the task when she dropped the towel. She knew another one was within her reach, but she didn't want to bother moving to get it; besides, she'd been able to pick some things up off the floor before, if she was careful. However, this time she reached just a little too far and lost her balance. She screamed as she hit the floor, then immediately panicked when she realized her helplessness. As accustomed as she'd become to her inability to stand or walk, she was still amazed at how thoroughly useless her legs were. Feeling that she needed Jon, she attempted dragging herself toward the door, certain her only chance would be to get to the porch and call for him. She lost her strength before reaching the door, and hit her fist on the floor in frustration. She tried to console herself in the fact that Jon was likely too far away to hear her anyway. But as she lay with her face against the floor, she was reminded of the day she'd been alone when the fire had started in the kitchen. She didn't know what had happened, only that the house was filling with smoke. The helplessness and terror she'd felt then came back to her now. Her breathing became shallow, and her pulse quickened until she feared she might pass out.

Convincing herself that she needed to calm down, Maddie turned her mind to prayer. She focused her entire being on asking her Father in Heaven that she be kept safe. Within a few minutes a marked peace began to fill her. She recalled how even in the face of that fire, the Lord had prompted both her mother and Jon to help her, and she had been fine. And now there was no emergency, nothing to be afraid of. She was simply faced with a rather unproductive morning, stuck as she was. She folded the towel, now within easy reach, and tucked it beneath her head, finding that she wasn't necessarily uncomfortable.

As she continued to pray and think, Maddie's mind wandered through the circumstances of her life. She'd found so much happiness with Jon, but as always, she felt an ever-present heartache with thoughts of her father's attitude. For more than an hour she prayed for understanding and forgiveness, and found that while she didn't fully understand his reasoning, she knew his motives had always stemmed from his love for her, even if it had gotten out of hand. She cried silent tears when it became evident that she'd found some forgiveness for the hurt he'd caused her. And with that added peace, she drifted to sleep.

Maddie's next awareness was Jon nudging her awake. "Maddie?" he said, his tone panicked. "Maddie? Are you all right?"

"I'm fine," she insisted, once she was coherent enough to get her bearings. "I just fell out of the chair and couldn't go anywhere."

He slumped with relief and admitted, "I thought you were unconscious. I thought something was really wrong and—" She couldn't help chuckling, and he demanded, "What's so funny?"

"I'm sorry," she said. "It's just that I was just as panicked when I first fell, but then I thought I might as well take a nap. You know the view of the house is a lot different from down here."

Jon chuckled and laid beside her. "Yeah," he said, "but I like it. We should do this more often."

Maddie laughed and kissed him, then she told him about her changing feelings toward her father. He helped her up, and together they prepared lunch and ate.

Autumn merged gracefully into winter. Maddie liked the way the cold weather kept Jon at home more, since Dave had no need for his help. He worked on some little extras in the house and did a lot of reading. Cold weather also increased the illnesses in the community, and Jon was called on frequently. Occasionally, when someone was terribly ill, he went out to the home, but more often people came to their home. They were both amazed at the miles some people would travel to seek his help. Apparently word was spreading of his expertise and willingness to help.

Jon taught Maddie how to avoid the spreading of infections when patients came. She made sure everyone washed their hands frequently, and she cleaned certain areas with soap and water once they had left. Once in a while he had to do some stitches, and he even removed a growth from a woman's foot. The first time he asked Maddie to assist him she was hesitant. But she found that she wasn't terribly disturbed by the sight of blood, and she actually enjoyed being able to help him.

"You make an excellent assistant," he told her one morning after a patient had left.

"Thank you," she said. "And you make an excellent doctor."

She was surprised when he almost smiled—a stark contrast to the usual scowl she received after such comments.

Jon couldn't help contemplating on Maddie's attitude about his medical profession. It hovered relentlessly in the back of his mind, forcing him to face up to feelings that were difficult to deal with. He really didn't *want* to be a doctor. But he had to ask himself if such feelings justified the estrangement between him and his father. Looking into the grateful faces of the people he was able to help, he couldn't deny that he was glad to be in the position he was in. And with time he felt a lessening of his darker feelings toward his father, although he found it difficult to define why. He had a desire to bridge the gap between them, but he wasn't certain how. And while he believed Maddie could help him make sense of his feelings, he still felt hesitant to talk about it. He knew she'd been able to somewhat come to terms with her feelings toward her own father, but he somehow believed his feelings were more complicated. He simply hoped that with time it would all make sense.

* * * * *

Maddie stared toward the bedroom window, contemplating the frost patterns on the glass while Jon exercised her legs. She wondered if her sensation of not feeling well could actually be an illness coming on, or if she had become just plain weary of the monotonous, and seemingly fruitless, exercising. No matter how much she willed resistance from the muscles in her legs, nothing happened; nothing changed.

"Please stop," she groaned. "I just can't take it anymore."

"I'm not going to give up that easy," Jon said in a high-spirited tone that only increased her irritation.

"I said stop!" she shouted, and Jon froze. He'd never imagined Maddie could be prone to such anger. But there was no mistaking the fire in her eyes as she silently dared a challenge from him.

Controlling his temptation to get defensive, he said calmly, "You know I'm only trying to help, Maddie. If you don't—"

"I don't want any more help!" she snapped. He set her leg down and moved away. "I'm sick to death of this ridiculous project. Why don't we both accept that it's just not going to work?"

"Maddie," Jon said gently in spite of his growing aggravation, "before we ever started this, you said very plainly that you wanted to try, and—"

"Well I've tried!" she retorted and turned away from him. "I've tried and tried and I don't want to do it anymore, so why don't you just admit that there's no point."

Jon chose his words carefully. "How can I admit there's no point when I believe that learning to walk deserves more effort?"

"Well, I *can't* walk, Jon. I can't!" She threw a pillow at the wall and groaned. "Oh, who knows? Maybe my father was right."

"About what?" Jon demanded, feeling the anger take hold of him.

"Everything!" she barked.

"Oh, of course," he countered with sarcasm. "After all, he did say I would only bring you misery, didn't he? And he did say it was wrong of me to get your hopes up over something that was futile and ridiculous. Is that what you're trying to tell me, Maddie? Would you prefer that I take you back to your father and—"

"Don't be ridiculous! You can't assume that I meant he—"

"What can I assume from your saying that he was right about *everything?*" Jon shouted. "Unless I'm mistaken, you'd do well to clarify yourself, Mrs. Brandt. Otherwise, I'm going to have to assume that you're having regrets about the choice we made—to be together in spite of the obvious challenges."

Maddie stared at her husband while echoes of what he'd just said reverberated through her mind. What had brought them to such harsh words and misconceptions? Knowing she had been the one to provoke the argument, she quickly determined that she needed to stop it. She closed her eyes and took a deep breath to calm her anger. "Forgive me," she said and looked him in the eye. "What I really meant was . . . maybe my father was right in the respect that I can't expect to live a normal life. Maybe I'm a fool to be trying."

Hearing the humility in her voice, Jon swallowed and carefully sat on the bed beside her, taking her hand in his. "Maddie, honey, in my opinion we have a very good life. And normal is relative. I can understand how discouraging this must seem to you right now. But I really believe you can walk." She shook her head adamantly, and he feared she would get angry again, so he quickly pleaded, "If we give up now, we'll lose all the strength you might have gained, even if you can't feel any difference yet." Seeing the deepening frustration in her eyes, he sighed and added, "But I'll leave it up to you. If you don't want to exercise anymore, I won't say another word. You know that I'll always love you, no matter what."

She relaxed visibly, and Jon wondered if he'd been pressuring her too much. As difficult as it was to let it go, he knew he couldn't force her to do something that she didn't believe in. Seeing her eyes become sad and distant, he touched her face and said, "You're missing your parents, aren't you?"

She squeezed her eyes shut and nodded while tears spilled down her cheeks. Knowing there was nothing he could say to console her that hadn't been said before, he attempted to distract her. "Why don't we bundle up and ride into town? Maybe we could buy some—"

"I don't want to," she said firmly. "I'm tired. I just want to rest."

Jon sighed, feeling concerned for her in a way he couldn't quite define. "Can I get you anything?"

"No," she insisted, then repeated, "I just want to rest."

Jon tried to keep his distance and let her rest. She ate the meals he took her, but she slept most of the day. He wondered if she was getting ill. When he crawled into bed that night she snuggled close to him and murmured, "I want to keep trying. I guess I just feel . . . worn out."

"That's understandable," he said.

He expected her to say something more, but a few minutes later he realized she was asleep.

Maddie woke up feeling rested but still tired, and again she wondered if a sickness was coming on. Still, she insisted on the usual exercises in the morning, knowing that as long as Jon was willing to work so hard, she couldn't give up. Once again she focused on the frosted window panes, trying to will her legs to heal and be strong.

"You all right?" Jon asked, noticing how pale she looked.

"I feel exhausted," she said. "And a little . . . queasy, perhaps. I hope I'm not coming down with something."

"I hope so too," he said, pushing his shoulder against her leg.

Maddie felt better later in the day, but the following morning she felt worse, and once again, Jon questioned her. When his questions became more specific and personal, she felt alarmed.

"You think something's wrong with me," she said. "You think that—"

"Calm down," he said with a chuckle. "I don't think there's anything wrong with you. In fact," he raised his brows and smiled, "I think you might be pregnant."

Maddie couldn't will even the slightest sound from her mouth. The joy that surged through her was beyond expression, but she had to ask, "How can you be sure?"

"It's not difficult to tell," he said and asked her more questions about her cycle and symptoms. He laughed with perfect delight after a brief examination, and stated firmly, "You're pregnant, Maddie. I'm absolutely certain of it."

Maddie held to him and cried, silently thanking God for giving her the life she'd once believed she'd never have. To be a wife and mother was all she had ever wanted. Seeing her joy mirrored in Jon's expression only deepened the serenity that sharing such a life had given her.

"I love you," she murmured.

He pressed a kiss to her brow and repeated firmly, "I love you."

They went that afternoon to tell Ellie the good news, and it was difficult to tell if she was laughing or crying. Ellie's happiness on Maddie's behalf helped compensate for not being able to share the news with her mother personally, but Ellie promised to see that Sylvia got the letter she'd written.

In spite of the worsening symptoms of pregnancy, Maddie felt happier than she'd ever dreamed possible. It was only the distance she felt from her parents that caused her any grief. Her father's continued absence at church made her ache, and the long gazes she exchanged with her mother across the room hardly seemed to count for much. She knew from her mother's letters that Sylvia feared even conversing with Maddie, for fear of what others might tell her father. Sylvia felt that for the time being it was important to stand by her husband. She had told Maddie many times that she'd been prayerful over the matter, and felt that a time would come when the Spirit would guide her to take another step. In the meantime, they had to endure and hope that something good would eventually bridge the horrible gap.

Maddie prayerfully decided to write her father a letter and tell him of her happiness and that she was expecting a baby. She expressed her love for him, and her desire to share her life with her parents. She copied the letter, knowing how much effort and concern she had put into her words. Fearing he might destroy it, she wanted to have her words recorded. Her fears were realized when her mother's next letter reported that he refused to read it, and had tossed it into the fire. Maddie cried on Jon's shoulder, but he reminded her that she had done all she could do, and the matter was in her father's hands.

On an extremely cold day, when Maddie felt more ill than she ever had in her life, Jon decided they would keep the exercising to a minimum. She wanted to tell him that it was pointless anyway, but he was adamant about not missing a day, and she couldn't deny her appreciation of his ongoing hope—especially when hers had gone dry. Maddie forced her mind to thoughts of the baby in order to get through the monotonous routine. She was startled to hear Jon gasp.

"What?" she demanded.

"Do that again," he said.

"What did I do?"

He chuckled with merry eyes. "You just moved your leg. Do it again."

Maddie held her breath, hardly daring to hope. She willed herself to move, just as she'd attempted thousands of times with no result. She felt her leg move against his resistance. She laughed as he pushed against it, suddenly filled with strength and energy. Some minimal effort proved the same with the other leg, and Jon declared firmly, "You're going to be able to do it, Maddie. It's just a matter of time if we keep doing what we're doing."

Maddie wept uncontrollably as the reality settled in. She realized now how deeply she had grieved when she'd lost her ability to walk, and that she'd never fully come to terms with it inside. When she finally calmed down enough to speak, she admitted, "I just don't know how much happiness I can manage."

"You're making up for lost time," he said. "I'm just lucky enough to share all that happiness."

He kissed her warmly, leaving Maddie humbled and in awe of all that she had been blessed with.

CHAPTER TEN
Clouds of Pride

While Maddie had been anxious to share the news of expecting a baby, she preferred the progress of her physical abilities to be kept a secret.

"I don't want folks in town keeping track of my every bit of progress," she insisted. "We'll work on it at home, and behave as we always have in public. When I can walk as good as you can, then I'll do it for the world to see."

"That could be an interesting day," Jon said with a chuckle. "You'll have people declaring that a great miracle has been wrought."

"It is a miracle," she said firmly. "It's just that, well, most people don't understand that miracles usually take a lot of hard work."

Jon wondered anew at her faith and positive outlook. Since the day he'd met her, he felt that being in her presence was like basking in the warmth of the sun following a long, cold winter. And her effect on him had not lessened with time. His happiness seemed to deepen with every passing day.

The only hovering cloud in his life was the issue with his father; it seemed to become weightier with time. He found it ironic that the same was true for Maddie. When he finally admitted to the thoughts he'd been having about his father, it became evident that her feelings toward her father were startlingly similar. They felt angry to some degree—with their fathers for behavior that was insensitive and sometimes appalling, and with themselves for the things they'd done to add to the problem. But in contrast to the anger, they both had to admit a deep caring for their fathers, and heartache for the circumstances at hand. And while Maddie could honestly say she'd done everything in her power to heal the wounds between her and her father, Jon had to admit he'd done nothing. While his regular letters from Sara had kept him informed of his father's well being and activities, Jon hadn't written a single word to his father directly. Maddie suggested that he write to his father now, even if it was only a simple letter expressing a general appreciation. Jon liked the idea, but his attempts to put his thoughts on paper always left him frustrated. He felt certain that eventually his confusion would settle and he'd be able to properly express all he was feeling. And perhaps, given some time, his father would write to him first.

As the new year began with extremely cold temperatures, Jon found genuine pleasure in the life he shared with Maddie. Together they worked to prepare the nursery for the baby, knowing that the warmer months would be busier. Maddie made curtains for the window, and Ellie helped her with some bedding, as well as a layette so the baby would have care and clothing essentials.

With the growing strength in Maddie's legs, and the progression of her pregnancy, Jon felt a deepening gratitude for his medical knowledge. Being able to care for her personally in both respects meant more to him than words could say. Living in a place with such limited medical help, the knowledge that he could see her pregnancy through assuaged his concerns immensely. It was one more reason that he felt the need to write that letter to his father, but it was as if some invisible wall stood between his desire and his ability to do it. And again he hoped that his father would take the first step and make it somehow easier for him.

With the coming of spring, life became too busy to contemplate the difficult matters concerning their fathers. Jon began helping Dave in the fields again, and he and Maddie prepared and planted their own garden near the house. He was amazed at how much work she accomplished in one sitting. She'd stay in one spot to break up the ground thoroughly, and then plant the seeds in perfect rows. When she could no longer reach he would move her to a new spot. By the time the new plants were sprouting and needed the weeds pulled from around them, Maddie had gained enough strength to move down the rows on her hands and knees, in spite of her well-rounded belly. She thrived on being outdoors and the work she accomplished in the garden. She also revived a row of rose bushes along the front of the porch that had been sorely neglected and grown wild over the years. As the illness related to her pregnancy passed, she blossomed with the added glow of motherhood and the innocent thrill of just enjoying the simple pleasures of life.

The day Maddie took her first steps Jon declared it a perfect day for a picnic, and a picnic was the perfect way to celebrate. They returned to the house only a few minutes before Ellie came by with a pie.

"Thank you," Jon said as she set it on the table. "You're so good to us."

Maddie giggled for no apparent reason and Jon couldn't keep from smirking.

"What?" Ellie said. "Have I got pepper in my teeth or something?"

"No, of course not," Jon said, and Maddie giggled again.

"Then what?" Ellie insisted.

"Nothing," Jon said with forced severity, but Maddie giggled again.

"I'm sorry," Maddie said. "It's just that . . . Oh, Jon. We have to tell Ellie. I just can't keep it to myself any longer. Ellie's no gossip. You won't tell anybody, will you, Ellie."

"Of course not, but what? I already know you're going to have a baby. What else could be so exciting?"

Jon grinned at Maddie as he stood before her and held out both of his hands. Maddie gripped them tightly and rose slowly to her feet. At the sight Ellie gasped and took hold of a chair.

"Merciful heaven!" Ellie muttered in a quivering voice as Maddie took two careful steps with Jon's help. She hurried to sit back down, knowing that was all she could handle without her legs getting shaky.

"It's a miracle," Ellie added, sitting down herself.

"Yes, it is," Maddie agreed.

"A miracle that Maddie has been working very hard at for several months," Jon said.

"I'm not the only one who worked hard." Maddie took hold of Jon's hand and squeezed it tightly.

"Why don't you want anyone to know?" Ellie asked.

"Oh, everyone will know eventually," Maddie said. "But, until I get a little more sure on my feet, we'd rather not have everyone speculating over my progress."

"That's good thinking," Ellie said, then she laughed. "I can't believe it."

"Now, remember," Maddie said, "you mustn't tell a soul."

"I promise," Ellie said. "Just make sure when you come out of hiding that I'm there to see it."

"I promise," Maddie repeated.

Ellie hurried home to put supper on for her family. Maddie felt anxious to practice her steps, but Jon suggested that she take it slower and continue to build stamina.

"You must think of the baby," he said. "You've got to keep up your strength and be very careful."

They worked on it a little every day, along with continuing the usual exercises. By the time Maddie was eight months along in her pregnancy, she could walk slowly from one room to the next, provided she didn't get too far from a wall or a piece of furniture to help support her. She loved the independence she felt, moving about her home freely, and the prospect of actually living like a normal woman increased her happiness tenfold.

Together, they decided that when she had recovered from having the baby, she would be ready to unveil her secret. About four weeks from the anticipated due date, Jon couldn't help pondering how full his life seemed—then the telegram arrived.

The knock at the door came early. Jon exchanged a surprised glance with Maddie across the breakfast table.

"Who on earth could that be?" she asked as he rose to get the door.

Jon pulled it open to see a young man he recognized, although he couldn't recall his name.

"Telegram for you, Dr. Brandt—from Boston." The excitement in his voice made it evident that such a thing was rare.

"Thank you," he said. Reaching out to take it, a sharp dread tightened his chest. The boy left. Jon closed the door and leaned against it. Regret for his procrastination descended over him as he attempted to open the envelope with trembling hands. He knew it was bad news intuitively, but it still took several seconds for the words to penetrate his clouded mind:

Father is dying. Come quickly if you can.

Sara.

"What is it?" Maddie appeared, leaning in the doorframe of the kitchen.

Jon took a step toward her and held out the paper, and she noticed it quivering in his hand as he did so. She met his eyes with concern, then took it and read. With a steady voice and firm eyes she said, "You'd better hurry. I'll help you pack."

"I'm not going anywhere without you," he said.

"I'm eight months pregnant, Jon. How can I—"

"Precisely," he said. "I'm keeping you with me so I can keep an eye on you. Besides," he added, moving toward the bedroom, "I need you. Don't think for a minute that I could ever get through this without your holding my hand. Come on. Let's pack."

When Jon had most of his things gathered, he said, "I'm going down to the station to find out when the next train east comes through. And I need to talk to Ellie."

"I'll get everything packed and put things in order."

"Thank you," he said and kissed her quickly. "I'll hurry so I can help you."

Jon went to Ellie's house first. He found her in the kitchen, her hands in bread dough. Her pleasure at seeing him clouded over when she absorbed his countenance.

"What's happened?" she demanded. "Is Maddie—"

"Maddie's fine. I just got a telegram from Boston. Your brother is dying."

"Good heavens!" she murmured, and sunk into a chair. "Do you know . . . what's wrong?"

"No. But we're leaving on the next train. Why don't you come with us?"

Ellie glanced around the room as if it might help her think more clearly. He could see her working things over in her mind, until she said firmly, "I can't, Jon. I'm in the middle of that Relief Society project, and Dave needs my help with the—"

"It's all right," he said. "I understand."

"Give him my love," she said with tears in her eyes.

"If I get there in time, I will."

"And we'll see that everything's cared for here," she said. "The animals and such."

"Thank you," Jon said. "We'll keep you posted."

Jon left Ellie's house wanting to cry himself. He felt certain that tears would relieve the horrible pressure in his head and chest. But the emotion wouldn't penetrate the numb shock that held it back. Jon sent a telegram to his sister to tell her they were coming. He purchased tickets, certain that the news of his telegram and subsequent trip east would be fodder for gossip and speculation. And that was fine, he reasoned. For the most part he knew people were simply curious and concerned. But no one could possibly know or understand the unbearable heartache that had taken hold of him. The very idea of his father dying before he had a chance to say what he needed to say seemed unthinkable. Thoughts that had milled around in his mind for months now became suddenly desperate, and the miles between here and Boston represented the harrowing chasm that had always existed between him and his father.

When he returned Maddie had everything nearly ready to go. And he was glad they were in such a hurry to get to the station—he didn't want time to think. Brother Cline, who worked for the railroad, helped unload their luggage onto the platform.

"All the way to Boston, eh?" he said.

"That's right," Jon replied, trying not to sound as distracted as he felt.

"Not taking the wheelchair?" he asked nonchalantly as they sat on the bench waiting for the train.

Jon noticed Maddie barely concealing a smug grin. His carrying her to the bench had been the first time he'd done so since last Sunday, only for the sake of keeping their secret.

"We didn't want to bother with it," Jon said. "Besides, I like carrying her."

Brother Cline chuckled. "Good thing you're a strong lad, now that you're carrying two around."

"Oh, that he is," Maddie said.

Jon's heart was pumping mercilessly fast when the train pulled in. He prayed that it would get them there on time, then he tried to distract himself from worrying. Carrying Maddie on board, he whispered teasingly, "The two of you are an armful, but it's still a pleasure."

Maddie laughed softly. "Well, this is the last time you'll ever get to carry me. I think it would be wise for me to come home on my own two feet."

"Perhaps. But don't think this is the last time I'll ever carry you."

Once they were settled on the train, Jon couldn't keep his mind from the reality setting in—*His father was dying!* Sorrow for his procrastination in making amends enveloped him so fully that he almost felt physical pain.

"Talk to me, Jon," Maddie said, startling him from his thoughts. He attempted an innocent expression, but she hardened her gaze on him and said firmly, "You're practically choking on emotion. I can see it. Talk to me."

Jon took a deep breath and resigned himself to getting all of it out in the open. "Oh, Maddie," he said, holding her hand tightly, "I can't count the times over the last several months that I've wanted to send him a letter . . . just to tell him that I . . ." He became too emotional to speak. She put her arm around him and urged his head to her shoulder. He was grateful that no one was sitting nearby.

"Everything will be all right," she assured him, running her fingers through his hair.

"Will it?" he asked, wishing he didn't feel so cynical. "If he doesn't hold on until I get there . . . if I can't have the opportunity to . . . just tell him I . . . I don't know how I can face it."

"Then we must simply pray that he'll hold on until we get there."

Jon took a deep breath, attempting to draw her faith inside himself. But each mile of the journey was marked by deepening regret. The only way he could find peace was to keep his mind in constant prayer. He prayed with all his heart and soul, harder than he ever had, that his father would hold on. He envisioned their reunion—the tears, the smiles, the sweet embrace of forgiveness and acceptance.

Just as on his trip out west, Jon felt mostly oblivious to the passing scenery. He lost track of days as he drifted in and out of sleep, plagued with intense emotion and frenzied, chaotic dreams. Maddie was always at his side, offering a silent support that eased his anxiety more than she could ever know. She was often absorbed with the view out the window, and were he not so absorbed in his grief, he would have enjoyed just watching her response to the broadening horizons of her world.

The awe in Maddie's eyes grew deeper when they arrived in Boston. He knew she was keeping most of her thoughts to herself, out of respect for his growing anxiety, but her excitement in seeing a city so large and advanced was readily evident. Jon had seen it all before. Little had changed in his absence. He'd never felt at home here, and he was glad for the life he'd found elsewhere. But his heart and mind were fully absorbed with the pressing reunion with his father.

When the cab pulled in front of the home where he'd grown up, Maddie gasped. "This is it?" she asked, her voice more alarmed than excited.

"This is it," he repeated dryly.

"It's so big and elegant."

"It's just a house, Maddie," he said, grateful that she didn't seem offended by his crisp tone. She had a way of understanding him, even the thoughts he couldn't put into words.

Jon helped Maddie up the steps by holding to her arm. She was a bit slow, but doing well. He set down the bag he carried and rang the bell while the cab driver deposited the rest of their luggage on the stoop. Jon settled with the cab driver and rang again, feeling as if his heart would pound right out of his chest.

"You all right?" he asked Maddie in a calm voice that belied his growing anxiety.

"Of course," she said. "How about you? You look as if—"

The door came open and Jon held his breath. Coming face to face with a woman he'd never seen before, it took him a moment to recall that Sara had written concerning their old housekeeper. She'd retired and been carefully replaced, but Jon couldn't recall the new housekeeper's name. When he said nothing, she asked stiffly, "May I help you?"

"Forgive me," he said, "I'm Jonathon Brandt, and this is my wife, Maddie."

"Oh, of course," her face showed a genuine smile, however faint. "Miss Brandt was hoping you'd arrive today."

Jon moved the luggage into the entry hall and the woman closed the door. He attempted to keep the anxiety out of his voice as he said, "Is my father—"

"Your sister's in the main parlor." She motioned with her hand. "I assume you know the way."

"Yes, thank you," he said and took Maddie's hand. His heart maintained a racing beat that he feared would kill him if he didn't get relief from the tension soon.

Jon was grateful to have Maddie's hand in his as he stepped into the open parlor doorway. His sister was slumped against the shoulder of a man he recognized, although he couldn't recall his name. Sara was sobbing, and the gentleman holding her had tears in his eyes as he turned to see Jon and Maddie standing there. He nudged Sara and whispered something. She sat up abruptly and turned toward them. She gasped and wiped frantically at her face as she rose to move toward them. Jon crossed the room to take her in his arms, where she resumed crying against his shoulder without having uttered a word. Her emotion tightened the dread in his stomach. Unable to bear the tension another moment, he took her shoulders into his hands and demanded softly, "Father? Is he—"

"He's gone," she said.

Jon felt as if she were suddenly far away while the words attempted to penetrate his clouded mind. "Gone?" he heard himself say in a voice that cracked. "When?"

"About . . . an hour ago," she sniffed and pressed a handkerchief beneath her nose.

Jon took a step back and dropped his hands, feeling as if he'd been hit square in the chest, the wind knocked from his lungs. *He couldn't believe it!* The strength drained from him and he teetered slightly, grateful to feel Maddie take hold of his arm.

He saw Sara glance toward Maddie just as her gentleman friend stood behind her. He knew introductions should be made, but he couldn't bring himself to think beyond the ache filling his every nerve.

"Where is he?" Jon asked, as if he could somehow find his father and prove that Sara was wrong. *He just couldn't believe it!*

"In his room," she said and sniffled, wiping at a continuing stream of tears. "They'll be coming for him soon, but . . . I couldn't stay in there any longer, and . . ."

Jon didn't hear the rest of what she said. He hurried out of the room and toward the stairs. He hesitated only a moment to meet Maddie's eyes. She seemed to understand that she wasn't physically capable of keeping up with the urgency he felt. Or perhaps she sensed his feeling of being torn between needing her and needing to be alone. She smiled faintly. "It's all right. I'll catch up with you in a few minutes. I think I can find my way around."

Jon nodded, unable to get his voice past the growing lump in his throat. He took the stairs three at a time then stopped abruptly outside his father's bedroom door. He felt suddenly terrified to step into the room, as if not doing so might prevent him from having to accept the possibility that his father was truly gone. Recalling that Sara had said they would soon be coming for him, Jon took a deep breath and pushed open the door. He had to steady himself before he approached the bed. Gazing at his father, for a moment Jon felt unexplainably better. Although he had become significantly thinner since Jon had last seen him, he looked completely at peace, as if he were only sleeping. But absorbing his appearance more fully, the gaunt, wasted appearance of his face and hands became evident. He reached out to take his father's hand, startled by its coldness. He held it tightly as if he could somehow will his warmth into it and bring his father back. But the warmth of his own hands turned cold as the reality crept into him. *It was true!* His father was gone, and he'd been denied the last possible chance to tell him that their differences didn't matter, to forgive and be forgiven, to let him know that he loved him.

Jon heard the anguish come from his throat, and he sunk to his knees beside the bed. "Oh, dear God! Why?" he murmured into the sheet that covered his father's body. *"Why?"*

Jon cried himself into exhaustion, and when he looked up, Maddie was there, sitting quietly in a chair near the bed, her hands folded over the top of her rounded belly. Their eyes met, and unspoken volumes passed between them. He wondered if she had any idea how grateful he was to have her in his life. He was attempting to find the words to tell her when Sara appeared in the room.

"Mr. Bentley and his assistant are here," she said in an unsteady voice.

Jon came to his feet and reluctantly let go of his father's lifeless hand. "We'll be able to see him again at the mortuary," she said. Then she disappeared.

Jon had no desire to watch them take his father's body away. He took Maddie's hand and led her to the room that had once been his. Their luggage had been put there, and he found that nothing had changed. Some of his clothes still hung in the closet, his books were on the shelf, odds and ends were in the drawers. Maddie tried to comfort him, but Jon barely heard her. He stared out the window to the beautiful yard below, where he'd played as a child with his parents sitting close by with books or a newspaper. Memories passed through his mind, intermittently assaulted by images of his father's countenance in death.

"Are you all right?" Maddie asked, touching his arm.

"No," he chuckled tensely, "but I think I'm in shock. Just keep talking."

She easily complied and he appreciated the normalcy of her voice, and the tangible evidence of her presence.

The housekeeper came to tell them that supper would be served in twenty minutes. Jon splashed cold water on his face and marveled at how calm he felt, but he sensed a storm threatening somewhere inside of him. A portion of his emotions felt familiar, not unlike what he'd experienced when he'd lost his mother. The shock. The grief. The reality that life would never be the same. But with his mother he had felt no regrets. He had done his best to care for her, be with her, always please her and make her happy. She had left this life with good feelings between them, and he'd been blessed with the opportunity to say good-bye.

But this was different. He felt somehow amputated; this was something that he hadn't been prepared to lose, and the regret was so deep and raw that he had to force it away in order to even consider sharing a civil meal with his wife and his sister.

"Do I look all right?" Maddie asked, smoothing her hair and her dress.

"You look beautiful as always," he said firmly, appreciating the distraction. "How are you feeling?"

"A little slow and awkward," she said, "but I'm fine. It's difficult to tell if I have trouble walking because I'm so new at it, or because this baby's occupying every spare inch inside of me."

Jon chuckled. "A little of both, perhaps."

He kept his arm around her as they went slowly down the stairs. Memories of the house surrounding him began to settle in, his most prominent being the day he'd left—without even saying good-bye to his father. The thought threatened to spark the explosive emotion bubbling inside of him, and he quickly repressed it. They entered the dining room to see Sara and her gentleman friend about to be seated.

"Good, you're here," Sara said to Jon. Then, more to Maddie, "You must forgive me for not introducing myself properly earlier. Needless to say, the circumstances we met under have been far from ideal."

"No apology necessary," Maddie said.

Jon added, "Sara, my wife, Maddie Brandt. Maddie, my sister, Sara Brandt."

Sara extended a hand and Maddie took it just as Sara bent forward and put a quick kiss to Maddie's cheek. "I've heard so much about you, my dear," Sara said. "It's a pleasure to finally meet you. I hope you'll stay long enough that we can get to know each other well."

"The pleasure is mine," Maddie said, seeming a bit in awe.

"Jon and Maddie," Sara said, "this is my dear friend, Harrison Hartford." She motioned toward him while her eyes betrayed the full depth of her affection for this man. "Jon, I know you've met before, but it was a long time ago, and—"

"It's wonderful to see you again, Mr. Hartford," Jon said, extending a hand.

He shook Jon's hand firmly, but his face remained sober. "And you," he said. He nodded toward Maddie. "Mrs. Brandt, it is an honor."

Maddie nodded and smiled in return. She was spared from having to speak when the housekeeper brought a tray into the dining room.

"Of course, you met Mona," Sara said, motioning toward her.

"Briefly," Jon said. He nodded toward her and added, "It's nice to meet you, Mona."

"Mona," Sara said, "you must know this is my brother Jon, and his wife, Maddie. I've told you about them."

"It's a pleasure to have you here," Mona said, ladling soup into their bowls from an elegant tureen.

Jon managed a smile toward her, feeling awkward with the formal service of their meal after being away for so long. Maddie's expression made it evident she was quite in awe of the situation, and even a bit nervous. He reached beneath the table to squeeze her hand, hoping to convey that there was no need for concern. They exchanged smiles, however faint. He thought of the circumstances that had brought them here and knew his emotions were blanketed by shock. He wished they could remain that way indefinitely, knowing that facing the reality of what he felt deep down would not be pleasant.

The meal passed mostly in silence, there was little to be said that wouldn't bring them back to the harsh reality of what they were facing. Jon knew that Sara's loss would be at least as difficult, but in an entirely different way. She likely had no regrets, but she had worked her existence around her father for most of her life. Surely she would be at loose ends with a great deal of adjustment ahead of her. In fact, Jon strongly suspected that her reason for never marrying had to do with feeling too obligated to her father to be able to commit herself elsewhere. Jon thought of the similarities between her situation and what Maddie had experienced with her father. He suspected that eventually the two of them would have a great deal to talk about, but at the moment, there seemed nothing to say.

Just before dessert was brought in, Harrison said to Jon, "So, what is it exactly that you do out in Utah?"

Something subtle in the tone of the question put Jon on the defense, but he forced an even voice. "I'm trying my hand at farming, actually."

"Really?" Harrison chuckled as if the idea was terribly amusing. "Why would an experienced physician digress to being a farmer?"

Jon swallowed carefully and fought back his anger. The question sounded so much like something his father would have said that it sent a shiver down his back. "I have my reasons for wanting to expand my horizons, Mr. Hartford. And a good farmer has no less knowledge or experience than a good physician; it's simply learned in a different way, and practiced in a different field—pardon the pun."

Sara laughed slightly as she apparently got the humor. And Maddie joined her. But Harrison's face remained stony. He started into a monotonous oration of the benefits of education, that once again, reminded Jon of his father. The feelings storming through him were so filled with confusion he could hardly think straight. He was relieved when they'd finished their meal, and he rose at the first break in Mr. Hartford's speech.

"It's been a long day," he said, "if you will excuse us. According to her personal physician, Maddie should get some rest."

Sara laughed softly. Maddie smiled and said, "Jon takes very good care of me."

"Oh," Sara said as they headed toward the door, "we need to meet with Mr. Bentley at ten in the morning to . . . make the arrangements." Jon turned toward her, feeling briefly disoriented. It all sunk in fully when she clarified, "For the funeral."

He nodded and hurried out of the room, suddenly feeling as if the full enormity of his emotions would catch up and smother him. He barely managed to keep from erupting as he guided Maddie slowly up the stairs.

"Are you all right?" she asked just as they reached the landing.

"Not really. Why do you ask?"

"I can just tell that you're upset. Is there a reason you—"

"My father just died, Maddie," he said more tersely than he'd intended. "Should I not be upset?"

"Of course, but—"

"I'm fine," he interrupted and attempted to push it all down inside once again. But with the door to his room closed, the emotions erupted, refusing to be held at bay any longer. Jon paced his room frantically, barely aware of Maddie's quiet gaze. He felt so thoroughly consumed with bitter anger that he wanted only to break something, or run away as far and as fast as he could go, as if he could stay one step ahead of the monster threatening to devour him.

"Jon," Maddie said gently, "I know this is difficult for you. Why don't you sit down and talk to me. If you—"

"I don't *want* to talk," he snarled. "An hour. One lousy, stinking hour. Why couldn't we have gotten here sooner? Why couldn't he have held on that long? I don't understand. I just *do not* understand!"

"It was beyond your control, Jon," Maddie said. Her calm, gentle demeanor frustrated him. "You did the best you could and—"

"It was not beyond *God's* control!" he shouted, shaking a fist at Maddie as if she could somehow take the blame. "I prayed with everything I have inside of me just to . . . to have a few minutes with him . . . to just be able to have him *know* that I love him. Was that too much to ask? Was it? Apparently it was." He raised his fists and shouted heavenward, "How could you do this to me?"

"Jon!" Maddie said in a strong, firm voice he'd never heard before. It got his attention. He turned to see her standing close to him, her eyes full of fire. "I will listen to you rant and rage all you want, if that's what it takes to get what you're feeling out of your system. But I will not tolerate your blaming God for this. Do you think you can put demands on Him to lay out the answers to prayers according to your desires? Do you think it's up to Him to undo the path you laid with your own pride?"

"Pride?" he echoed, her words barely penetrating the anger that refused to relent.

"Yes, pride, Jonathon Brandt. I understand that your father was a difficult man. Well, so was mine. But it was your pride, so much like his, that helped put the wall between the two of you. You laid at least half of the stones in that wall, Jon. And then you were just plain scared to break it down. You put off writing that letter for months. Don't try to lay blame at God's feet because you're too proud and scared now to admit the truth. There's no one to blame for the way you feel now, Jon, except you. And the sooner you realize that, the sooner you can come to terms with the way you feel." She took a deep breath and added more softly, "And don't talk to me like that. Be angry if you must, but don't take it out on me. I'm your wife, and I won't stand for it."

The full depth and breadth of her words began to sink in, dragging his pride and fear from hiding the regret at the core. Jon sunk into a chair and hung his head. Everything she'd said was true. *Everything!* He had no one to blame but himself.

"Oh, Maddie," he muttered, pressing his head into his hands, "I'm so sorry. I . . . I . . ."

"It's all right, Jon," she said and he felt her hand gently stroking his hair. "I know you're hurting. I know it's difficult."

Jon heard himself sob and clamped a hand over his mouth as if he could hold back the torrent of emotion bursting through a weakening dike.

"Go ahead and cry, Jon." She sat close beside him and urged his head to her shoulder. "Just cry if you need to. It's all right."

As if all he had needed was her permission, his efforts to hold back suddenly failed. He heaved and sobbed without restraint. He unconsciously slid to his knees, pressing his face into the folds of Maddie's dress, soaking it with tears while he held to her as if she could save him from drowning. He cried until there was nothing left in him but a spiritless ache.

"Will you be all right?" Maddie asked gently, awakening him to the realization that he wasn't alone. But shifting his hands he found them gripping her tightly. He lifted his head to see that her eyes were red and swollen. It was evident that she too, had been crying. Jon couldn't bring himself to answer. He knew he would have to be all right. He would have to go on. But at the moment he couldn't comprehend how that might happen.

"Come along," she said, urging him to his feet. "Let's get you to bed. You must be exhausted. I know I am."

Jon went silently through the motions of preparing for bed, if only to see that Maddie got her rest. He knew she wouldn't lie down if he didn't. When she extinguished the lamp and crawled into the bed beside him, the emotion began again, bubbling up from a source that he thought had gone dry. He focused on the feel of Maddie's lips on his brow, and her gentle fingers in his hair, and his next conscious realization was that he'd been asleep. He opened his eyes to see the room filled with a dim, rosy glow as the pre-dawn sun filtered through the sheer curtains at the windows. Recalling the events of the previous day, he wanted to curl up and never get out of this bed. But knowing what had to be done in the coming hours, he turned his face toward the rising sun and prayed that he could manage to get through. He felt Maddie shift in her sleep beside him. Her presence, combined with the light of a new day, made him believe for a moment that everything would be all right—somehow.

CHAPTER ELEVEN
Pride Reciprocated

Jon was relieved when Mona brought a breakfast tray to their room. He had no desire to endure another meal with his sister, even though Mr. Hartford would likely be absent for breakfast. Maddie didn't awaken until Jon nudged her and put the tray beside her. They sat together on the bed and ate, while he concentrated on how much he loved her, if only to distract himself from the impending doom he felt in facing the day.

"How are you this morning?" she asked, gently touching his face.

"I'm all right," he said, feeling as if he were lying. "How are you?"

"I'm not sure," she sighed. "I think I've overdone it."

"Not surprising."

A few minutes later she glanced around the room and said, "I really like your home, Jon. It's so fine." He didn't comment, and she added, "Your sister is such a lady, Jon—so elegant and refined. I feel so simple and backward when I'm with her."

"My sister is a fine lady," he said, "but no more so than you. The difference in your backgrounds does not make you simple and backward, by any means. Your mother is elegant and refined in her own right, and she taught you well." He took both her hands into his and kissed each in turn. "I'm proud to have you by my side in any situation."

She gave him a familiar smile that lit her eyes, and he knew that with her by his side, helping him to see reason, loving him unconditionally, he could face anything—even this. But after they'd finished their meal he was disappointed to realize that Maddie wasn't feeling well. The traveling and long days seemed to have caught up with her.

Being more than eight months pregnant her body could only take so much. She pleaded exhaustion and stayed at home to rest while Jon went with Sara to make the funeral arrangements. At least Mr. Hartford was busy with his work as an attorney, and Jon didn't have to put up with him.

Together he and Sara made a number of stops to see that everything was arranged for their father's funeral. Jon was grateful for the numbness coating his grief which made it possible to be matter of fact about discussing details that seemed too appalling to contemplate. It all came down to the same cold, hard facts. His father was gone. And their chance for peace was gone with him.

On the way home in the cab, Jon ventured to ask a question that had been tumbling around his mind since he'd seen his father yesterday. He didn't want to bring it up, but he had to know. "What happened to him, Sara?" She looked astonished, or perhaps uncertain of what he meant. Or more likely, she wanted to pretend she didn't know what he meant. Jon clarified carefully, "He looked horrible. He didn't deteriorate like that from some sudden illness."

Sara's obvious hesitance made his heart quicken. "He didn't want me to tell you," she said, glancing to her gloved hands as they fidgeted with the pleats in her skirt. "He didn't want you to run home, or even write, because you suddenly felt sorry for him. It started about a year after Mother died, and it wasn't long before he couldn't work. He turned all of his patients over to—"

"What was it, Sara?" he demanded crisply.

She sighed and gazed out the carriage window. "It was leukemia," she said.

Jon squeezed his eyes shut, trying to block out the image. While his father had been slowly deteriorating from a terminal illness, he had been ignoring repeated promptings to write him a simple letter and bridge the ridiculous gap between them.

Nothing more was said, and they returned home to find that Maddie had eaten lunch alone and was sleeping. Mona brought their lunch into the dining room and Jon helped Sara with her chair before he sat across from her.

"So," Jon said, searching for any conversation that would fill in the terrible silence of the mourning that filled the house, "I assume that you and Mr. Hartford are rather chummy. He is the gentleman you were seeing before I left, isn't he?"

"Yes, on both counts. I'm very fond of him, and he is of me."

"Has he asked you to marry him?" Jon asked.

"A long time ago."

"And don't tell me," Jon said, hearing a bitter edge in his voice, "you turned him down because Father needed you."

"That's right," she snapped. "And what's wrong with that?"

"I'll tell you what's wrong with that, Sara. It's possible for a woman to be a wife and mother, and still be a good daughter. She shouldn't have to choose." He thought of Maddie's situation and realized his convictions on the matter ran deep on behalf of both women. "What made you think you had to be everything for Father? I don't understand."

Her voice was void of anything but sadness as she answered, "I'm not sure I understand, myself. I just always felt like he needed me."

"Because he wanted you to feel that way, Sara. He wanted to be in complete control of both our lives. He was a difficult man. Why don't you just admit it?"

"I don't have any problem admitting it, Jon. I know our father was a difficult man. But he had his reasons, and he had a good heart. Why don't you just admit *that?*"

Jon sighed and forced back the rising emotions. "I don't have any problem admitting that, Sara. I realized a long time ago that, in spite of our differences, he only wanted what he thought was best for me. I know I was difficult myself; stubborn and proud, just like him." He sighed again. "I guess that's what is so hard. I wish I could have told him before he left . . . that I'd forgiven him, and . . ." Jon heard his voice crack and had to fight back the sudden urge to sob.

"Why didn't you?" she asked gently.

"Just procrastinating, mostly. I had intended to write him a letter for months. Maddie tells me I was too proud and scared. She's probably right. But now it's too late, and . . ." He bit his lip and squeezed his eyes shut. He felt his sister put her hand over his where it lay on the table. He opened his eyes and tried to smile, but the tears in her eyes prompted his own to fall.

A few minutes later he finally managed to get control of himself and he forced a change of subject. "So, now that Father doesn't need you, are you going to accept Mr Hartford's proposal?"

"Yes, I believe I will. In fact, we'll likely be getting married in a couple of weeks. It would be nice if you'd stick around long enough to be there. I was hoping you'd stay long enough to help see the estate settled, anyway."

"Yes, I was thinking the same. I can stay until everything's settled, and . . . well, I really don't think Maddie should be traveling any more until after she has the baby. I don't want to wear her down, and I certainly don't want to risk having it come on the journey."

"Oh, that would be wonderful for her to have it here," she said. It was the first hint of genuine happiness he'd seen in her since he'd arrived.

"And I would love to be here to see you married," he added. "Even though . . ." He chuckled tensely.

"What?" she demanded with a smile, then she guessed. "You don't really like him, do you."

"He seems like a decent man, Sara, even if I don't have much in common with him. It's that he's, well, he's just . . . so much like . . ."

"Like father?" she guessed when he hesitated, and Jon scowled at her, not liking his mind read. Before he could retort she added, "Yes, he is. And I don't know how you can sit there and say that you've forgiven our father, and then speak of him with such distaste. It seems to me you've still got some feelings to come to terms with, brother."

When he said nothing she went on. "You want to know what I think?"

"I have a feeling you're going to tell me whether I do or not."

"Only because it's for your own good. I think that you don't even know our father, Jon. You never allowed yourself to get close enough to really know him. Maybe when you learn what kind of man he really was, you can truly come to terms with how you feel about him. You have to realize that you don't have to see eye to eye with someone to love them and appreciate their good qualities. But you have to be willing to look past the tip of the iceberg in order to know him."

"How can I get to know him when he's gone, Sara? My desire to get to know him has come too late. That's the problem, sweet sister." The sarcasm in his voice provoked a frown from Sara, but he continued, "He's gone, and it's too late. I will never see him again. Never be with him again. If only I could tell him that our differences were petty. If only I *could* tell him that in spite of everything I ever said and did I still . . ." His voice broke. "I still loved him." He choked back a rising sob. "If only I *could* get to know him, Sara. But that chance is lost to me now, and I . . ."

"Not necessarily, Jon," she said gently. "Come with me."

Jon hesitated only a moment before he followed his sister into the hall and to the door of their father's study. It was a room Jon had hated and generally avoided. As a youth, Jon had always been called to the study for reprimands and lectures. Entering the room now, he longed to have his father seated behind the desk, even with the intention of scolding his only son.

Sara lovingly stroked the desk as she spoke with yearning in her voice, "He spent a great deal of time here once he became too ill to work. He'd sit in this chair for hours, reading, daydreaming. He often took his meals here. He was very stubborn about finally resigning himself to bed rest during the days." She stood behind the big leather chair and put her hands on its back, as if she'd done it a thousand times. He could well imagine her coming in here at regular intervals to see if he was all right, to express her interest in whatever he might be doing.

"Have a seat, Jon," she said, startling him from his own daydreaming. He gave his sister a reluctant gaze, but she repeated firmly, "Have a seat."

Jon sat hesitantly in the chair and pressed his hands over the polished desktop. He froze when he saw the photograph of himself prominently displayed in front of him, next to one of his mother.

"Where's *your* photograph?" he asked.

"He didn't need one of me here," she said. "He had the real thing." She sighed and added, "Our father wasn't prone to the written word, much. You know how he rarely answered Aunt Ellie's letters. Mother usually did it for him. Mother was very good at recording her thoughts and the events going on around her. In fact, her journals are really quite amazing." Sara set her hand on a small stack of leather bound books sitting on the desk to his left. "I believe Father read them all a dozen times after she died. I read them a few times myself. I learned things about my parents that surprised me, but not as much as I think they'll surprise you. Read, Jon. You've got plenty of time. Then we'll talk."

She hesitated with her hand on the door and turned toward him. "Oh, and Jon, your sweet wife told me that according to your Mormon beliefs, families can be together for eternity. If that's the case, you *will* see him again. Won't you?"

She left him alone in his father's chair with his mother's journals, and more guilt and confusion than he cared to admit to. He wanted to believe that he would see his father again, that they could be together forever. But he felt that his faith was shaken. There was a part of him that knew God was not to blame. At the same time, he failed to understand why it had to be this way, and he couldn't deny feeling that God had somehow let him down. Of course, Maddie would tell him it was the other way around. And she was probably right. But at the moment he had so many thoughts and emotions bubbling up inside of him that it was impossible to make sense of any of them.

Forcing his thoughts to the moment, Jon shuffled through his mother's journals. There were seven books in all, not necessarily thick, which covered her life from a few years before she met his father until her death. Her entries were not frequent, but they were filled with eloquent descriptions of the high points of her life and the feelings related to what was taking place. He decided to start at the beginning and was quickly drawn into the tale of her meeting and falling in love with Phillip Brandt. She was the daughter of an average middle-class merchant. He was the son of a sailor, the middle child of seven, who had suffered through childhood barely keeping his stomach full.

With the hours passing, Jon took the journal to his room to find Maddie. She was still napping. He reasoned that catching up on the poor rest she'd gotten through the journey was a good thing. When she woke up they walked through the house and the yard while he told her of what he'd read so far. After supper he returned to the book and read long after Maddie had gone to sleep. Carol Brandt told in brief detail of Phillip's one and only confession to her—his deep resentment toward his own father, for the harshness he'd used with his wife and children. She also told of his unfathomable sacrifices to get through medical school, wanting a better life for himself and his family. He had often managed to get by on very little sleep, since he worked half the night in order to pay his tuition, and it wasn't uncommon for him to sleep in an alley when he couldn't stay with friends or coworkers, because he simply couldn't afford rent and school at the same time. He had refused to marry Carol until he had his degree and a good job; he was determined to care well for her, and to raise their children with the best of everything.

Jon pressed a hand over his eyes, overcome with an emotion so deep he couldn't consciously define it. He thought of the fine home he'd grown up in, and the abundance he'd always been blessed with. His father had been one of the best doctors in Boston, highly respected and well paid. And Jon had reaped the benefits of that without ever giving a thought to the sacrifices that had made such a life possible. He'd worked for scholarships, and kept a job to pay the balance of his tuition. But he'd always had a place to call home and plenty to eat while he'd worked to get his degree—a degree that he'd fought against and resented every step of the way.

Jon fell asleep in the chair with the book in his hand. He dreamt that he was laying in an alley, too frightened to sleep, and shivering from the cold; then Maddie came and covered him with a blanket. He woke up to find her doing just that. He reached out to take her hand and pressed it to his lips.

"I love you, Mrs. Brandt," he said.

"I love you, Dr. Brandt," she replied. And he smiled.

* * * * *

Jon was dismayed to realize that he and Sara had an appointment with their father's attorney concerning the will and estate. Although Jon wouldn't have blamed him, he feared being omitted from his father's will. With the trip east, Jon realized that his financial reserve was running low. He could never make a living as a farmer without being able to invest in a significant piece of land and some farm equipment, and making a living as a country doctor was not necessarily prone to bringing abundant income. He wanted to provide comfortably for Maddie and their children, and he prayed that there would be some allotment left for him in his father's will.

The meeting barely got underway when it became evident the will had not been altered since it had first been drawn up when Jon and Sara were children. Since their mother was already deceased, Phillip Brandt's assets would be divided equally between Jon and Sara, except for a minimal amount set aside for each of his four siblings that were still living, and an allotment donated to a local hospital, specifically for the care of underprivileged children. It was also stated that the house was to be sold and the amount divided equally between Sara and Jon.

Jon and his sister were both silent on the brief cab ride back home. Jon was relieved to have the financial security his father had left for him; but he just felt so completely unworthy of it. He thought of the sacrifices his father had made to become so well off—not necessarily wealthy, but certainly amply comfortable. As Jon looked back over his own life, he couldn't see that he'd sacrificed anything—except his relationship with his father. If throwing away every cent he'd just inherited could bring his father back, or mend the chasm between them, he'd do it without a moment's hesitation. As it was, he just wished he could have the chance to tell him how very grateful he was for all that his father had done for him, in spite of their differences.

"Are you all right?" Sara asked as they stepped into the house together.

"It's hard to say," he admitted. "I feel . . . guilty."

"Guilty? Whatever for?"

"For coming away with so much . . . when I gave so little."

"There's no need for that, Jon. He really loved you. He would want you to have it."

"Yes, I know," he said, his voice quavering slightly. He didn't like the way the word *love* was used in a past tense.

Once again Jon found Maddie resting and didn't want to disturb her. He went to his father's study to read from his mother's journals, but he'd only been there a few minutes when Maddie came in.

"I thought I might find you here," she said.

"How are you feeling?" he asked as she kissed him in greeting.

"I'm fine. How are you?"

He made a noncommittal noise and was glad when she didn't press him.

"Jon, there's something I feel I need to ask, but . . ."

He could see that she was nervous, and he prodded gently, "What is it? You know you can ask me anything."

"I know, but . . . I'm afraid it might sound selfish or . . ."

Jon actually laughed. "You're the least selfish person I've ever known. Now what's on your mind?"

"Well . . . your father is a very well-known man in the community."

"Yes," he drawled inquisitively; this was not what he'd expected.

"And many people will be attending his funeral—fine upstanding people."

"Yes."

"Well," she said, "I am his daughter-in-law, and even though I never knew him, I want to feel like I fit in with the family, and . . . I want you to be proud of me, and in my condition I feel so unattractive and awkward as it is, but . . ."

"What's the problem, Maddie?" he asked when she hesitated too long.

"I know we don't have much money left, but do you think I could get a new dress for the funeral? I really don't have anything appropriate, and—"

"Oh, Maddie, my darling," he said, easing her onto his lap, "you may buy anything you want. I told you before, and I meant it, that I am proud to be your husband under any circumstances. You can go to my father's funeral in calico, for all I care. But if having a new dress will make you feel more comfortable, by all means, you should have one."

She sighed deeply. "You're so good to me, Jon, but can we afford it? I've never bought a ready-made dress before. I know they're expensive. But I don't have time to make one, and—"

"Yes, Maddie, we can afford it. In fact, maybe you should buy two or three new dresses, and a few things for the baby. Buy whatever you want."

"But, how can . . ."

"Maddie, we're receiving a significant inheritance from my father's assets." She gasped softly and he continued. "I feel guilty for even taking it, but I want to give you a good life, and, well . . ." He smiled and smoothed a hand over her face. "I believe he would have loved you, Maddie. I only wish I had thought to bring you here months ago, so that he could have had the privilege of knowing you, and you him. I think he would be pleased to know that his money was being spent on you, even if he didn't believe that I—"

"Oh, there you are," Sara said, peeking into the room. "I've got to go downtown and pick up a few things. Do you need anything?"

"I don't," Jon said, "but Maddie could use some new things; a dress for the funeral, most specifically. Would you mind taking her along and—"

"Oh, I'd love to!" she said eagerly. "We'll have such fun. When can you be ready to go?"

"Anytime," Maddie said with a delightful little laugh.

"Have a good time," Jon said.

"Oh we will," Sara said, taking Maddie's hand to lead her toward the hall.

"And watch out for her," Jon added. "Don't let her get too tired."

"I promise," Sara called, and Maddie waved at Jon just before they disappeared.

Jon sighed deeply, inhaling the serenity he felt in seeing the women he loved developing a bond, in spite of the stark differences in their upbringing. A poignant gratitude filled him, momentarily bringing reprieve from his grief. He returned to his mother's journals and immersed himself in the recounting of the significant points of his and Sara's childhood. According to his mother's account, his father left most of the guidance and discipline to her during their younger years, but he was continually concerned for his children's welfare. She wrote more than once that she knew work was his way of showing his love for his family, that every hour he worked provided a security for them that he'd never known in his own youth. He'd seen his mother and siblings go without, and he would die before he would see the same with his wife and children.

Jon turned from the books and deeply contemplated the new layers he was discovering of the man he'd struggled to tolerate most of his life. He drifted to sleep in the chair and woke abruptly at the sound of the front door closing in the distance, followed by excited chatter from the women. He came into the hall to see Maddie and Sara burdened with packages and full of smiles.

"It would seem you had a good time," he said.

"Oh, the most wonderful time," Maddie said. She laughed as he took the packages from her and carried them up to the bedroom.

Sara followed, saying, "You must try them on and show Jon. Of course, there are a few that won't fit until after the baby comes, but you must try on the other two."

Jon briefly forgot his pain and regrets as he watched Maddie emerge from the sitting room. She was wearing a lavender day dress that made her glow all the more, if such a thing was possible. She went back and returned wearing an elegant black dress, lace gloves, and a smart little veiled hat.

"You look beautiful," he said, feeling as if he'd just fallen in love with her all over again.

"I feel like a queen," she said and pressed her hands over her belly. "Even with as big and round as I am, I still feel like a queen."

"You *are* a queen, my dear. And you get more beautiful every day—even as big and round as you are."

Once Maddie changed back into the dress she'd worn shopping, she dropped into bed and only came around long enough to eat supper in their room before she slept through the night. Her shopping had obviously worn her out, but he thought on how incredibly wonderful it was that she could go shopping without being carted and carried. She'd made amazing progress, and he had to remind himself that they were extremely blessed. Recalling his indignation toward God not so long ago, he felt suddenly guilt ridden. For the first time since his father's death, Jon knelt down by the bed and poured out his heart in prayer. He cried and prayed until his knees ached, then he crawled into bed and cried and prayed some more. Somewhere in the darkest hours of the night, he clearly recalled Ellie once telling him, *It's been my experience that God's answers are for the best good. And we must remember that He sees a perspective of our lives that we can't possibly comprehend.*

Jon knew in his heart that he couldn't possibly understand why his father had been taken before he could rectify his mistakes, but he had been greatly blessed in his life despite those mistakes, and he had to trust in the Lord to help him get beyond this. He prayed that he would be able to come to terms with his father's death, although he felt certain that finding peace with it was simply something that would never happen in this life. But if he believed in eternal life, he had to believe that eventually he would be given another chance, provided he did his best to live right and earn such a privilege. With that hope prominent in his mind, he finally drifted to sleep.

* * * * *

Phillip Brandt's funeral passed by like a dream for Jon, while mottled images of the past flitted sporadically through his mind. The glimmer of peace he'd felt the previous evening became distant and obscure as his memories were drawn to a countless string of arguments, and a tension ever present when he and his father had occupied the same room. He'd come to understand and know his father in a way he'd never imagined. He was able to see that he'd been a good man, in spite of a crusty exterior difficult to break through. The funeral speeches were filled with sincere praises for his father; he had done much good in his life. Jon had no trouble accepting that he'd had a distorted perception of his father, but he could also see that his father had been far from perfect, and being dead didn't make him suddenly beyond reproach. Jon felt at ease knowing both; he could accept his father for being human, just as he could clearly see his own faults and strengths. The problem was simply the hole in Jon's heart. A hole that could only be healed by knowing that his father had forgiven him. There was just so much he wished he could have said. And it was too late.

When the burial was completed, the blanket of numbness that Jon had felt protecting his emotions began to dissipate. He shut himself in his father's study, sometimes crying, sometimes staring at nothing while his mind tried to make sense of what he was feeling and why. In spite of occasional inquires from Maddie and Sara, Jon stayed alone through the night, going without food, and dozing in between his prayers and meditation. He finished reading his mother's journals, amazed at the overall love and commitment they shared through their lives—one not readily evident in the way Jon had seen them behave together. He learned something of the long-term reality of what marriage was really all about. He thought of Maddie's parents, and Sylvia's commitment to standing by her husband in spite of his difficulties. He wondered what kind of sorrows and hardship were masked by Glen Hansen's fear and pride.

He felt somehow more wise and mature to be able to look at his parents and see their faults beside their strengths—to still know that he loved them and appreciated them for the people they were. His mother was meek and loving, almost to a fault. But she had been completely without guile. His father hadn't been a warm man; he'd been overprotective and controlling, but with reason. But Jon had seen in Maddie's father that it could be much worse. And he knew now that his father had been a man of integrity, honest and hard-working. And Jon loved him.

Some measure of peace came in the early morning hours when he was able to know beyond any doubt that God had forgiven him for his stubbornness, his pride, his anger. And he knew that he had truly and fully forgiven his father for the harsh, stubborn attitude that had caused him grief. Now if he could only forgive himself for his adverse response to those attitudes, and for putting off something that was now too late to rectify. He finally came to the conclusion that he had no choice. He had to put it away. He had to go on. And God willing, with time, he would find peace over the matter.

But days later Jon still felt unsettled. He couldn't expect much help from his wife either. Maddie stayed close to their room and in bed much of the time as the baby suddenly demanded all of her spare energy. Although she did enjoy being able to play the piano, something she'd not been able to do since they'd married. It was practically all she did beyond eating and sleeping. Sara joined her a few times, and Jon enjoyed hearing them play duets, or going back and forth with different pieces of music. Mingled with the music was chatter and laughter, and Jon wished the women could live closer to each other. They each seemed to have found the sister they'd never had. But Sara's life was so completely different from theirs. It simply wasn't possible. He did, however, make a mental note to order a piano after they got home and settled. Hearing Maddie play made him realize how much they had both missed it.

Maddie's time at the piano became less frequent as she began to feel exhausted and constantly uncomfortable, and she often commented that she was counting down the days. Sara's company helped her immensely, especially when Jon knew he was distracted by his own feelings. He did, however, try to be sensitive and see to her needs, and he too was looking forward to the arrival of their child. He couldn't deny that his life was good and he had much to be grateful for. But that in itself almost added to the unexplainable guilt and sorrow that continued to plague him.

Jon wrote a long letter to Ellie, explaining in detail all that had happened. He'd already sent her a telegram to let her know of his father's death, but he knew she'd be longing to know more. He sent it off feeling a distinct ache for Utah. It had definitely become his home.

With his father's estate settled and all his business matters closed, Jon worked with Sara to go through their father's personal papers and clean out his office. He had been very organized, and as Sara had once said, he wasn't much for writing. There were practically no papers that could be considered personal. But at the back of one of his desk drawers, tucked between some photographs of family members, Jon found a sealed envelope. His own name was written on it in his father's hand. His heart quickened and he sat down hard.

"What is it?" Sara asked, turning her attention from a different drawer that she was sorting through. Jon held it out to her but said nothing. She took it from him, sighed deeply and said, "Only once he said he wanted to write you a letter, but he kept hoping you'd write first. I told him he should go ahead and write it, and he could send it when he heard from you."

"Oh, help," Jon said quietly, and pressed a hand unconsciously over his heart. It was one more aching piece of evidence that he'd been a fool. And how much like his father he was! Both of them waiting for the other to take the first step, too proud and stubborn to get past their fears and admit to their true feelings. Jon took the envelope back from Sara, afraid of what the letter might say. If the words written here were bitter and resentful, as they often had been when they'd spoken, he wondered if he could swallow them despite his newfound forgiveness.

"I think I'll leave you alone," Sara said as she left the room. He wanted to beg her to stay, to hold his hand. But he knew she was right. He had to face this alone.

Jon took a deep breath and broke the seal on the envelope. He pulled out a single page, unfolded it and closed his eyes, willing himself to open them and face his father's words. He first noted the date was about the time he'd been married, a little over a year after he'd left Boston. Sara had said his father became ill about a year after his mother's death. Had his father's illness prompted a change of heart? He forced himself to read on.

Dear Jonathon,

I must confess that I am missing you greatly. I know that we had many differences, but I'm learning with the passing of time that I was to blame for many of them. You're just so much like me, son. And maybe I saw in you the traits that I didn't like about myself. Whatever good you have in you, I suspect it came from your mother, and from her careful love and guidance. She was very good at loving both of us in spite of our difficulties.

I want you to know, Jonathon, that I'm proud of you. I know you didn't want to follow in my footsteps and become a doctor, but you did it anyway, and I know how hard you worked. I hope that whatever you choose to do with your life, you'll eventually appreciate the knowledge you have—that you can save lives and help those in need. I pray that all is well with you, and I look forward to the day when we can be together again.

With love and affection, your father,

Phillip Brandt

Jon read the letter three times before he tossed it onto the desktop and wept. He was startled to feel a hand on his shoulder, and looked up to see Sara standing beside him.

"May I?" she asked, motioning toward the letter.

"Of course," he said, his voice raspy.

Sara sat on the edge of the desk and read, while Jon wiped his face with his handkerchief and managed to get his composure. When she was finished, she asked gently, "So how does it make you feel?"

"Well," he sighed, gazing toward the window, "it's wonderful. I can't deny it. Those are the words I always wanted to hear from my father—that he was proud of me, that he loved me, that it was difficult. But . . ." Emotion caught his voice and he felt his chin quivering.

"But?" Sara pressed.

"I just wish I could have told him the same."

"Well, you can, can't you?"

"What do you mean?"

"You do believe in life after death, don't you?" she asked. "Maddie's talked to me more about your beliefs than you have—you've been distracted, I know—but, well, I can't say that I would ever embrace another religion as you have, but I admire you for doing it, and I must say that some of your beliefs feel very . . . right. So, if our father's spirit lives on, then . . ."

"It's a comforting thought, Sara, I admit. But the prospect of being reunited with him one day doesn't really help at the moment. I intend to live a long life. I have to live it out knowing I put off something that I will always regret."

"We all make mistakes, Jon. Surely you can accept that and move on."

"I'm going to have to," he said.

"All right, but the point I was trying to get to was that you *can* tell him how you feel now, can't you? I'm not saying that he's right here looking over our shoulders; I don't begin to know how this veil between life and death idea works, but . . . couldn't you write him a letter? Or talk to him? It might make you feel better. Think about it. You know where to find me."

Jon *did* think about it. And he prayed about it. And he talked to Maddie about it. He finally concluded that it was the only way he would ever begin to come to terms with how he felt. He considered writing his feelings down, but then, what would he do with the letter? If only mailing a letter to heaven was possible. He concluded that he just wanted to talk to his father, and he prayed that somehow God would make it possible for him to hear. He left home early one morning and went to the cemetery. The newly carved marker stood out among those surrounding it, but Jon couldn't bring himself to speak aloud to the piece of stone. He was completely alone and had no reason to feel self-conscious; but he also knew that his father's spirit wouldn't necessarily hover near the grave. He walked for a long while with no particular destination in mind, contemplating the thoughts he wanted to express. He was surprised to find himself at the waterfront. He walked aimlessly along the pier, recalling the habit he'd once had of coming here for solace. He loved to watch the ships, all sizes, sitting magnificently at the dock. He stopped in a place that was peaceful beyond the occasional cry of the sea birds, and without any premeditation, the words began to flow. He talked aloud as if his father were there in front of him. Tears flowed as he told his father the full extent of his feelings, pouring out his heart with soul and purpose.

He worked toward a conclusion by saying firmly, "I love you, Father. I do. And whether I end up being a farmer, or a miner, or a shopkeeper, I'll always be glad that I'm a doctor. I want to thank you for pushing me to do it. I can see now that you actually sacrificed our relationship for the sake of seeing that I got my education, and developed a skill that would actually mean something to me, and to the people I can help. I'm grateful for that, and for the sacrifices you made to give me a good life." The words suddenly ran out and he finished with, "I just wanted you to know that, and I would give anything if I could just know . . ." He became so emotional that it took him a full minute to be able to say, "To know that you had forgiven me for being so proud . . . and so slow to come around." He swallowed carefully and gained his composure, knowing that he'd said what he needed to say. He took a deep breath and added, "Either way, I believe we'll be together again someday. Take good care of Mother. I love you."

Jon turned and walked away, a gesture that put a finality to the conversation, if only for him. He returned home to find Maddie up and about more than she had been in days. She met him in the hall and wrapped her arms around him, holding him tightly. He returned her embrace, grateful beyond words for the love and understanding she gave him.

"Are you all right?" she asked.

"I think so," he said. "Let's just say I'm doing better."

"Good," she smiled. "Let's get something to eat. You missed lunch and you know me; I can eat six times a day."

"You are eating for two," he said.

"Yes, and as you once told me, my stomach's being crowded out by the baby. I can't get very much in it at one time."

While they were sharing soup and sandwiches, Maddie said, "You know, Jon, a thought occurred to me this morning that, well, it's so obvious I don't know why I didn't think of it before. I guess there's just been so much going on, and . . ."

"And you haven't felt well," he reminded her.

"Yes, but anyway, with you're father gone, given some time, we can do the temple work for him and your mother. They can be sealed together, and you can be sealed to them."

Jon absorbed what she was saying, and the peace that had begun to fill him expanded. He smiled and squeezed her hand across the table. "What a splendid idea, my dear. It's something we can look forward to."

She smiled in return and came to her feet in order to kiss him. And Jon silently thanked God for all that he'd been blessed with.

CHAPTER TWELVE
The Veil

Two weeks after the funeral, Jon sat in his father's study rereading certain sections of his mother's journals. Hearing a knock at the open door, he turned and called, "Come in."

He was surprised to see Harrison Hartford step into the room. The man had come and gone a great deal during Jon's stay. Occasionally they all shared supper, but for the most part he had visited with Sara privately, and that was fine. They had very little in common, and even less to talk about.

"Mr. Hartford," Jon said, coming to his feet. "Sara's not at home right now. I could tell her that you—"

"No, that's fine. I knew she wouldn't be here. I would like to talk with you, if I could."

"Of course," Jon said, motioning him toward a chair. Mr. Hartford sat down, but remained at the edge of his seat. Jon returned to his own chair behind the desk. "Now, what can I do for you?"

"Mr. Brandt," he said, and Jon thought it was odd that they'd never risen to a first-name basis. But then, the formality seemed to suit their relationship. "There are a few matters that I wish to discuss with you."

"Go on," Jon said, motioning with his hand.

"The first being . . . well, in your father's absence, I would like to officially ask for your sister's hand in marriage."

Jon chuckled, then wished he hadn't when Mr. Hartford didn't so much as crack a smile. "There's really no need for that," Jon said. "Sara is a grown woman with a mind of her own. She's perfectly capable of making her own choices."

"I'm aware of that," he said, sounding subtly offended. "I simply want to do the appropriate thing and ask for your blessing."

"Of course you have it," Jon said. "It's evident she cares very much for you, and you for her. I know you'll provide well for her. I only hope that you will also be sensitive to her emotional needs and treat her with the utmost respect."

"Of course," he said, actually seeming to appreciate the admonition. "We would like to be married next week, here at the house. Quiet and simple; just close friends and family. I believe it would be appropriate for you to give the bride away, if you're willing."

"I'd be honored," Jon said, and waited for him to get to the next point. He honestly didn't know what Sara saw in the man, but as he'd just said, she was a grown woman with her own mind.

"Also," he went on, "I would like to make a proposition. I understand your father's will specified that the house should be sold, and the profit divided. However, Sara dearly loves this house, and I would like to see it remain her home. I would like to purchase your share, if that would be acceptable. I have the cash readily available."

Jon only had to think a minute before he said, "I don't think that's necessary, Mr. Hartford. My sister did a great deal to care for our father. I think she's entitled to the house. I'm perfectly content with the inheritance I've got."

Mr. Hartford turned visibly red. "Mr. Brandt," he said, "I can appreciate your wanting to be generous with your sister, but this is between you and me. I can assure you that the income I receive from my occupation is more than adequate to meet the needs of a wife and children. I have a significant inheritance of my own, and I wish to own the house, free and clear. If you're not willing to accept my offer, then the house will simply have to be sold, and we will find something equivalent."

Jon stared at the man, marveling at how very much he *was* like Phillip Brandt. Proud and firm and not to be trifled with. Jon just smiled and said, "Have it your way, Mr. Hartford. I'll expect a check in hand before the wedding." He thought of the fine piece of land he could purchase with the money. Maybe some sheep. "Was there anything else?"

"No, I don't believe so," he said, coming to his feet and extending his hand. Jon rose and shook it firmly. "Thank you for your time, Mr. Brandt. I believe I'll be seeing you at supper."

"I'll be looking forward to it," Jon said, grateful the man didn't know him well enough to catch the mildly sarcastic undertone. He hoped his sister would be happy. In terms of her marriage, he was glad that he and Maddie would be living far enough away that they wouldn't have to socialize often.

Plans for the wedding were discussed that evening at supper, and Sara seemed deliriously happy. Maddie quickly became caught up in the plans, and over the next few days she stayed busy helping Sara in ways that wouldn't tire her out. Jon loved to see them together, and the genuine friendship and sisterhood they had come to share in such a brief time.

Sara's wedding was, as Mr. Hartford had said, quiet and simple. Jon held Maddie's hand through the ceremony, and his eyes were often drawn to hers. They exchanged warm smiles and a deep gaze, and he knew that she was remembering, just as he was, the day they had been married. And he appreciated all the more just how blessed he was to have the gospel in his life, and to have had the opportunity to be married in the temple. He knew there was no place on earth so beautiful, and the eternity it represented made it doubly so.

The house became especially quiet when Sara left for a brief honeymoon. Maddie caught up on her rest, and worked occasionally on her crocheting, while Jon did a lot of reading in his father's study. While his father hadn't written letters or kept journals of his personal life, Jon had discovered that he'd kept extensive medical journals of his experiences and cases. And Jon found himself entranced by his father's knowledge and natural gift. He couldn't help being grateful for the opportunity to glean from his father's wisdom.

Sara returned from her honeymoon bright and cheerful. Even Mr. Hartford seemed a little less dull. But Jon wasn't especially pleased with having to live under the same roof with him; he had no choice, however, until the baby was born and Maddie recovered enough to travel safely.

"You know," Maddie said when he mentioned his feelings, "if Mr. Hartford reminds you of your father, well, perhaps learning to get along with him might be . . . I don't know, healing somehow. Coming to terms with your feelings for your father doesn't mean that he would be any easier to live with now than he used to be. It's just a thought."

Just a thought, Jon echoed silently. A thought he didn't necessarily like, but he couldn't manage to put it out of his head. He finally decided that Maddie was right. If his father was still alive, would he be able to overlook their differences? Could they have learned to accept and enjoy each other's company? Praying for some fortitude, Jon considered it a personal challenge to be in the same room with Harrison Hartford and not be annoyed. Amazingly enough, within a few days, he actually got Harrison to laugh a few times. They progressed to a first-name basis, and Harrison admitted that he was rather partial to gardening and could understand Jon's desire to work the land.

When Maddie's estimated due date arrived, she was so swollen and miserable that they all prayed it wouldn't be much longer. That same night Jon came awake in the dark; he realized in his effort to snuggle closer to Maddie, that she was gone. He turned and attempted to adjust his eyes to the moonlit room, and then he saw her silhouette standing near the window.

"You all right?" he asked and she turned toward him.

It took her a long moment to answer. "I've been counting the seconds between the pains. They're less than three minutes apart."

Jon stood beside her and held her tightly. "Everything's going to be all right," he said, sensing her concern.

"I believe it will," she said. "You've told me what to expect. I feel as prepared as I possibly could be, but I still know it will be hard and . . ." Her voice quavered and she held to him tightly. "I'm so grateful you know what you're doing, Jon—that you can deliver the baby yourself; I'm so grateful."

"So am I," he murmured, and pressed a kiss into her hair while he silently asked God to thank his father for him.

Jon urged Maddie back to bed and held her as the pains became more frequent and intense. He checked her regularly to be certain all was well. When they missed breakfast, Sara came to their room.

"She's in labor," Jon said quietly. "The pains are less than two minutes apart now. Her water broke a few minutes ago."

Sara rushed to Maddie's side and sat on the edge of the bed, taking her hand. "Everything's going to be just fine," she said. "I'll stay with you every minute, if you like."

"Oh, I would," Maddie said, and grimaced with another contraction.

"Sara's helped deliver lots of babies," Jon said when the pain subsided.

"Really?" Maddie was obviously surprised.

"She worked on and off assisting our father for years."

"I didn't know that," Maddie said, but the pain came again before she could inquire further.

By late afternoon the pain became so constant and intense that Maddie screamed and cried, insisting that she couldn't do it any more. Jon was grateful for his sister's calming presence, fighting his own urge to cry. He'd delivered many babies, but it had never been like this. Her physical state and emotional reaction were familiar, but the fact that he loved her, and that this was his child, made it difficult to remain unaffected by her suffering. He did his best to soothe and assure her, intermittently praying that they would both make it through this. He knew well enough that even with the best medical care things could go wrong, things that were beyond any human control. He began to imagine some of the horrible things he'd seen throughout his career happening to Maddie. He wondered how it would feel to write Ellie and tell her the worst had happened. He could never go back to Utah and face Maddie's parents. His life would be over. Jon shuddered at the thought of anything happening to Maddie. Everything that mattered to him was contingent on her making it through this safe and well, and he forced doubts and fears from his mind, praying constantly that he would be guided, and that she would not be plagued with complications.

It was nearly midnight before the trauma finally ended. Maddie's exhausted groans were muffled by the baby's strong cries. The hearty wails began before she had even fully emerged into the world enough for them to know it was a girl.

Jon laughed at her tiny hands and angry face, and his hands trembled as he lifted her up for Maddie to see. "She's beautiful," he murmured in a shaky voice

"A girl." Maddie's laugh was exhausted, and she slumped back onto the bed.

Jon had to blink the tears out of his eyes to see clearly enough to cut the cord. He was grateful to have Sara close by, and grateful for her efficiency in handing him everything he needed just before he needed it. She provided a blanket to wrap the baby in, and Jon held the little one close a moment before he rose to give the baby to Maddie. The baby stopped crying and looked toward him with wide eyes, as if to say, *So you're my father.* In the same moment, Jon's heart began to pound as a second thought appeared in his mind, *I'm proud of you, Son. All is forgiven.* Jon gasped for breath and held the baby close to him, in awe at the tangible, undeniable warmth spreading through his every nerve. He closed his eyes in order to hold the moment close, knowing beyond any doubt that his father was standing beside him.

"Jon?" he heard Maddie say, as if from a distance. "Is she all right? Are you—"

"She's perfect," he said, and looked down at the baby again. He didn't realize he was crying until he saw the tears drip onto her little blanket. He placed the baby in Maddie's arms. "She's perfect," he repeated. "Everything's perfect."

Maddie cried through her laughter as she absorbed her infant daughter. "Oh, she's beautiful, Jon," she said, looking up into his eyes. Her expression told him that she'd sensed something deeper in his emotions. He just smiled and touched her face. Then he put his arms around both her and the baby, and wept with perfect joy. Just as he'd told her, *everything was perfect.*

* * * * *

While Maddie slept peacefully, Jon sat in the chair near the bed, holding his infant daughter against his chest. In spite of his lack of sleep, he felt replenished, rejuvenated, and full of life. He contemplated over and over the experience he'd been blessed with, when the veil between heaven and earth had momentarily been lifted. He marveled at God's mercy and wisdom. While Jon had believed he'd been denied the answer to his prayers, denied the miracle of having his father hold on long enough to see him, he knew now that he'd been blessed with an even greater miracle. The inner turmoil Jon had been through in the weeks since his father's death only strengthened his appreciation of what he'd experienced. He leaned his head back in the chair and closed his eyes, silently thanking God for more miracles than he could count. Yes, he thought, lightly running his fingers over his daughter's wispy hair, everything was perfect.

* * * * *

Maddie recovered quickly and felt relatively well. Sara was thrilled with the opportunity to help Maddie with the baby, and the two women became even closer. Jon knew it would be difficult for them to part when the time came, but he felt grateful for the time they'd been able to share.

During Maddie's recovery, Jon and Sara worked to appropriately divide their parents belongings, especially those with any sentimental value. Jon boxed up his father's books and medical journals, along with some other odds and ends, and had them shipped to Utah. He also packed up and shipped the remainder of his own belongings, previously left in his rush to escape. He sent Ellie a telegram, telling her to expect the packages and have them put in the house, and he also told her when to expect their arrival.

Elizabeth Brandt was two weeks old the day they set out for Utah. It was incredibly difficult to say goodbye to Sara. Tears were shed during the farewell, but they all promised to keep in touch through letters, and Harrison said that one of these days they just might have to come to Utah for a visit. Jon actually felt pleased by the idea.

The journey was long and tedious, but Elizabeth slept a great deal and proved to be a good baby. Maddie actually felt better than she had on the journey east, and Jon felt completely at peace. Returning home now, with peace and forgiveness warming his soul, he knew that life could be no better.

Knowing that Ellie had been informed of their return, it was a surprise to step off the train and not find her and Dave waiting. They were generally punctual. Standing together on the platform, it quickly became evident that all faces were turned toward them, gaping in stunned silence.

"Maddie," Jon said quietly, "I think we overlooked something."

"I forgot all about it," she answered just as quietly.

Jon took in the expressions of the townspeople he'd come to know so well and chuckled softly. "You'd think they had just seen the Red Sea parted."

"Maybe they did," Maddie said, and took the baby from him, obviously feeling self-conscious with the way people were staring and whispering. "Get the luggage. I'm sure they'll be here soon."

Maddie took a few steps and sat down on a bench. Jon moved toward the baggage car, then stopped and turned. He waved his hand toward Maddie and said loudly, "She can walk. She didn't just suddenly stand up and do it. She's been working very hard at it for several months. If you want to hear all about it, come by later and we'll talk. Bring a pie or something."

A quick glance showed that Maddie was smiling and more relaxed. A low chuckle went through the small crowd before people moved on with their business. Dave and Ellie arrived before Jon had the luggage together on the platform. Maddie walked over to join him. Dave turned from helping Ellie down and gasped. "Merciful heaven! It's a miracle."

Ellie just laughed and ran to embrace Maddie and the new baby. Jon paused a moment to watch them, grateful for all he'd been blessed with.

Through the ride home, Ellie demanded to hear details of all that had happened, things that Jon hadn't included in his letters. She commented over and over how beautiful little Elizabeth was, and declared that she would be doing her fair share of tending the baby.

"Thank you," Jon said as he shook Dave's hand at the door of their home, "for the ride and for taking care of everything while we were gone. I owe you."

"Nah," Dave laughed, "maybe we're even now. You've helped me more than you'll ever know, and I still can't get you to take a red cent."

"Why should I? You put me up and kept me fed, and—"

"And you took care of everything while I was sick and you—"

"Oh, for heaven's sake," Ellie interrupted. "We're family. We're not keeping score. Now I'm sure the two of you are tired from the trip. We'll catch up more later. Why don't you come over for dinner tomorrow after church."

"Thank you," Maddie said, "that would be nice."

"We'll see you tomorrow then," Dave said, helping Ellie back onto the wagon seat.

"Oh," Ellie called, "those boxes you shipped are in your spare bedroom."

"Thank you," Jon called back.

They drove away and Jon opened the door. Maddie walked in first and gasped.

"What?" he demanded, coming beside her, certain something was wrong. The table was set for two, with thick sliced bread and butter, and a pot of stew sat on the stove.

"No wonder they were late," Maddie said and laughed softly. "We could never get even in our entire lives."

"Well, maybe," Jon said. "Maybe when they're old and decrepit, we can take care of them."

"That's a nice thought," Maddie said.

"What?" he chuckled. "Dave and Ellie being old and—"

"No," she laughed, "all of us being here together for the rest of our lives."

Jon sighed and agreed, "Yes, it is." He took the baby and put his arm around Maddie. He pressed a kiss to her brow and added, "Yes, it's perfect."

"Not quite perfect," Maddie said, and Jon saw the ache in her eyes.

"You've done everything you can, Maddie. If your father—"

"No, I haven't done everything I can," she said. "Time has passed and things have changed. And as soon as we eat and get this stuff unpacked, we're going to go pay my parents a little visit."

"Really?"

"Really," she said. "I think it's time they met their grand-daughter."

"Indeed," Jon said with a chuckle.

"Is something funny, Dr. Brandt?"

"No, Maddie. Not funny. I just love the way you, well, the way you've learned to take charge of your life." She smiled, and he added, "I must disagree on one point, however."

"What's that?" she asked, as if she dared him to defy her.

He laughed again. "We're not waiting until we unpack. We can do that later. I think we'd better get to them before the gossip does."

Maddie laughed with him and they sat down to eat.

"So," Jon said as the horse pulled the buckboard toward the Hansen home, "are you nervous?"

"I'm terrified," Maddie admitted.

"Well," Jon said, "you do have the advantage of surprise."

"Yes. Showing up at their door when I've been ostracized from the family ought to surprise them."

"Yes, but what I meant is the fact that you will be *walking* up to the door."

Maddie laughed. "Yes, that's true."

Jon pulled the buckboard up in front of the house. He and Maddie both let out a heavy sigh, then chuckled at the evidence of their mutual anxiety.

"Here goes," he said, jumping down. He took the baby, then held up a hand to help Maddie come to her feet.

He attempted to walk toward the door, but she held his hand tightly, forcing him to stop and look at her. "What?" he asked, noting the tears showing in her eyes. When she said nothing, he added, "I know this is difficult, but you're going to do just fine. And if it doesn't go well, you'll know you tried, and—"

"I know all of that, Jon," she said.

"Then what's wrong?" he asked.

"Nothing's wrong," she said. "That's just it. The last time I was here it was the morning we left to get married, and look at me! Look at us—at how far we've come . . . all we've been blessed with. I love you, Jon." She touched his face and he turned to press a kiss into her palm. "And no matter what happens in there, as long as I have you by my side, I will never have cause to complain."

Jon sighed and quickly kissed her lips. "The feeling is mutual, my love." He kissed her hand again, took a deep breath, and escorted her to the front porch.

"What if they're not home?" she asked.

"Then we'll come back."

"What if they don't answer?"

"Then we'll come back," he said again.

"What if—"

"Let's just do this and worry about it later," he said, and knocked loudly on the door.

Sylvia pulled the door open and for a long moment the world seemed frozen. She stared, open-mouthed, at her daughter, seeming to absorb the evidence that she was holding a baby—and standing. A sharp noise came from Sylvia's throat before she clamped a hand over her mouth and huge tears brimmed in her eyes.

"Hello, Mother," Maddie said, her voice shaky and broken. "We just got in from Boston a while ago. We wanted you and Father to meet Elizabeth." Her voice became more steady. "If he doesn't want us to come in . . . well, what can we say? But . . . we thought you should at least see the baby and . . ."

Sylvia encircled both Maddie and the baby with a tight embrace as they both cried. Then Jon eased the baby away so they could hold each other more tightly. Sylvia leaned back and touched Maddie's face, then she glanced down at her legs. Her expression betrayed her amazement and joy, but she couldn't speak. Her tears turned to laughter as she turned toward Jon, holding the baby. She touched the baby's hair and face and cried again. Jon put his arm around Sylvia and she wept on his shoulder.

"It's all right, Mother," he said, wondering when Glen would appear and disrupt their tender reunion.

Sylvia stepped back and wiped at her face. "Oh, good heavens," she said. "I've missed you so much, and I knew the baby should be here by now. I just don't think I knew how much I missed you until now and . . . here you are. I'm so glad you came. Come in. Sit down. We need to talk."

"Are you sure that's a good idea, Mother?" Maddie asked. "I mean, I want to see Father, but—"

"Who's there, Sylvia?" Glen bellowed just before he appeared in the hall. He looked more shocked than angry as he froze where he stood, much as Sylvia had done. Maddie took advantage of his obvious astonishment. She took Elizabeth from Jon, walked toward her father and put the baby in his arms. Glen gasped and looked down at what he was holding as if it might break.

"Hello, Father," Maddie said. "I hope you won't be angry, but . . . we wanted you to meet Elizabeth. And we wanted to let you know that we're doing well and . . ." She glanced toward Jon, as if for support. He nodded firmly to let her know she was doing just fine. She turned back toward her father and added, "We'd love to have you come over for supper sometime soon, and—" Glen abruptly handed the baby back to Maddie and turned to leave the room.

"Father," Maddie said. Glen stopped walking but didn't turn around. "I want to thank you for everything you've ever done for me. I know you always tried to be a good father. You also have to know that Jon is a good husband. He's the best thing that ever happened to me, Papa. And I love him. I want to share my life with both of you. I don't want to have to make a choice." Her firm voice finally faltered when she finished with, "I love you, Papa."

He barely glanced over his shoulder and took another step. He stopped again when Jon said, "When are you going to lower your pride enough to admit that she's happy?"

Jon held his breath, fearing an angry eruption, but Glen simply left the room. All was silent until they heard the back door and knew he had left the house. They all exchanged concerned glances, then Jon said, "Well, he didn't yell and kick me out. I think that's progress."

Maddie forced a smile and nodded, then tears showed in her eyes.

"May I hold her again?" Sylvia asked, and took the baby from Maddie. "Oh, she's so beautiful. I do believe she looks like you, Jon."

He chuckled. "Hopefully she'll grow out of that. Although, I must admit she is beautiful; almost as beautiful as her mother." He smiled at Maddie, then put his arms around her while she got her emotions under control.

"So," Sylvia said, sitting down near the piano, "how did everything go in Boston? Ellie told me your father passed away, Jon. I'm so sorry."

"Yes, well, it's been difficult but I believe I've come to terms with it. Beyond that, everything's fine, as you can see."

They sat down when she started asking questions about Maddie's learning to walk again. She cried once more, then asked questions about the baby's arrival. Jon noticed Maddie's eyes being drawn to the piano more than once. He made up his mind to order one right away.

"You know," Maddie said, coming to her feet abruptly, "we probably should be going. We don't want to give Papa any cause to be angry and . . . well, perhaps it would be better if we leave while we're ahead."

Jon stood also. "You know, Mother," he said, "we have a spare room if he gives you any trouble."

Sylvia smiled and said, "Thank you, but I'll be fine. And believe it or not, so will he. I'm so glad you came. And I hope to see you soon."

On the way home Maddie took Jon's hand and squeezed it tightly. He turned to see her smiling, with tears on her face. "My prayers were answered," she said. "I was able to say what I wanted to say to my father without him getting angry, and I was able to visit with my mother. I don't know if anything will change, but as you said, it seems that we've made some progress."

"Yes," he said, pressing her hand to his lips, "I believe we have."

At church the following morning, people weren't as surprised to see Maddie walking as they had been at the train station. It was obvious the news had spread quickly. People oohed and aahed over the baby, and they were asked many questions about Maddie's condition on the way in. When it became evident the meeting was beginning, Jon said to the people gathered, "I'll tell anyone who cares to listen all about it after church."

When the closing song and the benediction were done, a crowd quickly gathered around Jon and Maddie. Jon gave a brief explanation of his initial diagnosis of her condition, and the slow grueling process they'd gone through to make it possible for her to walk again. He finished by saying, "As many of you have said, it is a miracle, and like many miracles, it took a great deal of hard work. But we're grateful, and we appreciate your concern and support."

It took them another half an hour to get away while people hovered to visit and fuss over the baby. They went straight to Dave and Ellie's house where dinner was just being put on. Jon couldn't help thinking how good it felt to be home, to have his daughter here, and to have Maddie living a normal life.

When they were nearly finished eating, Jon said to Dave, "So, what can I help you do tomorrow?"

Dave chuckled and leaned back in his chair. "You know, Jon, you really don't need to help me. You know I can't afford to pay you and—"

"It's not about getting paid," Jon said. "I'm learning. Besides, I enjoy it."

"Well, that's fine, and I'd always welcome your help, but honestly we're managing just fine. I suspect that once word gets around that you're back, you'll be plenty busy being a doctor."

Jon sighed. He glanced at Maddie and saw her thoughts plainly in her expression, *You might as well just accept it.* He turned to Ellie and saw exactly the same look on her face.

"I really like farming," he said with overt exaggeration, like a spoiled child who wanted his way in spite of all logic. Everyone laughed and the tension was eased. But on the way home, in the late afternoon, Jon had to admit that was how he felt. Was that how it appeared to everyone but him? Was he simply a spoiled child with an idea stuck in his mind that defied all logic? Was his wanting to be a farmer just a ridiculous leftover from the ill feelings he'd had toward his father? He found the question difficult to look at and forced his mind elsewhere. One look at Maddie and the baby reminded him of all he had to be thankful for. He felt compelled to count his blessings and found there was hardly room in his heart to hold them all.

They'd only been home a short while when a knock came at the door. Since Maddie was feeding the baby, Jon went to answer it. He laughed aloud to see Sylvia, a large basket hooked over each arm. "You're moving in?" he asked.

"No," she laughed softly, "I just have some things for the baby. Is Maddie—"

"She's feeding the baby. Come on in. She'll be thrilled to see you."

Sylvia followed him to the bedroom, where Maddie was sitting in the rocker, nursing the baby. "Mother!" she said with that delightful little laugh Jon loved so thoroughly. Nothing made him so happy as to see and hear the evidence of *her* happiness.

"Hello, darling," Sylvia said, setting the baskets on the bed. "I have some things for the baby. I was going to have Ellie pass them along to you, but under the circumstances, I thought I'd just deliver them myself so I could get to hold her again." She laughed. "Oh, it's so good to be with you—both of you." She laughed again. "All three of you."

"And it's all right with Father that you're here?" Maddie asked.

"Well, he hasn't said much. He's been in a rather foul mood, but he's kept quiet. I told him I was going to visit my daughter and her family, and if he had a problem with that, I could just move in with them. I told him a new mother needed her own mother to guide her and help her, and I was not going to watch my granddaughter grow from a distance. I also told him you offered your spare room, but I'd prefer to stay in my own. I suggested that he might prefer it that way too, since he'd starve to death without me."

Jon and Maddie both laughed. "You've come a long way, Mother," Jon said.

She reached out and took his hand. "Yes, I believe I have. And I love the way you call me that." He impulsively hugged her, loving the way she returned his embrace. From the first time he'd met Sylvia Hansen, she'd had a way of soothing the loss of his own mother, and now her presence was even more comforting, with the recent loss of his father.

Sylvia turned her attention to the things she'd brought. She pulled out a wide assortment of clothes and bedding for the baby, reciting with each item when she had made it. She'd been working little by little for years, with the hope of Maddie having children. She admitted tearfully, "In spite of what seemed obvious, I could never rid myself of the feeling that I would be a grandmother. Funny how things work out."

"Isn't it, though," Maddie said, and smiled toward Jon.

* * * * *

Early Monday morning, Jon went to visit Ellie and found her alone in the kitchen.

"Hello," she said brightly. "What brings you here so early?"

"I wanted to give you this," he said, holding out an envelope. "I've been anxious to give it to you, but I wanted you to be alone."

"What is it?" she asked, wiping her hands on her apron before she hesitantly took it.

"It's something your brother wanted you to have. It's a pleasure to deliver it personally."

Ellie opened the envelope and gasped. "Good heavens!" she said and dropped into a chair. "Why in the world would . . ."

"It was stipulated in his will," Jon said. "Your other siblings received equivalent."

"But . . . you should have this money," she insisted. "You should—"

"I received much more than that," Jon said and sat down beside her. "In fact, I got much more than I deserved. You should use this to get some things you've been needing around the house, and you should get something just for yourself. And maybe put a little away. However you choose to spend it, it's yours."

Jon stayed a long while, sharing with her all he'd learned about his father and the experiences he'd had that brought him peace. He left feeling closer to Ellie than he ever had, and looking forward to the day when she could go with him and Maddie to the temple to see that the work for their family was completed. And then, one day, they would all be together again.

CHAPTER THIRTEEN
Dancing with the Doctor

Dave proved to be right as Jon was inundated with patients over the next few days. The parlor became the waiting room, and the kitchen served more as an examination room than a place where they had time to cook or eat much of anything.

"You know," Maddie said, while she was scrubbing the kitchen table for the fifth time that day, "the money you got from your father would add some nice rooms onto this house. You could have a clinic with a separate front door and plenty of space."

Jon scowled at her and said, "That money is to buy some land and—" He stopped when she gave him that look again, and he found himself wanting to stomp his foot and insist that he would be a farmer.

"Go ahead and say it, Maddie."

"Say what?" she turned away, her voice dripping with false innocence.

"I know what you're thinking, so why don't you just say it and get it over with?"

"There's no reason for me to say anything, especially if you already know what it is. Why don't *you* say it?"

"What?" he retorted. "That I'm stubborn and proud, just like my father, and I'm too blind to see what everyone else is so certain of?"

Maddie smiled. "You were right, Jon. You *did* know what I was thinking." She walked out of the room, leaving him alone with the silence of his own thoughts, and the growing realization that she was probably right. After being alone with his thoughts for a few more minutes, he found Maddie outside taking laundry down from the line.

"You know," he said, removing the clothespin at the other end of the sheet she was taking down, "my father and I rarely saw eye to eye, but there was one thing he often said that I admired."

"What's that?" Maddie asked, and kissed him quickly as their folding brought them face to face.

"He said that when you're married to a good woman with a good head on her shoulders, you'd have to be a fool not to pay attention to what she has to say."

Maddie smiled. "I do believe I would have liked your father."

Jon chuckled. "Yes, I do believe you would have. You would have been able to worm past his crusty exterior, not unlike Sara, and find all the love that he was so good at keeping hidden. And you know what, Mrs. Brandt? He would have loved you. I know I do."

She smiled and turned her back to take down a long row of diapers that looked so white in the sun they hurt Jon's eyes. "So," he said, putting his hands in his pockets, "I'm asking."

"Asking what?" She stopped and looked directly at him.

"What do you think we should do with the money? And don't tell me what you think I want to hear. I want to know what you *really* think."

"First of all," she said, putting her hands on her hips, "I've never told you anything just because I thought you might want to hear it, and secondly, it's not *my* money. It's *your* money."

"No, Maddie, it's *our* money. This is a big decision, and I think we need to talk about it, think it through, and then take it to the Lord. So, I want you to tell me what you think."

"All right," she said, "I will." She sighed and looked around, as if the hills surrounding her could help her come up with the right words. "Farming is an honorable profession, Jon. And to most of the people who came west and settled here, there weren't many other options. The people needed to work the land in order to live. My father makes furniture, and he's fairly good at it, but he still has to run a fair piece of land to make ends meet. I like the way you admire the simple professions of these people, because if there's one thing they know, it's how to work hard. And so do you." She looked directly at him. "But there are plenty of farmers around here, Jon. And there is a short supply of doctors."

Jon looked at the ground and shuffled the toe of his boot through the grass. "I bet if you asked any one of the men around here who make their living working the land, they would say you'd have to be downright crazy. Why would a man with your education and experience invest so much in something that would only guarantee you a lifetime of hard work and uncertain income?" She sighed. "So, you want to know what I think? I think it's been good for you to learn what you've learned about farming. It's been good for you to walk in the shoes of the hard-working people of this community. And now that you've gained some empathy for these people, I think you can best serve them by using the gift that God has given *you*. In my opinion, we have plenty of land." She looked around again. "We have a large, beautiful garden, plenty of room for the horses to run; we have fruit trees and a big yard for our children to play in. You have plenty of opportunity to be close to the land, Jon. And plenty of farmers around here who could always use a helping hand. But I believe the money would be best spent in providing a place for these people that won't infringe so greatly on our family life. I would be more than happy to spend the rest of my life assisting you in any way I can with helping these people. I will drop whatever I'm doing in an instant to help you heal wounds, and save lives, and care for the sick and the needy. But I'd like to have supper on the table and keep it there." She stepped toward him and lowered her voice. "And we are so blessed, Jon. We have the means to make that happen." She took his face into her hands and kissed him. "There. That's what I think. So, you pray about it, and we can talk about it all you want. But I want you to know that whatever you decide to do, I will stand by you without question."

Jon sighed and pulled her into his arms. "You're too good to be true, Maddie. What did I ever do to deserve stumbling upon such an incredible woman?"

She drew back and smiled. "I thought it was the other way around."

"What?"

"I'm always asking myself what I ever did to deserve having you walk through my front door." Her eyes became serious as she added, "You saved my life, Jon. Perhaps not physically, but in a very literal sense, you saved my life. My spirit and my heart would have eventually shriveled up and died like a plant denied the light of the sun, and the kiss of the rain, and the richness of the earth. And I love you, Jon."

"I love you too, Maddie."

She returned to taking down the wash and Jon went inside to check on the baby. She didn't say anything else about their conversation, but her words became deeply ingrained in him as they turned over and over in his mind. He knew in his heart what he needed to do, and he also knew it was only that remaining crust of pride that made him resist.

On Wednesday Jon returned from a quick trip to town to find Maddie bubbling with excitement.

"Come see," she said, practically jumping up and down as she took his hand and urged him to the parlor. He entered to see the piano that had once been in her parents' parlor, situated neatly against the far wall, with the remainder of the furniture having been rearranged to accommodate it. Before he could even get a question out, she said brightly, "Several men from the ward delivered it not long after you left. They just said that my parents wanted me to have it. Isn't it wonderful?"

"It certainly is," Jon said and laughed as she sat on the bench and began to play. He was glad he hadn't yet found the time to order one. It was heavenly to hear her play, and to see how happy it made her. But without a word spoken, they both knew that this meant some measure of softening from her father. He prayed that it was the first step in a direction that Glen Hansen would take toward reuniting with his daughter.

Late in the week Jon finally found some free time with no prospective patients. He went out to help Dave in his north field, only to find Dave had taken the boys to town for supplies. While he worked, his mind wandered once again through Maddie's words of wisdom. And the more he thought about them, the more wise they became. Combined with his change of heart toward his father, he couldn't deny that the things she had said were beginning to settle almost comfortably.

Jon sunk the shovel into the dirt, pausing to wipe the sweat from his brow when he realized he wasn't alone. He turned abruptly to see Glen

Hansen watching him contemplatively. His heart quickened, and it actually crossed his mind that the man had purposely found him alone in order to do him harm. While Jon pushed the thought from his mind and tried to think of something to say, Glen looked down at the shovel, then back at his face. With a voice as sober as his expression, he said, "When are you going to lower your pride enough to admit that you're not a farmer, you're a doctor?" He paused and something genuine—almost soft—came to his eyes as he added, "And a fine one at that."

Jon was so stunned he couldn't move, couldn't speak. Had he heard him right? Had the man just complimented him? Had his question been a roundabout way of admitting that *he* had lowered *his* pride enough to be here? When Glen just stared at him, obviously expecting some kind of response, Jon cleared his throat carefully and said, "If you must know, I think I've already managed to figure that out. I've had some memorable lessons in pride lately." He looked down and put his hand on the shovel handle. "I was just helping Dave out a little." Jon sighed and looked around himself. "I actually enjoy this sort of thing—within reason."

"Well," Glen said, glancing around as well, "that would give us something in common."

Jon felt tempted to pinch himself, just to be sure he wasn't dreaming. Glen Hansen had just admitted that they had something in common. The silence grew long and Jon wondered what he might say to break it.

Glen finally said, "I wonder if I might talk to you, son."

Son? Jon echoed silently. Was this encounter as miraculous as it seemed? Were months of prayers on his behalf finally being answered? He reminded himself not to jump to conclusions, or let his hopes distort reality. "Of course," he said.

They wandered idly across the field as Glen began by saying, "I've spent a lot of time on my knees since I saw you last Saturday . . . a place I haven't once been since I first met you. You remember that day, don't you?"

"Oh," Jon chuckled, "I remember it well."

"I was afraid of that," Glen said. "I was really hoping you'd forgotten."

"Forgiven, yes," Jon said. "Forgotten, never." Glen looked surprised, and Jon couldn't hold back a little laugh. He couldn't believe they were having this conversation, and that he didn't feel the least bit uncomfortable with a man who had clearly hated him.

"Well, I do appreciate that, the forgiving part, at least. Because I was hoping to get around to that—asking your forgiveness, that is."

"That's not a problem," Jon said.

Glen was silent for a minute, and Jon realized he was struggling with his emotion. They arrived at a shady spot just past the edge of the field, and Glen sat down on the grass, as if he'd lost his strength. He set his forearms on his knees and gazed toward the distant mountain peaks to the southwest. Jon sat beside him and did the same.

"So," Glen finally said, "it stands to reason that if I was too angry to get on my knees and talk to the good Lord, I wasn't seeing things clearly. But I think I'm seeing things clearly now, or at least I'm beginning to. So I guess what I want to say is . . . well, I was going to work toward asking your forgiveness, but you've kind of thrown me off." He laughed in an obvious effort to control his emotion. Jon just waited. "I guess it would be good if you understood what you were forgiving me for, or maybe if I tell you what I'm thinking, I might understand it a little better."

"Either way," Jon said, "I'm listening."

Glen nodded but was silent again for a minute or two. "When I was just a kid," he finally said, "five or six, I believe, my parents and my older sisters joined the Church. They were all baptized except me; I was still too young. But I remember how I felt that it was true. I remember the conviction in my family members, and how there seemed no remorse or concern about leaving everything behind to cross the plains with a handcart company. For me it seemed like an adventure. Of course, I had no idea what we were in for, or how horrible it would be, but . . ." Jon put his focus fully on Glen as his oration took such a painful turn.

"I never doubted that it was true," Glen said. "In spite of all that happened, I remember feeling angels with us as clearly as I can feel you beside me right now. My father baptized me while we were living in Salt Lake, after I had turned eight. The thing is, it was just him and me by then."

Jon's heart quickened unexpectedly as he began to realize what was coming. Still, he never would have dreamed. . .

"My sister was the first to die from exposure. She was eleven. She was buried in the snow because the ground was too frozen to dig a grave and we had to move on. A week later we lost my mother, and she too was left without a grave. My other sister got frostbite so bad that it turned to gangrene. Both her feet were amputated, but it never healed right. She always suffered in pain. She died just before my eighth birthday, some infection or something."

Glen Hansen wiped the tears from his face with his shirt-sleeve. He sniffed and went on, "The thing is, I never doubted it was true. I knew what I'd felt, and I saw my father continue to serve the Lord until he died an old man at fifty-four. But I also saw the heartache that never left him. He was never the same after we lost them. And even though I knew we would all be together again, and whole again, this life can be awfully long and difficult without someone you love."

He took a deep breath and seemed to be gathering his words. "When I met Sylvia she filled so much of that emptiness of losing Mama and my sisters. Then I came real close to losing her when she had Maddie. It's a miracle she made it through, and even though I would have loved having more children, I was relieved that it would be impossible for her, because I didn't want to risk losing her. And Maddie was such a joy to me." He laughed softly and the nostalgia in his eyes softened his grief. "But oh! She was such a wild child, always getting bumped and bruised, always climbing and getting into mischief. Every time I turned around I heard myself telling her to be careful. I was terrified that something awful was going to happen to her. And then . . ."

Again he fought for composure. Jon impulsively put a hand on Glen's shoulder. He nodded and coughed before he went on. "I saw her fall out of the tree. I thought she was dead before I got to her. Of course, she wasn't, and I was grateful, but when she couldn't stand or walk . . ." Glen lost all control of his emotions and wept openly. Jon offered him a clean handkerchief which he accepted eagerly. "It broke my heart to see her suffer. But as hard as it was, I couldn't deny that little bit of relief I felt that she wouldn't ever get hurt again, because she couldn't run and climb and . . ." Again he cried while Jon just waited patiently.

"Once she stopped having pain and could sit up without any trouble, we started taking her to school again. But she'd cry every day; some of the children teased her. She couldn't run and play with them. So, we kept her home from school and Sylvia taught her. We were taking her to church and into town occasionally, but then she caught the influenza and we nearly lost her. Me and Sylvia didn't have it, so we knew she'd gotten it from being around others. Soon afterward that young man came courting her. He was from a fine family, and they grew to care for each other, but when he told her he just couldn't live with her not being able to walk, it broke her heart. It took her months to get over it. It made me so angry. I think that was the final straw. I became so terrified of losing her that I decided no one or nothing was ever going to hurt my little girl again."

Glen took a deep breath as if he'd just set down a huge load he'd been carrying. He blew his nose into his handkerchief and went on. "Now that I've talked it over with the Lord in and out for a number of days, I know now that I let my fears get the better of me. I was having trouble understanding what I'd done wrong until . . . I remembered learning as a young man about the war in heaven. It was Lucifer's plan to take away our free agency and force us to go back to our Father in Heaven, but . . ." Glen pressed his face into his hands and wept. Jon put a hand on his shoulder and kept it there. "I was such a fool . . . so wrong . . . I don't know how I could have been so blind . . . such a fool."

"Well then," Jon said, "that would give us something else in common."

Glen looked up and mopped his eyes. The blatant hope and amazement in his eyes nearly prompted Jon to tears himself. He turned away and forced back his emotion before he said, "Now maybe I could tell you something." He sighed and clasped his fingers together. "I grew up with every possible comfort, everything a boy could ever want. My mother was an angel, much like your good wife. My father was a hard-working man with integrity and a good heart. He was also intolerant, controlling, and extremely stubborn and willful. He was also a very good doctor. I became a doctor because he wanted me to, and I hated every minute of it. I had been here for quite some time before I began to realize that I was at least fifty percent to blame for the estrangement between me and my father. A hundred times I thought that I needed to write him a letter, just to tell him that I loved him, that I'd forgiven him for his weaknesses, and to ask his forgiveness of mine. But I put it off, always talked myself out of it. Pride. That's all it was. Stubborn pride. And then we got word that he was dying. I prayed with all my heart and soul that he would hang on long enough for me to tell him what I had to say. But he didn't."

Jon heard his voice crack and took a moment to compose himself. "Little by little I've come to appreciate my education and my upbringing, but I was never so grateful for the skills I had acquired as when I was able to deliver my own baby. That, along with seeing Maddie walk again, made me realize that I was meant to be a doctor. And my father had seen something in me that I had been too foolish and stubborn to see. He had sacrificed our relationship in order to push me to become what I am, and I never got the chance to thank him face to face."

He sighed, and chuckled to fight off his emotion. "But everything's okay now, I believe. I felt him with me when Elizabeth was born, and I know that all is forgiven. I'm going to do his temple work when the time is right, and I believe we'll be together again. But I think it's important that you know I've had my own share of pride and fear, and I hope you can forgive me for my anger toward you for those very reasons."

Glen looked into Jon's eyes and smiled. He said with a firm voice, "All is forgiven."

It reminded Jon so much of the moment he'd heard those words in his mind, knowing his father had somehow spoken them through the veil, that he was moved to tears. He quickly wiped his face and turned away, wondering if this reconciliation with his father-in-law had somehow added another layer of healing in his feelings toward his own father. *Thank you, Lord,* he prayed silently.

"I don't know about you," Jon said, coming to his feet, "but I think my stomach's telling me it's past lunchtime. And I'd wager that pretty little daughter of yours has some of last night's stew simmering on the stove. I doubt anything could make her happier than to feed you a bowl of it." He held out a hand and Glen took it, coming to his feet and sharing a firm handshake at the same time.

"Thank you, Doctor Brandt," Glen said, still holding his hand firmly. "She was right. You're the best thing that ever happened to her—and to me, I believe. Thank you for sticking it out with her, in spite of me. There is no way to express my gratitude for all you've done for her—and me and Sylvia, as well."

"She's easy to love," Jon said. "Beyond that, the rest was just as easy. She's a fine woman with a lot of fine qualities. I know you raised her well, in spite of the difficulties."

Glen sighed and they walked together toward the house.

* * * * *

Maddie sat down to eat her lunch when Jon hadn't come by the usual time. She knew they were going to have to get one of those triangle bells that Ellie had so she could call him in if he was needed. When she heard the back door, she called lightly, "You're late. It's all gone. I ate every bite of it."

"That's too bad," Jon said, "because I brought a friend with me, and I told him you'd be happy to feed him, too."

Maddie came to her feet, wondering who might have come in with him. There were many people in the community who might have stopped to chat with him; perhaps it was someone in need of some minor medical assistance. Jon appeared in the kitchen, wearing a complacent grin.

"Hey, honey," he said, "remember that first day we met, and you introduced me to Ellie as if we were dear friends?"

"I remember," she said, "but then, we were, weren't we?"

"I think so," Jon chuckled. "Well, I want you to meet my new dear friend." Jon motioned with his hand and a man stepped into the kitchen beside him, but it took Maddie a long moment for her mind to accept what her eyes were seeing.

"Papa?" she barely breathed, pressing a hand over her pounding heart. "I can't believe it!" she said, her vision of him blurring with the mist in her eyes. She blinked them onto her cheeks and saw him open his arms.

"Hello there, princess," he said, and she rushed into his arms. She cried harder at being in his embrace. "Oh, Maddie Jo," he said close to her ear in a voice that betrayed his emotions, "can you ever forgive me for being such an old fool?"

"Oh, of course. Of course," she murmured and looked into this face. "I've missed you so much, Papa," she said.

"And I've missed you," he said, "more than you could possibly imagine."

Maddie wanted to know what had brought about this miraculous change of heart. While she was searching for the words to ask, he seemed to read her mind. "Your good husband can tell you later about the talk we had. Right now, I think I'd like a bowl of that stew. I must confess I haven't eaten since yesterday sometime, and—"

"Oh, of course," Maddie said and hurried to get him some. They sat together to eat, and Jon offered a blessing on the food, expressing gratitude for the healing they had found, and the chance to be together as family. After the amen had been spoken, Maddie took her father's hand across one corner of the table and Jon's hand across the other. "Perfect," she said.

* * * * *

Over a leisurely lunch, Glen asked at least a hundred questions about Maddie learning to walk, their trip to Boston, and the baby coming. Elizabeth woke up, and Maddie nursed her with a blanket thrown over her shoulder while they visited. Her father asked Jon about his background and his family. Then he finally said, "Well, it's a pleasure to have you in the family, son."

"The pleasure is all mine . . . *Papa,*" Jon said with a sparkle in his eyes that prompted Maddie to laugh. She watched her father playfully slap Jon on the shoulder and they all laughed together.

"I've got a little something for the baby," he said. "If you're going to be here, I'll run along home and get it."

"Oh, of course," Maddie said. "We're not going anywhere."

Once her father had left, Maddie hugged Jon tightly and cried again. "I can't believe it," she said. "It's a miracle."

"Yes, I believe it is," he said.

"But I wonder what would make me so deserving of so many miracles in my life," she added.

"You worked hard for them," Jon said and pressed a kiss into her hair.

"Now you must tell me what happened," she insisted. They sat down together and he repeated all that her father had said to him.

"I never knew," she said. "I mean, I knew he'd lost his mother and sisters. But I never knew more than that. It makes so much sense now, the way he felt."

"Yes, it does," Jon said.

A short while later her father returned with her mother. Maddie embraced her mother and they both laughed, then they had to move aside for her father to carry the cradle into the house.

"Oh, it's beautiful," Maddie said as he set it in the parlor.

"I didn't know if you had something for the baby to sleep in, but—"

"We don't, actually," Jon said. "She's been sleeping with us most of the time. We ordered a crib but it's been slow coming."

"And that'll work fine when she gets a little bigger," Glen said. "But a cradle's nice when they're needing to be rocked."

"Oh, Papa, I love it," Maddie said, running her fingers lovingly over the polished wood surface.

"Well, I've had a lot to think about this last week, and I kind of holed myself up in the barn to do it. I just sort of found myself making a cradle for little Lizzy."

"Lizzy," Maddie repeated, glancing toward the baby against Jon's shoulder. "I do believe that suits her well. What do you think, Jon?"

"I think it's perfect," he said.

* * * * *

At church on Sunday the harvest ball was announced for the following Saturday. On the way home, Jon eyed Maddie mischievously, "Will you go to the dance with me, Mrs. Brandt?"

Maddie laughed and felt giddy inside as it occurred to her that she'd actually be able to dance. "It would be an honor, Doctor Brandt. But you might have to give me a few lessons in the meantime. Learning to walk is one thing, learning to dance is quite another."

"It would be an honor," he echoed, and she laughed again.

They'd not been home long when her parents arrived for dinner, and Ellie's family came as well. Somewhere in the midst of the meal, Maddie took Jon's hand across the table and glanced around at their families—talking and laughing as if it had always been this way. *Thank you, Lord,* she uttered silently, then laughed just for the sake of it.

* * * * *

Jon sat with Lizzy on his lap, watching Maddie being waltzed by her father. He pondered the last two times he'd attended this traditional affair, and he marveled that life could change so drastically in so short a time. Two years seemed like a lifetime, and yet they had their whole lives ahead of them. The music came to a stop and everyone applauded before another set began. Glen took the baby and Jon held Maddie close to him while he waltzed her around the room for the fifth time this evening, and he loved every minute of it.

On the way home, Jon put his arm around her shoulders and said, "I talked to Peter Carter a couple of days ago."

"Really? How is he?"

"He's good, and so's the family, he says."

"Good. I don't think I've seen any of them since he took that job in Manti. But it was only temporary, wasn't it?"

"That's right. He's nearly finished with the job he's working on there, and they'll be moving back next week. He said he could get started on our addition right away, and probably get quite a bit done before winter sets in."

Maddie turned toward him, eyes wide. He chuckled, having gotten just the reaction he'd hoped for. "What addition?" she demanded.

"Well, we need to talk about what exactly, but I thought a sewing room would be nice. You've said you'd like to do more sewing. And another bedroom or two wouldn't hurt, with all those kids we're going to have. And of course we need the clinic. I liked your idea about that. It can have a separate front door, but it will be connected to the house so we can go between. From what Peter tells me, I think we've got plenty to build it and get everything we need to stock the clinic, and still have a good amount set aside to fall back on if we have hard times ahead. So, what do you think, Maddie Jo Brandt?"

"I think it sounds marvelous, Dr. Brandt," she said and laughed. How he loved to hear her laugh!

They arrived home, and Maddie took the baby inside to put her to bed while Jon unharnessed the horse and saw to its needs. He went in to find Maddie brushing her hair down. She was still wearing her dress, but her feet were bare.

"Come along," he said, taking her hand.

"Where are we going?" she asked, tossing the hairbrush down.

"It's raining," he said, lifting her into his arms just after they passed through the front door. He carried her to the lawn. She laughed and lifted her face heavenward as he set her on her feet and they waltzed in the rain. *Yes,* Jon thought, *life was absolutely perfect.*

PHOTO BY "PICTURE THIS . . . BY SARA STAKER"

ABOUT THE AUTHOR

Anita Stansfield has been writing for more than twenty years, and her best-selling novels have captivated and moved hundreds of thousands of readers with their deeply romantic stories and focus on important contemporary issues. Her interest in creating romantic fiction began in high school, and her work has appeared in national publications. *Where the Heart Leads* is her seventeenth novel and fifth historical work to be published by Covenant.

Anita lives with her husband, Vince, and their five children and two cats in Alpine, Utah.